MINE TO HONOR

When your best friend asks you for the biggest favor of her life.

Eva
Things were finally looking up for me. I was my own boss; I owned my own house—and I recently was contacted by an older sister I didn't know I had. Everything was perfect... until tragedy struck. All the things that had come into my life were suddenly gone—except for one thing: my niece.

Levi
I was a confirmed bachelor. I was married to my work and committed to nothing more. No woman was going to change that. Eva is my best friend and needed a life-changing favor: marry her so she could gain custody of her niece. A marriage of convenience that would only last a year, tops. But there were stipulations we hadn't planned on. Things got blurry—lines got crossed. I would honor my commitment...I just hope I can walk away.

BOOKS BY NATASHA MADISON

SOUTHERN WEDDING SERIES TREE

Southern Wedding Family tree

Mine To Have
Travis & Harlow
Charlotte
Theo

Mine To Hold
Shelby & Ace
Arya

Mine To Cherish
Clarabella & Luke
Unborn Unnamed Baby

Mine To Love
Presley & Bennett
Cici
Unborn Unnamed Baby

Mine To Take
Sofia and Matty

Mine To Promise
Stefano & Addison
Avery

Mine To Honor
Levi & Eva

Mine To Keep
Grace & Caine

Southern Family tree
Billy and Charlotte
(Mother and father to Kallie and Casey)

Southern Chance
Kallie & Jacob McIntyre
Ethan McIntyre (Savannah Son)
Amelia
Travis

Southern Comfort
Olivia & Casey Barnes
Quinn (Southern Heat)
Reed (Southern Sunshine)
Harlow (Mine to Have)

Southern Storm
Savannah & Beau Huntington
Ethan McIntyre (Jacob's son)
Chelsea (Southern Heart)
Toby
Keith

Southern Sunrise
Emily & Ethan McIntyre
Gabriel
Aubrey

Southern Heart
Chelsea Huntington & Mayson Carey
Tucker

Southern Heat
Willow & Quinn Barnes

Southern Secrets
Amelia McIntyre & Asher

Southern Sunshine
Hazel & Reed Barnes
Sophia

Cover Design: Jay Aheer
Editing done by Jenny Sims
Editing done by Karen Hrdicka
Proofing Julie Deaton by Deaton Author Services
Proofing by Judy's proofreading
Cover picture by: Britt & Bean
Interior Design by Chrisatina Parker Smith

mine ♡ to
HONOR

Southern Wedding Series

NATASHA
MADISON

Prologue

Dearest Love,

Spring is in the air, which means wedding season is rapidly approaching us.

Brides and grooms preparing to take the leap and walk down the aisle.

Or.

A woman asking her best friend for a huge favor.

Just for a year.

A fake wedding.

Except.

What happens when they have to live with each other?

What happens when they have to share a bed?

What happens when everything starts to get blurry?

Will the vows they said to each other be real?
Will they honor those promises?
Time will tell!
XOXO
NM

One

Eva

I step out of the bathroom in my office, tucking the white T-shirt into the blue jeans I just slid on. The crash of the waves hitting the rocks fills my room, giving you a nice Zen feeling. If it isn't waves playing in the background, it is the lull of the soft instruments. I make my way over to my desk at the same time my phone beeps on top of it. Looking down at my phone, I see I have a text from Levi.

Levi: *Running a touch late, max five to ten minutes. Order me a beer.*

I shake my head and roll my eyes at the same time, not surprised at all by this text. "Shocking," I mumble to myself before picking the phone up as I slide one foot into my nude, sky-high shoes, then the other, until my feet pinch from being in the shoes.

Me: When am I ever not waiting for you?

I press send before tossing the phone into the purse that is on my chair. Levi and I have been friends for the past ten years, I met him through my cousin, who I had no idea I even had, also ten years ago. Needless to say, Levi and I, we just clicked. We had the same humor and found each other annoying, but not so annoyed we didn't always text the other person. Either way, our friendship just grew and grew. He is one of, if not, my very best friend. There is nothing I can't say and vice versa. Trust me, nothing is off-limits between us. The two of us get together at least once a week, if he's not traveling for work, or every two weeks just to catch up. It was something we started after we went a whole month without seeing each other and we spent four hours catching up, and that was only for one week.

I walk over to one of the pink cushioned chairs facing my desk, picking up my long, black sweater. I slide my arms into it and push the sleeves up to my elbows. Turning toward the mirror that hangs by the door, I take one long look at myself before I head out to meet him.

My tight, light-blue jeans mold my legs with a white V-neck T-shirt. Simple, casual, and with the red-bottom shoes, a little bit classy and very, very sassy. Very different from how I walked into the salon this morning, wearing the black-pants-and-top uniform everyone wears in my business, with the name of the salon stitched on the right side. I tuck the right side of my brown hair behind my ear and see the wave I did this morning quickly after I walked in, is still holding up. "It pays to own your place." I smile to myself. Leaning forward, I see that the makeup is still lasting, even after eight hours of being at work. "The tricks you learn from your trade." I smirk as I take a big inhale before I grab my bag off the chair and head out of my office, closing the door behind me. The door to my left is open and some of the washers are going in the laundry room. I stick my head in to see if anyone is there, but it's empty.

To my right, the lights in the hallway to the men's and women's bathrooms are dim, and music plays softly in the background.

As I walk down the hallway to the front of the salon, the music gets louder and is very different from the back. It's today's hits and it's upbeat. Even the lights are different from the spa area, where it's dimly lit in the back. Here in the front, it's like the more lights the better.

My shoes clicking on the tile floor fill the empty room as I look around to see all six hairdressing seats empty, my reflection following with me as I walk through the room. I hear voices coming from the color area and stop to stick my head in when I see Keira and Chloe are both in there, cleaning up after the day. "See you two tomorrow." I smile at them as I wave with the tips of my fingers. I pass by the men's hair station, seeing Saverio and Isabelle both sweeping their stations. Black leather barber chairs face full-length mirrors. "Night, guys," I say and they both look up and smile.

It takes me a couple of more steps to walk out into

the waiting room. This is one of my favorite rooms in the place. I knew what I was going to do. I wanted it to be warm and welcoming, so I stuck to the neutral tones with, of course, pink, because everyone secretly likes pink, and if they tell you otherwise, they are just plain bald-faced lying to you. Raquel, our receptionist and office coordinator, sits behind the white rounded desk that is facing the glass door when you walk in. Behind her is a brown, tan, and beige wall with exposed bricks. A huge crystal vase with fresh light pink roses sits at the corner of the counter. "I was just coming to see you." She looks up from her desk, her blond hair tied in a ponytail high in the middle of her head. "Here you go." She lifts her hand holding a green mesh bag. "This is the deposit for tomorrow."

I walk toward her desk. "You're a lifesaver," I praise. "I was going to come in early tomorrow morning and do it, but now I get to sleep in until six forty-five." I glance over to the right, through the open wall that shows the little café we added this year. The tables and chairs are all clean and ready for the next day. Moving my head a bit to the side, I see past the café into the nail part of the salon. Three people sit side by side as they get their nails done, conversations flowing. I can't help but smile when I take a look around at what I've done here.

"Also." She gets up from her chair. "I just checked the calendar, and I'm happy to announce we are booked solid for the next six months."

"For real?" I believe it, but also don't believe it. "That's amazing. Thank you, by the way." She tilts her head. "If it wasn't for you, we would be all over the place. I'll see you tomorrow." I look up and see the name that I came up with. It took me so many months of throwing names around. Literally going word by word in the dictionary until I got to the word—Envy Spa & Salon—and as usual, I can't help but smile. In reality, I wanted to be the envy of all spas out there, and looking around, I really hope I am.

"I will be here," she confirms, and I turn to walk toward the front door, passing two pink chairs with a fake but very expensive cherry blossom tree between them. Looking over my shoulder one last time, I smile at her, holding up my hand and wiggling my fingers.

My car is parked on the side, chirping crickets in the air fill the night. The wind softly blows my hair as I make my way from the commercial building to my car. Grabbing the keys, I unlock the doors, sliding into the driver's seat and placing my purse in the seat beside me. Turning the car on, I buckle myself in, looking back at what hard work has gotten me.

When I was sixteen, I got a job at a hairdresser in town, washing hair and sweeping it up. But I was always more interested in the back of the salon where they did skin facials and waxing. After a year in the salon, I got to work more with Sandra, who did all waxing, peeling, and everything that had to do with the skin. I soaked it in, and I was good at it, so right out of high school, I opted to forgo college and head straight to aesthetician school.

School just made me even better than I was. I was at the top of my class, so when it was time for my internship, they sent me to the best salon there was out there. I meshed well with the owner, and when I got my hours in and graduated, she offered me a job. I jumped at the chance, especially since it was in a nice area and the clients were high-paying and high-tipping. A year later, I asked if I could rent space in her salon instead of working for her. She was apprehensive at first, but she wasn't getting any younger, and none of her daughters even wanted to work with her. So that is how it started. I rented my space, and slowly, little by little, I worked up to afford to hire someone under me. It was a considerable risk, but I was putting my money on myself. It was amazing until the owner passed away, and her daughters decided to close up shop. I took out a small business loan and bought the building from them. Most of the hairdressers stayed and rented their chairs from me. It took five years of busting my ass to make it to where we were, one of the most sought-after salons. I hired the best hair color people. I hired a couple of massage therapists and even had makeup on the weekends. It exploded when we were featured in a bridal magazine.

Then last year I found this building for sale, but it would be really tight. Especially since I had just bought my house, but I ran the numbers and figured it would be doable. It was a one-stop shop, we set up spa days— complete with hair and makeup—which was our biggest seller. Last month, I finally put in the café and it was a hit. People who would come and do their hair or nails could stop and get a bite to eat with a friend. It couldn't have been going any better and I was so proud of myself.

I mean, no one else was proud of me, so I had no choice but to give myself a pat on the back. My mother was always in and out of my life. She, in her words, couldn't be tied down. She had to see the world, spread her wings, which she did multiple times. I didn't even know who my father was. I'm not sure my mother knew, but she pretended she did. He was so handsome, every single time she would pop in for a visit—which wasn't frequent—she would tell me stories about him. In the beginning, I would sit and listen intently until I think I turned eight, and I learned early on not to believe anything she told me.

My grandmother is the one who raised me, and lucky for me. She lasted until I was eighteen years old and she knew I would be able to take care of myself. I believe that she finally let go and passed away in her sleep. Six months after my grandmother died, so did my mother.

I was literally all alone, and then one day I saw this advertisement online about tracing my ancestries. *Why not,* I thought, what is the worst that can happen? So as I was swabbing my inner cheek, I never expected the results. I matched with a family in Greece, that didn't shock me since my mother mentioned meeting a man in Santorini with the bluest eyes, which is apparently where I got my blue eyes from.

It was the strangest thing to go from being all alone to then having over twelve connections of close family members, on the other side of the world. I wasn't sure if I should reach out to them, but they reached out to me. They were both shocked and happy to find me. More shocked than anything for sure. Unfortunately for me, my father had passed on the year before from cancer. Right after I found that out, I got a phone call from Stefano, who was—of course—forced by his family to reach out to me. We were shocked to find we were in the same state, so we decided to meet up. All it took was one time and his father and mother came down to meet me. His father was my father's nephew and he and his family have been very, very nice to me. They've included me all the time. It's a little bit weird but I've attended a couple of functions, of course bringing Levi with me since he knew them also.

The phone ringing makes me come out of my daydream. I look at the Bluetooth and see it's Levi calling.

"You'd better not be canceling on me." I don't even bother saying hello.

His laughter fills the car. "Would I do that?"

"Yes," I immediately answer him. "You would and you have."

"Never." He gasps but doesn't stop chuckling.

"There was that leggy brunette who you pegged as soon as we got into the restaurant the last time and you bailed after appetizers," I remind him.

"She was in town for the night," he snaps in his defense, "she was a nanny."

I can't help but laugh now. "She was not a nanny. She showed you a random picture. I asked her how old the kids were and she said, 'Um, about three to four months old.' The kid was walking."

"She was confused." He tries to plead her case, and I roll my eyes as I pull up next to his Mercedes. "English wasn't her first language."

"I'm about to be confused right now and bail on your ass," I remark, looking at him. He turns his head, and his face fills with a smile. He disconnects and leans over to grab his suit jacket before getting out of his car. His cuffs are rolled up to his elbows. On his left hand is the silver Rolex with the black-braided bracelet I got him for Christmas last year, and he holds his jacket in his other hand. He walks around the back of my car and opens my door.

"And they say chivalry is dead." I laugh as I lean over and grab my purse before shutting off the car. He holds out his hand for me to grab it, but I smack it away. "I don't even know where that hand has been."

"I just got back," he huffs, putting his hand in his pocket as he watches me get out of the car.

Even with my heels, I still have to tilt my head back. "Hi," I greet him, going in for a hug.

"Oh, you can hug me, but you can't take my hand." He wraps an arm around my shoulder.

"I'm assuming when you had sex you were naked, so technically your clothes are safe." I step back, and my face goes into a grimace. "Eww, unless you did it in the bathroom."

"Jesus, Ev." He calls me by a nickname he gave me one day when he was hungover and found it impossible to say two syllables. "I'm thirty years old, I think I have enough sex self-control that I can wait to get to a bed."

I fold my arms over my chest. "Six months ago, you were getting head in your car."

His head drops. "Forgot about that one."

"I bet you did," I tease as we turn to walk toward the restaurant.

He holds up his hand. "But foreplay isn't sex."

I roll my eyes because, of course, he would be the one who would find a loophole in anything, "I'm surprised you can squeeze me in with all those ladies."

He puts his arm around my shoulders. "You know, I always make time for you, Eva," he assures me as we walk into the crowded restaurant. "Now." He playfully shoves me away. "Get away from me in case I see someone who might come home with me tonight."

Two

Levi

$\mathcal{W}$e walk up to the hostess stand side by side, and instead of glaring at me, she just laughs. "You think I put on these shoes for you?" She points down to her nude, sky-high heels. Heels that just scream *fuck me* in them. "I'm not wasting an opportunity," she retorts, holding her purse in both hands.

"A table for two, please," she tells the hostess, who looks down at her iPad.

"Can I stand next to you?" I ask. "Wouldn't want people to think—you know—that we are together and you miss your shot."

"Shut up." She rolls her eyes at me and I have to laugh, I'm always laughing when I'm with her. It's why she's my best friend. "Also." She leans in and doesn't even bother to whisper. "Dinner is on you."

"When isn't it?" I huff as the hostess turns and tells us to follow her. I wait for Eva to walk first before following her into the restaurant.

The hostess stops by a booth, putting the menus down. "Your server will be right with you," she says as Eva slides into the booth. I start to slide in beside her and she pushes me out with her hand.

"Nice try," she notes, grabbing the menu and looking down at it, while I slide into the booth across from her, tossing my jacket in the corner.

"We come here all the time and you always look at the menu," I state, putting my hands beside me on the bench.

"They could have updated their menu, and you know me, I like to try different things."

"Oh, I know." I take a look around the bar. "You usually hate everything you try and end up eating my food."

She throws her head back and laughs as she shrugs off the black sweater. "It's like watching *National Geographic*," I tell her as the server comes to our table.

"Hi," she greets, "I'm Ashley. I'll be your server. Can I start you off with something to drink?"

"I'll have whatever you have on tap and she'll have a Pinot Grigio." I point at Eva, who just nods.

"I'll get that started for you," Ashley says as she walks away.

"You look tired," Eva observes, looking at me. I stare into her crystal blue eyes, and I don't know if she's fucking with me or not.

"I am tired," I admit. "I'm also fed up with traveling so much." I stop talking when Ashley comes back with my beer and a wineglass for Eva.

I pick up my beer as Eva mumbles, "Thank you," to Ashley and asks if she would give us another minute or two.

Putting the beer to my lips, I look at Eva as she glares. "Really?" She tilts her head to the side as I pull the beer from my lips. "Ten years and you do this every single time." She holds up her glass. "Cheers." She looks into my eyes because it's bad luck if you don't say cheers while looking into the other person's eyes. Something we fought about at the beginning, and when we both googled it, it said we could have seven years of bad sex. It was something neither of us were willing to tempt fate with so—it's eye contact every single time.

"Cheers," I grumble, hitting her glass with mine and finally taking a pull of the beer. I groan and she just puts her glass down.

"So what's eating at you?" she questions, her perfectly manicured nail tapping the bottom of the wineglass.

"Just tired, I guess." I shrug. "Spent the past month traveling back and forth to New York. I just want to be home, in my house, for longer than four days."

"Have you spoken to Stefano about it?" she asks of her cousin and my partner. We started our company about ten years ago, maybe a little more. Time just keeps passing us by. We started our firm when it was just him and me. Two kids out of college, with lots of computer knowledge. We started a small company, just the two of us, and it grew so much now we have a whole slew of people working for us. I'm a forensic accountant, which sounds a lot cooler than it actually is. What it is, has me sitting behind a computer for sometimes twenty hours a day following trails. They hire me to investigate financial inconsistencies, misappropriation of funds and irregularities with the company, and to investigate fraud and cybercrimes. Our contracts vary from private companies to the government. Every single time I show up, I have to laugh at how people use their computers without a second thought, thinking that things can be deleted. News flash—they can't. So we go in and find out what's wrong, and they either change it or people get fired. Also, no one likes when we show up. It's like when you throw a big party at your house, and everyone is having a great time, then the cops knock on your door. It's not fun.

"I haven't yet," I reply, and she lifts her eyebrows. "I know, I know, but he's a bit busy at the moment."

"Okay, well, what about you?" She grabs her wineglass and brings it to her mouth. "How long are you planning to wait?" I grab my own drink and bring it to my lips. This has to be why she's my best friend, because she gives it to me when I don't want to hear it. She is also the first person I call when something happens. Once, I was with a girl and I didn't know she was married. When her husband showed up, I had to literally jump from the second-floor apartment, breaking my ankle from the leap. I belly crawled across the grass and hid out until she came to save me. I mean, she did hold it over my head for about a year, but there is no one else I would call.

"I'll tell him next week when he's coming to town," I finally say and stop talking when Ashley comes back, asking if we have any questions about the menu.

"I'll have a burger loaded with bacon and fries," I order, not even looking at the menu. She looks over at Eva, who looks down at her menu. "She's going to have—" I start and earn a glare from Eva.

"He thinks he knows me, but he doesn't," she tells Ashley, who just smiles at her. "Kale salad," we both say at the same time, "and fries on the side."

"I don't know her at all," I tell Ashley. "Also, if you can bring some calamari over and some of the boneless wings." I look at Eva, who is still glaring at me.

"You are so annoying." She glares, handing her menu to Ashley.

"Did you not want calamari?" I ask and she refuses to even answer me, instead grabbing her glass of wine and looking around. "And do you not like to eat the boneless wings with your salad?" I laugh at her. "You could say thank you."

"Whatever," she says. "Also, three o'clock, two brunettes staring at us." I don't turn right away. "One is my client," she states with a smile, "and the other is glaring, so I'm assuming that one is for you." I put my head back. "This is why you don't shit where you eat."

"For the record." I hold up a finger. "I've never picked up a woman in this place."

She claps her hands together and roars out with laughter. "Okay, fine, it was one time, but again, what was I supposed to do? You left with Fabio." I pretended to flip the long hair off my shoulder because he had a man bun.

She laughs. "His name was Richard and he was a nice guy." I raise my eyebrows.

"You said he didn't even go down on you," I point out.

"It's not all about that," she returns, and now it's my turn to throw my head back and laugh.

"It's always about that," I remind her. "You get one shot to please a woman."

She holds up her hand. "Are you telling me that you pleased every single woman you've been with?" she asks, and I honestly have to run my hands through my hair.

"If I didn't, it wasn't intentional," I tell her, "or I was in a rush." I stop talking when Ashley comes back and puts the calamari and boneless wings in front of us in the middle of the table.

"You are so full of shit, Levi, and you're lucky I like you most days," Eva fires back as the calamari comes to the table. "And you are buying me dinner."

"Okay, so what do you think I should tell Stefano?" I ask as I grab a piece of calamari while she tells me what I should do. We spend more than three hours in the restaurant and, as always, it feels like twenty minutes.

"Call me when you get home," I remind her as I open her car door for her. She gets on her tippy-toes and kisses my cheek.

"Are you even going to be alone?" she asks and I nod. Usually, I would try to meet up with someone, but not tonight. I am legit dead on my feet.

"I'm going home and I'm going straight to my shower," I inform her as she gets in the car. "Drive safe."

"Will do," she confirms, and I close the car door as I step away for her to back up. I hold up my hand and watch her as she drives away, getting into my car and making my way home.

When I get to the parking lot, I enter the code as the black garage door slowly opens for me. I advance my car and drive to my assigned parking spot. I pop the trunk and take out my black bag before slamming it shut and heading to the door on the side where the elevators are.

I press the up button and wait for one of the two doors to open. The phone beeps in my pocket, so I pull it out seeing a text.

Marianna: *Hey, you free tonight? Was thinking we could hang out.*

That is code for she wants to hook up. Marianna and I have been hooking up for the past two years. Not frequent enough to call us a couple, but often enough for me to know that she is in the mood. I'm about to answer her when I hear a ping telling me the elevator is here. I step in and press the forty-four button.

I'm about to pull up the text thread and answer Marianna when the elevator door opens, and I see a couple of my neighbors who live in the building. We say hello to each other and chitchat about the weather right before they get off on the floor below me. I put my phone in my pocket when the elevator door opens finally at my stop. Grabbing the keys from my bag, I walk all the way down the hall to the end. Sliding my key inside the big brown door, I unlock it before I push it open.

The beeping alarm has me stop to put in the code. I toss the keys on the glass table at the door before turning on the lights. I walk into the open-concept condo, kicking off my shoes. The whole wall facing me is all windows, it's why I bought the place. The sun comes at just the right time during the day and it has a wraparound terrace. The furniture is very modern, something that came with the place, which is another reason I bought it. The only thing I brought into this apartment was my bed. I walk to the right, heading into my room and turning on lights.

The king-size bed sits in the middle of the room in front of the black wall, the beige material headboard sticking up in the back. I walk over to the walk-in closet on the side, dumping my bag in there. The phone beeps again in my pocket and I take it out as I head back out to my bed, sitting down on it. I'm about to answer the text when Eva's name comes on the screen that she's calling. I press the green button. "Did you miss me that much?"

"Levi." Her voice has me standing, shivers running up my back. My heart pounds faster than it was a couple of seconds ago and the only thing running through my head now is getting to her. I rush back to the front door. "Levi," she says my name again, this time her voice cracking.

"Where are you?" I ask, running as I put my shoes

on, the fear shooting up my spine. "Eva," I call her name when she doesn't answer me.

"Oh my God, Levi," she chokes out again, and I'm grabbing my keys and slamming the door shut behind me. I pull up her contact on my phone and press location, seeing she's at her house.

"I'm coming to you," I assure her. "I'll be there in ten minutes."

"Okay," is the only thing she says and all she does is sob quietly in my ear.

Three

Eva

I hear the car door closing from the phone and sit down on my couch. "Eva." I hear his voice, tight and worried, my hands shaking uncontrollably. "Where are you?" I shake my head. "I'll be there in ten minutes," he reassures me softly. "It's going to be okay." The tears just pour down my cheeks without a way to stop them. "Everything is going to be okay. Whatever it is."

"No, it's not," I whisper the words.

"What happened?" he asks and my stomach gets tight.

"I got a call from Lisa's neighbor," I start as my eyes close and two tears run down my cheeks, dripping off my chin.

"Your sister?" His voice is calm. "Is she okay?"

"I don't think so," I say, getting up. "Where are you?"

"Around the corner," he states, and I grab my bag and rush out of the front door, down the two steps toward the street. I look right and left until I see two headlights turn onto my road. He pulls up to the curb, putting the car in park, and rushing out of the driver's seat. His black hair looks like he ran his hands through it. His blue eyes that are usually clear look like they are clouded over, no doubt with his worry for me.

He pulls me into his arms without even thinking twice. "We have to go to Lisa's house," I sob into his chest, my arms by my sides.

"Let's get you in the car," he mumbles as he puts his arm around my shoulders and walks me to the passenger side of the car. He opens the door for me and slowly puts me in the seat, reaching across to buckle me in. "Put her address in the GPS." All I can do is nod at him as I look over at the middle part of his dashboard and press buttons while he walks around to the driver's side.

He gets in and all I can do is look at him. "Thank you," I whisper, my voice cracking. He grabs my hand in his, not saying anything. I turn my head to look out the window, replaying the past twenty minutes. "The police are waiting for me," I say, not turning my head. "They need to talk to me." The lights go by in the distance as my eyes try to focus on one, but it zooms by. "It can't be good." He never lets my hand go, and when we pull up to Lisa's apartment complex, I see two police cars parked in front.

"No lights are on," I observe when his hand slides out

of mine and he turns off the car. "That's good, right?"

"Let's get in there," he urges, getting out of the car and jogging to my side to help me out. He puts his hand in mine again as we walk up the sidewalk. The same walkway I use every other Monday night when we have dinner. It's every other week because we take turns. We also do it on Monday because it's my day off, so I don't have to rush.

I pull open the glass door with my free hand before walking up the stairs on the right. I make it to the fourth floor before I stop and look at her door. The mat in the front says Welcome. I look over at her neighbor's door, wondering if I should go there first. I don't have time to ask before the door is pulled open. Her neighbor, Gwen, stands there, her face streaked with tears, pretty much how mine looks.

"Eva," she whispers, "come in."

I walk in, looking to the right where the living room is. Two uniformed police officers are standing up, while two officers wearing suits are sitting down. A woman who has a briefcase in front of her sits at the table. "This is her sister," Gwen states, and my feet move without me even knowing they are moving.

"Ms. Crinkle," one of the suited police officers says, getting up. "I'm Detective McCaby."

"Ms. Meyers," I correct him, while Levi squeezes my hand in his. "Where is my sister?"

"I'm afraid we have bad news." The detective puts his hands in his pockets, staring down at the floor before looking back up. "There was an accident involving your sister."

"Is she at the hospital?" I ask hopefully, but even my brain knows it's worse than that. My brain is aware of why they are here. It's my heart—my heart is not sure I can survive another heartbreak. The other three officers avoid looking at me. Levi drops my hand and steps closer to me, putting his arm around my shoulders.

"There was an accident," the other detective starts. "Drunk driver sideswiped her, and she lost control of her car. The truck didn't see her." I gasp, but my ears start to buzz at this point, and I'm not sure I'm hearing what I'm hearing. "She didn't make it."

"Where is Cici?" I ask of my nine-month-old niece, her full name is Selena but since she was four hours old we've called her Cici, my knees getting ready to buckle with the news. Gwen quietly sits sobbing beside me with her hand in front of her mouth. The sound of a baby fills the room, and I wonder if I'm having an out-of-body moment. I wonder if I'm hearing things. I look around the room and Gwen rushes to her bedroom.

"She was alone in the vehicle." I don't even know who says it, my eyes go to Gwen's room.

"Oh, thank God," Levi says from beside me. I watch Gwen come out of her bedroom with Cici in her arms.

Her cheeks rosy from sleeping, I walk out of Levi's arms and go to Cici. "Hi, Stinky," I say to her and her face fills with a smile before she reaches out for me. I grab her under her arms and bring her to me, kissing her neck like I know she likes. "Someone is stinky," I lie. She smells like the lavender baby lotion I know Lisa always puts on her.

"Ms. Meyers." The woman who is at the table stands up. "My name is Josephine and I'm with Child Protective Services." My hand goes to Cici's back as she says this. "I'm going to have a few questions for you."

"Okay," I answer her as Cici puts her head on my shoulder, snuggling down.

"From what we found in the system, there is no father listed on the birth certificate." I don't know if she is asking me or telling me.

"No, there wouldn't be," I confirm, "she went through the sperm bank and did IVF." I rock side to side with Cici and I'm not even aware I'm doing it. "I didn't think it was a good idea to put his case file number on there, so she opted to leave it blank." The memory comes back to when she was filling out the papers in the hospital. She looked like she went through war, but she also never looked more beautiful and happier in her life. "Why are you asking this?"

"The law requires that the baby be placed in CPS care until things are straightened out," Josephine explains, and it's Levi who steps up.

"What do you mean, things are straightened out?" he asks for me.

"Well, does your sister have a will?" Josephine asks me.

"She must have a will." I defend Lisa. "She wouldn't have had a baby without a father and then not have a will."

"Since there is no father," Josephine starts, "it's the

law that a will is produced to see what the wishes were of the parent."

"I'm the only one she has," I say and I know they must know. "My sister was in the system her whole life. In and out of foster homes. You must know this, obviously." My tone is of anger, at everyone.

"Right," Josephine agrees. "The good news is that once the will is processed and we can affirm it is the only will on file, then we can proceed. But until then—" She wrings her hands. "We are going to have to place the baby in emergency foster care." The minute the words are out of her mouth, I feel like I'm going to be sick.

"There has to be something we can do," Levi argues for me because all I can do is rock back and forth. "She's her sister. Her only next of kin. There has to be something we can do. I don't know, maybe give us a couple of days."

"I'm aware of that," Josephine says, "but the law." Her voice trails off, and I can't even imagine how hard her job is.

"How long?" I look at Josephine. "How long until I can get her? How long until all of this is taken care of?"

"It's hard to say," Josephine sidesteps, "it could be a month." I gasp, holding Cici even closer to my chest. "Or longer."

"What about shorter?" Levi asks her. "There has to be, I don't know, some fast pass somewhere."

"The best thing to do would be for you to get the will. She would have had a lawyer," Josephine advises.

I look over at Gwen, handing Cici back to her. "She

has a bag," I say to Josephine, knowing it's not her fault. It kills me to admit this, but I will have to let her go, but I tell myself it won't be for long. I look over at Gwen. "Is her door open?" She nods, and I walk out of the room. Of course, Josephine isn't far away from me. But right behind her is Levi, who is watching everything. I walk into the house and see the toys on the floor mat, knowing Lisa probably said she would clean it up later, right before she walked out only to never return. I go to the nursery, turn on the light, and see the pink room come to life. I walk to the corner of the room and grab the diaper bag from the closet. "She has special pj's and a sleep sack." I grab the white folded sack that is hanging over the crib. "She has a stuffy she likes to hold on to when she is rocked, but don't put it in the crib because she could suffocate." I take the stuffy from the bed and put it in the bag as tears flow down my face. I wish I could stop them. I wish I could be strong, but I'm not. I have to get through this, then I can have my breakdown. "She takes a bath every night before bed," I tell her. "And she puts on this lotion. It's supposed to make them sleep longer." I hold up the purple bottle. "I don't know if it works, but we do it anyway."

"Eva." Levi says my name softly, and I look over at him. "I can get the stuff." He comes to me, putting his hand around my waist. "You can sit with Cici for a bit."

"She has a special formula," I continue, walking out of the room to the kitchen. "We don't know if she's lactose intolerant yet, but the other formula gave her tummy aches," I inform her, grabbing the can that is right beside the fridge and putting it in the bag. I walk over to the fridge and grab the two cans that are on top of it.

It's when I'm grabbing the second can that I see the lawyer card in the middle of the fridge. I put it in the bag and look at Levi. "Can you take this card?" I ask, motioning with my chin toward the fridge. He walks over to it and grabs the card, putting it in his pocket.

We walk out of the apartment, going back over to Gwen's place. She is holding Cici in her arms. "Is there a car seat?" Josephine asks me and I look back at her.

"In the car," I state, and she just nods.

"I'll go and get mine," Josephine says to us, "and give you a chance to say goodbye." I glance over at Levi, who looks at me.

"You want to make a run for it?" I ask, and he nods.

"I'm game if you are." He puts his arm around my shoulders.

Gwen comes to us and hands me Cici. I walk over to the side with her, looking outside. "I know you miss your mom," I soothe as she looks at me and smiles with a big old dollop of drool. "It's going to be weird for a bit, you'll be with people you don't know, but I promise you that I'm going to get you back. I'll do it as fast as I can, but you've got to be tough, baby girl." I pull her to me and she sinks into me. "Promise you, I'll come and get you."

When I turn around, I see Josephine is there with a car seat. Gwen is sobbing into a white tissue and Levi looks like he's about to literally take the baby and run. I walk over to the car seat and put her in as her feet start to kick in excitement. "Be good," I tell her, leaning and kissing her cheek.

"Where will you be taking her?" I ask Josephine and she smiles tightly.

"I'm not allowed to disclose that," she shares, walking over to her bag, "but this is my number and that is the case file." I nod, looking down at the card in my hand.

"The lawyer will call you tomorrow," Levi assures her. "We'll also be getting our own attorney."

"Good idea," she says, picking up the car seat.

I pick up the diaper bag and look over at Gwen. "I'll pass by tomorrow sometime." She just nods at me. "Call me if you need anything."

Levi takes the bag from my hand as we follow Josephine down the steps toward her car. We buckle Cici in and watch her drive away.

"Are you okay?" he asks and I just shake my head.

"I'm one hundred and seventy-five million percent the opposite of okay." I wipe my nose. "Jesus Christ, what the fuck?" I look over at him and ask him, "Like what the fuck have I done in my life that this shit keeps happening to me?"

"Let's get you home," he urges me, ushering me to his car. It's only then that I notice the police cars are gone. "I have three cards to give you," he says once he's driving me back home.

"Do you want me to stay?" he asks when he pulls up in my driveway.

"No," I tell him, reaching out to the door handle. "I need some space."

"Call me if you need anything."

I nod at him as he hands me the three white cards. My hand grabs them as I get out and walk back into my house. I walk straight to the kitchen, open the freezer, and take the tequila out. I don't even bother with a glass; instead, I take a gulp, swallowing and choking before looking down at the cards.

I take my phone out of my pocket and pull up one of my clients who has been with me since the very beginning, she is the one I go to for any law questions.

Me: *Hey, it's me, can you call me tomorrow from the office?*

I press send, looking down to see it's just after midnight and I'm wondering if I should have just waited until the morning.

I take another sip of tequila before my phone pings, and I think it's Levi. Picking it up, I'm surprised it's Alice.

Alice: *Is this official business?*

Me: *Sure is.*

Two seconds after I send the text, my phone rings. "Hello," I answer, closing my eyes. "I'm so sorry, did I wake you?"

"Yes," she answers honestly, "but it's a part of the job." I hear the sheets rustle from her side of the phone as I walk over to the couch. "Are you home or have you been arrested?"

"I am home," I tell her and the tears come. "There was an accident and my sister died."

Even saying the words are surreal.

Alice hisses, "Oh my God, I'm so sorry. Shit."

"I have a nine-month-old niece," I inform her. "What would it take for me to get custody of her?"

"Does she have a will?" is the first question she asks me.

"Probably, she was on top of things," I tell her. "There was a lawyer card on the fridge. I'm assuming she left it there in case of…" I close my eyes and lean back on the couch.

"We have to see what it says in the will," she advises. "Where is the child now?"

"CPS has her," I tell her, and this is when Alice groans.

"Fuck," she curses. "She's going to be in the system now, no matter what."

"What?" I say, sitting up shocked. "She didn't tell me that."

"Well, of course she isn't going to tell you that," Alice says. "They have to look at the will and see what that says, but…" She trails off. "Now that she's with the State, there will be follow-up and spot visits to make sure the child is okay. Listen." Her voice goes lower. "I love you. You know that, right?" I don't say anything as I wait for her to finish because nothing good can come from a "you know I love you but" chat. "Off the record, and this is not me talking, but

it would sure look better if you were married on paper."

I sit up and shriek, "What?"

"Listen, I know it's the twentieth century and all that, but you go into this married, it's just easier." I put my hand on my head.

"She went to a sperm bank!" I yell. "She was able to do it all alone, and now you're telling me that if I was married, it would be easier for me to get my niece from the State? Even though there is no other family?" I shake my head. "This makes no sense. That's crazy, there are single moms out there. Trust me, I know, half of them come to my spa."

"There are, but those single moms out there," she says, "weren't granted a baby through their family members. They created them with whatever means they chose." Okay, fine, she has me there. "Just think about it."

"Think about what?" I ask, shocked that maybe I misunderstood and laugh bitterly.

"Is there an app out there I don't know of that has a husband for hire?" I don't know if it's the booze I drank, the shock of losing my sister, or I'm just going insane.

"Oh, that could be a good idea," Alice replies. "I bet it would be successful."

I close my eyes, knowing I might regret asking the next question. "Okay, let's talk about the husband idea. What does that entail?"

Four

Levi

As soon as I open the door, my body does a sigh of relief. I toss my keys and wallet onto the glass table by the door before I kick off my running shoes. I dump my gym bag at the door before turning to walk into the kitchen. After tossing and turning all night, I got up. It's Saturday and I still went in to work today. I've been gone a couple of weeks, so it was easier to get in there when no one else was there and do some paperwork. After I spent five hours in the office, I decided I would hit up the gym. Big mistake there since it's been a couple of weeks since I've stepped in the gym, every single part of my body is now screaming at me. Even though I took a shower at the gym, I know I'm going to take another hot one before going to bed.

I go straight for the fridge, expecting by some miracle there is something in there I can eat. Opening it, I let out a huge breath seeing that there is, in fact, nothing for me to eat in there. Instead, I grab a bottle of beer from the door before reaching for the freezer door to see if maybe there is something in there I can put in the oven and doesn't take a million years. It isn't much better in there.

Pulling a box of frozen pizza from the shelf, I make my way over to start the oven. I tear open the paper box before grabbing a knife to slide through the plastic wrapper and placing it on a rack. Shutting the door, I then set the timer to twenty-three minutes.

Twisting off the cap to the beer and taking a pull of it, I grab the phone out of my pocket. I go immediately to my text thread with Eva, pulling it up.

Me: How are you holding up?

I send the text and decide I am going to give her thirty minutes before I call her. I had tried to call her earlier today but all I got back was a text that said:

Eva: Sorry, on the phone, call you in five minutes.

That was this morning at seven and nothing all day. I put the phone to the side as I grab the bottle of beer, taking another pull when I hear the soft knock of the door. Putting the beer back down on the counter, I look over at the hallway to see if maybe I made a mistake when the knock comes even harder this time. I round the corner and unlock the door, pulling it open without looking into the peephole. My mouth hangs open when I see her standing there. She's wearing jeans and a white

T-shirt. Her hair is piled on top of her head, not a stitch of makeup on her face. Her eyes are red from crying, no doubt, and she looks like she hasn't slept all night, but she still looks beautiful as she holds two brown takeout bags in her hands.

"Hey," Eva greets softly as she walks into the house.

"Hey." I open my arms for her and she walks into them as I wrap my arms around her shoulders. "I was worried about you."

"Sorry." She steps out of my arms. "I was going to text you, but one thing led to another and another, and well, here I am." I watch her eyes as she blinks them really, really fast, right before I know she's going to cry. I put my arm around her as I walk her toward the kitchen. "I brought you dinner."

"You are a godsend," I tell her as my hand drops from her shoulders as she walks to the island, putting the bags on top of it. "What did you get?"

She looks over her shoulder, smirking. "You really think you need to be picky right now?" she asks with a chuckle, and I can't help but put my hands on my hips.

"I'm not being picky." I tilt my head. "I was being excited." I clap my hands together. "What did you get?" My chipper voice sounds fake.

"Ass," she mumbles, turning her attention back to the bags. "I'm going to just eat all this food myself."

She looks over her shoulder at me. "You can have that frozen pizza in the oven. That probably has been in your freezer for the past six months."

I pfft out at her. "No, it hasn't," I retort, not even sure

I believe myself since I don't think I've been home more than twenty days in the past four months.

She takes the brown containers out. "That's a lie and even you know it." She looks down at the four containers she has taken out of the bags. "Now because I'm the best friend and bessst person you've ever met." She drags out the word best as she smiles sweetly, before turning and walking over to the drawers to grab a couple of forks and knives. She pushes the drawer closed with her hip. "I will share with you the food I bought for you." She moves over to the oven and turns it off. "Don't forget to throw that out later or else it'll still be in there at Thanksgiving."

"I'm not that bad." I roll my eyes at her and she just raises her eyebrows as she comes closer to me. I pull out one of the two stools for her to sit on before pulling out the second one for me. We sit down at the same time and I reach out to grab the first closed container. "This one is light," I note, opening it and seeing that it's a salad. "Eww." I toss it to her. "That's yours for sure."

"There is nothing wrong with a salad, Levi," she declares as she takes the container from me and I grab the other one.

"Now this one must be mine," I decide, feeling how heavy it is as I open it and see it's chicken parm with a side of pasta. "Yup, mine."

"You didn't even see what is in the other ones." She points at the other two that are on the counter. "What if that was mine?"

"Then I would say I really hope there's another one

of those that has this in it." I point down to the container in front of me.

"You're the worst," she says, leaning forward to grab the other one and when she opens it my mouth waters. "This is not for you." She side-eyes me, putting the shrimp scampi on pasta to the side of her salad. Grabbing the other one, I watch to see what was behind door number three that, apparently, I lost. My mouth waters even more when I see that it's a huge meatball smothered in sauce with a side of ricotta.

"That's to share." I grab a fork and knife from beside her. "No way can you eat all that meat."

"I can eat plenty of meat," she retorts, snickering as I stay still when I look over at her. "I might not like balls in my face, but I'm very okay with meat."

"Eeew." I fake vomiting while I cut a piece of chicken. "I never want to have a picture of you with balls in your face and meat."

"The balls are not in my face," she reminds me, grabbing the shrimp plate, "they are usually on my chin." She twirls the spaghetti on her spoon. "Unless it's like upside down and the balls are in my face."

"Are you trying to make me give up this chicken parm?" I ask as I put a piece in my mouth. "Because it's not working." I grab another piece of chicken, looking over at her. "How are you doing, for real?"

"I think I'm still in shock." She avoids looking at me. "It's strange, I know. It's not like we grew up together or anything like that." She shrugs.

"She was still your sister," I say softly.

"I know," she murmurs and I see her pushing her food around in front of her, "and she was really an amazing person, even with all the shit that was thrown at her." Her fork drops from her hands, and she wipes a tear away from her cheek. "My heart is broken for Cici because she'll never know."

I drop my own fork and put my arm around her shoulders, bringing her to me as I kiss her temple. "I have no doubt you are going to make sure she doesn't forget her." I put my head on top of hers.

She takes a deep inhale and I let her go, picking up my fork again. "I met with my lawyer today."

I stare at her. "Why didn't you call me?" She just shrugs and I know this shouldn't surprise me since she is always used to doing things on her own, but I'm pissed I couldn't be there for her. "You should have called me."

"It's okay." She avoids looking at me. "She's a lawyer who is also my client."

"That's good." I twirl some spaghetti on my fork. "What did she say?" I ask before I put the forkful in my mouth.

"Well," she says, smiling when she turns to me, "she has a will, so that is a good thing. She had everything taken care of." Her voice gets thick. "And I mean everything. Her lawyer already contacted the funeral home where she will be cremated tomorrow. She doesn't even want a service. She just wanted to be cremated and put in the urn she picked out herself." I know that she is babbling in an effort not to cry or freak out. "And she is to be placed in her final resting place that is in a mausoleum." She swallows the lump in her throat. "She left me Cici, so that should be easy, but…" Her voice is happy as she trails off.

"But what?" I ask, not sure what she is going to say. "It's in her will. She is giving you Cici. There is no but, right?"

"Funny you should ask." Her voice sounds really weird, making me stop chewing. "I need a favor."

I don't even hesitate, never, not with her. "Anything," I say, grabbing my beer and taking a pull.

"Good, glad you said that." She puts her hand on mine. "Makes this easier," she mumbles. "Even though she has a will and I get Cici without anyone contesting it. There is still just a little bit of a hiccup." She closes her finger and thumb together. "A little bit of an issue." She turns to me and all I can do is stare at her and hold my breath. She puts on the fakest, biggest smile I've ever seen on her face. I have no idea what the favor is, and not going to lie, I'm a little scared right now. I don't know what I was expecting her to ask me, but I will say I was definitely not expecting the words that came out of her mouth. "Will you marry me?"

My hand is in the process of putting the bottle of beer back down on the counter when it stops mid-action. I shake my head. "Excuse me?" I say, not sure I heard what she said. I laugh nervously. "I could have sworn you said." I put the bottle of beer down or maybe it just falls out of my hand, landing with a thud. "You said marry you." I shake my head again and laugh, thinking how ridiculous that sounds. When I don't hear her laughing, I turn back to look at her. "You have got to be kidding me." My voice goes higher than I want it to go, almost shriek-like. "What the fuck?" my mouth spits out, and my heart beats so fast in my chest I think it's going to come out. I push my stool away from the counter, jumping off it. "Are you insane?" I walk around the counter, the nerves filling my body. I open the oven and take the pizza out. "Are you joking?" I ask as I toss the soggy, half-cooked, half-defrosted pizza in the trash. "Are you going to jump up and say gotcha anytime soon?" I stand here waiting for her to say it, waiting for her to tell me I didn't hear what I think I did. Waiting for her to tell me anything.

She pushes the container in front of her away and I put my hands on my hips, the buzzing starting in my ears. "Come on, Levi," she urges, "I would do it for you." She throws her hands in the air as if she is asking me to take her laundry to the cleaners or borrow my car for a month.

"You would do it for me?" I say sarcastically. "You would marry me?" I put my hand to my chest. "I'm honored." I'm hoping like fuck she gets that this is me in the middle of having a mental freak-out.

She smiles at me. "You're welcome."

I stare at her, waiting to see when the joke will be up. I count to five in my head, even with Mississippi. After five I scream, and this time I know it's a scream because she grimaces. "I was joking with you."

"Oh." She laughs nervously. "Well, I guess we know who the better friend is." She puts her hands on her hips and my hands immediately go up to hold my head, expecting it to feel like it's going to explode like a ticking time bomb.

"Are you insane?" I ask again, because all the other words feel like they are jumbled in my head. She has to be insane. This is probably shock, she's in shock and becoming delirious.

"I'm not insane." She holds up her hand before I yell. "Hear me out." She walks around the counter and comes to stand next to me. "It'll just be for a year." My hands are still on my head. "Then we can annul it." She tilts her head to the side and smiles. "You know, since we actually won't be." She picks up her hand, puts her thumb and index finger in a circle, then takes the other hand and inserts her forefinger into the circle's center. "You know." She moves her finger in and out. "Going to Pound Town." All I can do is stare at her, and all she can do is continue moving her fucking finger.

"Stop that." I finally knock her hands away from each other. "What are you... twelve?"

"We get married." She ignores my question. "Then the judge sees that I'm married on paper." She smiles at me. "To a good guy." I glare at her. "To a great guy. The best guy."

I really hope my glare is like the look that kills. "Don't try to fluff my ego," I bark out and put my hand on the counter next to me, not sure if I'm putting it there to help hold me up if my knees give out as she tells me about this ridiculous plan.

She rolls her eyes at me. "Fine, he sees I'm married to just an okay guy, then." I shake my head. "I get my niece." She points at herself, then to me. "And you get a cool story to tell the boys."

"Tell the boys?" I repeat what she just said.

"I don't know what to call men who are friends. Are they not called boys? Is that not the term? Or is it bros now?" she rambles on. "I could never keep up with the cool kids or their sayings."

"They are just called friends," I inform her.

"Okay, fine." She folds her arms over her chest. "You get to tell your 'friends'"—she uses her fingers in quotation marks when she uses the word friends—"what a cool guy you are. Is that better?"

"We don't do that," I refute between clenched teeth. I'm irritated about this whole thing and that she is really not backing down on it. She's actually serious.

"Okay, fine. I'll tell your friends what a cool guy you are." She stares at me. "Is that better?

I'll hold meetings monthly just to tell them how cool you are, if that is going to help."

I close my eyes. "You can't really be asking me this?" I say softly, looking at her and seeing her eyes are now filled with tears.

"You said anything." Her voice is low, and I hear it trail off.

"I said anything, like lend me money?" I reply to her. "Or, can I borrow your couch?" I watch her. "Can you drive me to wherever? I did not mean get married to me."

"Oh, please." She throws up her hands. "It's not like you have anything going on." Her voice gets louder. "And I'd be the best fake wife you've ever had. I would even turn a blind eye and you can keep doing what you're doing."

I roll my eyes at her. "And what is that?" Now, I'm the one folding their hands over my chest.

"I've been here ten minutes." She looks from the kitchen that leads into the living room, where all my furniture is black and leather. "And I feel like I've stepped into a sex dungeon."

I'm shocked at this, turning toward what she was looking at. Okay, maybe the leather couches and the dark-brown dining room table, that to be honest, I've never eaten food on but I have done other things on there. Even the tray in the middle of the black coffee table hides condoms, just in case. "I'm a bachelor," I mumble to myself, thinking that this is how we live, isn't it? "Seriously?"

I turn back to her and this time she drops on her knee in front of me. "Levi Mathison," she states my full name, grabbing my hand. Her blue eyes fill with tears and fear. The smile on her face is fake as can be. But it's her hands that are shaking under mine that I look at while she says, "Will you marry me?"

Five

Eva

$\mathcal{M}$y hands are literally shaking, my whole body is tense and strung out. My head is screaming at me that this is the worst idea I've had in my whole life, and believe me, I've had some of the worst fucking ideas in life. Like, for example, when I thought I would be able to sew my own clothes. It took me over six months of saving to buy a secondhand sewing machine, only to figure out I fucking hated every single second of it. Then I thought I would knit a sweater, except all I knew how to knit was a straight line so I did scarfs. I wish I could say they were nice, but they were not. There were big holes in them, and that went away quickly. Now this right here standing, well actually, on my knee in Levi's kitchen is at the top of that list. It is the dumbest thing I've ever done, but it is also the only thing I can control. "Cat got your tongue?" I ask Levi, trying not to laugh in his face. The nerves are now running through my body. His face has gone from shocked to pale, and I hope he won't faint on me.

"Oh my God, Eva," he groans, and I drop my hand when he steps away.

"Okay, how about," I start to say, "we just meet with my lawyer?" I hold up my hand to stop him from talking when he opens his mouth. "You can ask her any questions you want." I don't know if I hold my breath or not, but every single second that ticks by feels like an eon.

"I can't believe I'm even discussing this," he finally relents and all I can do is jump off the floor and launch myself into his arms. My arms go around his neck and his arms go around my waist as I give him a hug. I bury my face in his neck, feeling safe as always in his arms.

Before putting my hands on his shoulders, I look into his eyes. "Thank you, thank you, thank you." My hands slap his shoulders with each word, before pushing off him and being put on my feet.

"Don't thank me just yet," he mumbles, "we still have to meet with the lawyer." He rubs his face with his hands.

"Oh, come on." I place my hip against the counter. "It's not going to be that bad." Even though I say the words out loud, my head screams, *it's going to be so much worse than just this.*

"I don't know about that." He looks down and back up.

"Listen, I know it will be hard for you to even think of committing yourself for a full year. That's three hundred and sixty-five days. To someone who never, ever had a relationship longer than a four-day weekend fuck fest, which was only because your flight kept getting canceled, this is like eighty-four years." I fold my arms over my chest as he glares at me. "But I promise I will make it as easy as I can." I hold up my three fingers. "Scout's honor."

"One, it was three and a half days, and if it had been a second longer, my dick would have fallen off." He holds his hand up with one finger.

"Barf." I fake vomit at the thought of his dick falling off, or of his dick in general. There is something to be said about being best friends with a guy who you don't find at all attractive. I mean he's hot, sure, and I can appreciate the view, but the mere thought of doing anything sexual with him makes me want to gag. It could also be because I know if we cross that line, we can never get what we have back. And I'm not willing to lose that for a thirty-second orgasm.

"And two, if I wanted to be in a relationship, I would be." He puts up another finger and my eyebrows go up. "I don't want a relationship because I don't have the time to put into a relationship right now."

"Okay, there." I nod, saying sure, but not pointing out that he makes time for me whenever he's in town. He texts me at least once a day, even if it's to send me a stupid video.

He tilts his head to the side, and I know he can see

through me. "How are you doing though?" His voice goes soft, and I roll my eyes and look away from him as I try to blink away the tears that are dying to come out. Tears I know that once one falls, it'll be a while before they stop. All day long, I've done what I needed to in order not to let my brain stop and think of what happened.

Of course, he would ask me this. I take a deep inhale as I try to get my heart under control so I don't lose my handle on the tears but then I just collapse. "I don't know really." I put my hand on the counter as I look over his shoulder toward the window. "I'm a bit all over the place," I finally get out. "I went to work today just so I wouldn't sit down and have to think about it." I look at him and see his eyes stare into mine. "If I stop and take a minute, I'm afraid I'm going to completely fall apart." I blink away quickly as my eyes start to burn. "And no one has time for that." I see him take a step toward me and I hold up my hand to stop him. "If you go soft on me, I'm going to take back my marriage proposal."

He takes a huge inhale before he looks at me. "Make the appointment."

I smile so big. "Tomorrow morning at ten."

He stares at me as his mouth hangs open, then closes when he presses his teeth together and hisses out, "Fine, text me the address."

"Will do. Do you mind if I get out of here?" I ask, motioning with my head to the front door. "I need to just…"

"Go." He pushes off from the counter. "Text me when you get home."

"You literally have my location on your phone," I remind him as he walks me to the front door. He opens the door for me, and I get on my tippy-toes to kiss his cheek. "Thank you for tonight," I tell him, "and also, you should open a couple of windows; it smells like a frat house in here. Like feet and Doritos."

He huffs again. "It's my gym bag." He points at the bag beside our feet.

"It also smells like—" He puts a finger on my lips.

"I haven't had sex here in over a month, if not longer, so now I know you're lying." His eyes shine bright.

I push his finger away from my mouth. "I was going to say it smells like Axe body spray." I turn to walk out of his place and to the elevator.

"You can stop watching me now," I call over my shoulder.

"I'm just making sure that you get in the elevator safe." He leans against the doorjamb. "Besides, if you end up on *Dateline,* I'm not going to be the asshole who didn't watch you get into the elevator."

The elevator pings, and I step into it, pressing the L button before looking at him. "You can close your door now. If I get murdered, you'll look like a bang-up guy who didn't even walk me to my car." He looks at me, shocked. "After my sister died," I toss out right before the doors close and see him racing toward the elevator. I can't help the tears from rolling down my cheeks as I swallow down the lump in my throat. Today has, without a doubt, been the hardest day I've ever had, and even when I buried my grandmother, this is ten times worse because of Cici. I went to work thinking everything was going to be okay, but it wasn't. I told Raquel, and she told me she would take care of everything. For once, I let her, and I spent the rest of the time on the phone with Lisa's lawyer and then my lawyer. I wasn't surprised Lisa had everything in place. That was just the thing she would do to make sure she was taken care of and so was Cici. She never wanted to be a burden to anyone, not even in death.

I don't even know how I make it home. I don't even know what route I took or if there was traffic. All I know is I walk into my house and go straight for the stairs to my bedroom. My house. A house I worked my ass off to buy. A house that is small but perfect. A house I've wanted all my life.

I walk through my bedroom to my bathroom, turning on the water in the tub before sliding out of my jeans and T-shirt. The room is in darkness still, the only light is from the outside coming into the open shades. I sink into the deep tub I had put in after I moved in, because the tub before was small and I wanted to be able to sink into the water. I submerge into the water, wetting my hair. I tilt my head back before coming out of the water. This time I don't know if it's my tears that are wetting my face or if it's the water from the bath. I look to the side as memories of my sister run through my head like a movie over and over again. Staying in the water until it's ice cold, I slip on my robe and head straight to my bed. Tossing the covers back, I don't even bother taking off the throw pillows before putting my head down.

Sleep doesn't come, or if it does it's in spurts of ten to fifteen minutes. I toss from one side to the other before finally giving up and walking downstairs. I grab one of my coffee mugs before putting a pod into the machine and pressing the button. I wait for the last drop before moving to the stainless-steel fridge and grabbing the milk. Once I fill the cup with the right amount of milk, I walk back upstairs to get ready for the day.

I put my cup of coffee down on the side table, right near the frame of Cici and myself on the day of her christening. I smile down at it as one lone tear falls down my cheek. I grab my phone and google how long a nine-month-old can remember things. I press enter and start down the rabbit hole to make sure that in the amount of time Cici will be without me she isn't going to suffer a trauma from being ripped away from her mother. I'm in a sobbing fit by the time I put the phone down and walk over to get ready for the lawyer.

I pull out a black pair of capri pants that are tight on the hips and go wide on the way down. Slipping my sleeveless, black silk top off the hanger and putting it over my head, I'm tucking it in when I hear the front doorbell ring and the door open. "Eva." I hear Levi's voice.

"Upstairs, in my room!" I holler and hear his footsteps come closer and closer until he stands at the entrance to the bedroom. He's wearing blue jeans and a baby-blue button-down shirt rolled from the wrist to his elbow.

"Hey," he says, looking at my face, "you okay?"

"I'm fine. I just—" I look down and let the tears come.

"I just don't want her to think I just gave her away." I wring my hands together.

"Eva." He says my name and comes to me, taking me into his arms. He smells like soap and his aftershave. "She's not even going to remember this."

"It takes a month," I inform him. "At six months, they forget after two weeks. Nine months it's a month and a half." He looks down at me. "Google." I put my head back on his chest as he rubs my back. "Good news is they don't understand the concept of time. It could be six hours or six months to them, it's all the same."

"How about we don't google anything for a while?" he suggests.

"Good idea." I step away from him and wipe my eyes. "How do I look?"

"Amazing," he replies, and I can't help but laugh when I know he's lying. "A little rough, if we're being honest." He picks up a strand of my hair. "Are we brushing our hair or is this the new look?"

"Are we going for the slicked-back mobster look?" I ask of his hair that is pushed back and combed to the side.

"Ummm." He puts his hands on his hips. "I got this look from your salon two weeks ago." He pats his hair. "It was all the rage."

I nod before going to the bathroom and looking at my hair. It's all over the place because I went to bed with it wet. I don't have time to tame it, so instead, I brush through it before separating it in the middle and putting it back at the nape of my neck in a ponytail. I walk out of the bathroom seeing Levi sitting on my bed, his head down, looking at his phone. "Better?" I ask, and he looks up.

"You look like a mom," he responds to me and I smile sadly. "Let's go so I can get you some coffee."

I nod, grabbing my phone and the coffee cup before walking back down to the kitchen and putting the cup in the sink, then sliding on my black heels at the door. I grab my purse while Levi holds the door open for me, and the two of us make it to his car. I get in, and neither of us says anything. I'm sure his head is spinning as much as mine is.

When we get to the office, he puts the car in park, looking over at me. "You ready?" he asks.

"No." I reach out to the door handle. "You?"

"Absolutely not," he returns, reaching out and opening his door. I wait for him to join me before walking over to the glass door.

I pull open the door and step in, seeing Alice there waiting for us. "Welcome. Sorry, it's Sunday, so there is no one here but me."

"It's more than okay. Thank you for making time," I tell her as I step in. "This is Levi." I introduce her, and he extends his hand to her.

"Pleasure," he states, shaking her hand.

"Come with me." Alice turns and walks down the hallway to her office. "Sit anywhere you like." She waits for us to step into her office before she follows us in.

Levi puts his hand on the lower part of my back, ushering me to the two chairs that face her big mahogany desk. I sit down and look over to see Levi sitting beside me. Alice walks around the desk and sits down in the big brown chair. "Okay." She smiles sadly at me. "The good news is we didn't find another will, so what they have is the only one."

"That's good, right?" I ask and Alice nods.

"Does that mean she doesn't need a husband?" Levi asks, and she looks at Levi.

"Like I was telling Eva," she starts, "Cici is in the system, and even though she will gain custody of her, the State will still have visits. Eva will still have to go through all the steps in order to make it official to be her primary caretaker. Now keep in mind, there are many single parents out there, but it just looks better on paper when it's a couple and not a single lady, who just bought a house. Her business is taking off, but still, it's paid off."

"Okay, so say we do this," Levi says. "What does it entail?"

"Well, usually, after a year, things die down. So worst case, you stay married for a year," Alice explains. "If things move faster, then you get divorced faster."

"Does he need to move in with me?" I ask Alice.

"Obviously, the two of you have to move in with each other. So it shows you are married. It's what married people do."

"I have to move in with her?" Levi now asks, confused. "What about my place?"

"You can still keep your place," Alice replies, "there isn't any law against that."

I don't even hear what else Alice says, I'm more

focused on Levi and wondering how he is feeling. "If you have any questions," Alice offers and I look over to see her standing up and Levi following her.

I get up and walk out, thanking her again. "I'll call and let you know what we decide," I tell her as I follow Levi out.

We walk to the car and I look over at him. "You can say no," I tell him, "I can always just get her when I'm single."

He turns and looks at me. "You know what pisses me off the most?" He puts his hands on his hips. "If the roles were reversed and you came to me, and I asked you to marry me for whatever reason…" He looks up at the sky. "You would do it without thinking twice."

"Well, yeah. Obviously. You need my help, I'm there."

I wait, holding my breath as he paces back and forth in front of me, no doubt having a whole conversation in his head about this. "Fine," he huffs. "What's the worst that can happen?"

Six

Levi

I look over my shoulder at the door we just walked out of, my head trying to process all the information Alice just gave me. I then look back at Eva as she stands there, her face pale, her eyes a bit puffy from probably crying all night long. I look up to the sky right before I start pacing back and forth. *You can't do this,* one part of my head says, while the other part of my brain tells me, *you have no choice but to do this.* This is insane and totally crazy. This is never going to work. *You can do this,* the other part of my brain says. *You have to do it. She would do it for you.* I stop and look over at Eva, knowing hands down if the roles were reversed, she would have already been married to me. It would have been instant, and it would have been without a second thought. I would not have to talk her into it. I would not have to have her jump through hoops. I would not have to do any of that because that's the friend she is. "Fine," I huff, my heart hammering in my chest so much it's about to explode. "What's the worst that can happen?"

"Well." She folds her arms over her chest. "Worst thing that can happen is I'm the best wife in the world. And I have to force you to divorce me." She winks at me, the smile on her face is so big. "Then it gets awkward and I have to tell the judge that you just don't do it for me. And you came up short in the bedroom."

"There is nothing short in my bedroom." I semi-glare at her and she just shrugs her shoulders.

"So you say," she mumbles to herself.

I chuckle at her. "We should do this before I change my mind." I walk over to the car, opening my door and stop to look over the hood at her. "We really are doing this?"

"Yes." She nods before taking a deep breath in, but I don't see her exhale as she holds it in. The wind picks up and her ponytail flies to the side.

"Should we go to Vegas?" I ask, looking at my watch and seeing it's almost eleven. If we got on a flight in the next two hours, it would take six hours to get there, wasting a lot of time.

"Vegas might be good. I mean, that is where everyone else I know goes to elope."

"Who is everyone you know?" I ask, pulling out my phone, looking down at it when she starts talking and I have to look up.

"Britney Spears." She holds up one finger. "Kourtney Kardashian." She holds up another finger. "Joe Jonas. Jennifer Lopez and Ben Affleck."

"You don't know those people, Eva," I remind her, "those are celebrities."

"You don't know everything about me, Levi." She glares at me. "I have other friends."

"Shall we invite your friends to our wedding, then?" I ask, trying not to laugh.

"No, because they don't know you," she chuffs as she opens the car door and gets in, slamming it, and all I can do is laugh.

I open my own door and get in, starting the car and putting the phone on Bluetooth. As soon as it's connected, I look for the contact and call the only person who, sadly, will know what to do in this situation. I mean, he might not know what to do exactly, but he's with someone who would know. I click the phone button and Eva looks at the middle console; her eyes go big as she grabs on to my arm and squeezes when he picks up.

"Hey," he answers after the second ring and before Eva can talk me out of calling him.

"Hey," I greet back quickly, "how are you doing?"

I look over at Eva, who shakes her head and mouths, "I'm not here," as she motions to her neck with her hand and shakes her head. "Can't complain," he replies. "What about you?"

This whole conversation is strained and I have no doubt Stefano feels it as well. "Yeah, yeah, it's good," I say. "Are you home?"

"I am," he confirms. "Is everything okay with you?"

"Um, yeah," I say, glancing at the screen, then looking out my window. "Listen, Eva and I are going to come visit with you tomorrow."

"Eva," he says her name, "and you"—his voice stops—"are coming to visit with me tomorrow?" He repeats my words and I close my eyes thinking maybe I should have just shown up at his place.

"Yeah," I state as if it's nothing and look over at Eva, who just shakes her head and mouths, "Idiot."

"Is something wrong?" Stefano asks, his voice going low, and I hear he's walking fast. "Should I come to you guys? Where is Eva?"

"She's—" I start to say when I roll my eyes as I think of an excuse but nothing, and I mean nothing, is coming to me, my mind is a blank canvas. Actually, the only thing that is coming to me is I will probably be married by this time next week. Married. I open my left hand to see my finger. Will I wear a ring?

"I'm right here," Eva pipes up, smacking my right arm to snap me out of my freak-out.

"You're next to Levi, and you guys are coming down tomorrow?" he questions. I hear ringing and look down at my phone to see he's trying to FaceTime us.

"What do I do?" I whisper over to Eva, who grabs the phone out of my hand.

"You're the worst," she whispers back, pressing the green button. She waits for the white circle to go around and say it's connecting and Stefano's face fills the screen.

He brings the phone close to his face. "Why does she look like that?" he grinds between clenched teeth. "Levi, did you do something?" I glare over at the phone, putting my head back on the headrest. "Listen, it's too much to explain right now," Eva explains, "but I know you, and you'll go all apeshit crazy."

"Batshit crazy," I correct her, "it's you who is going batshit crazy."

"Really?" she growls between clenched teeth. "Now you want to correct me?" She doesn't even let me answer. "Anyway, before you alert the whole Greek family and they start descending on me, I'm fine, he's fine." She motions with her head toward me. "But there is something we need to talk about, and we will do it tomorrow when we get there." She looks over at me. "Anything you would like to add?"

"Nope," I reply, unsure of saying anything really. Stefano is the closest thing I have to a brother. Being an only child to parents who had me a lot later in life, who actually just had me so they could say they had me. They did their duty, but when I moved out and went to college, we drifted apart. They did their thing, I did mine. We would talk a couple of times a year but it was nothing like Stefano had with his parents. It was only when I was around Stefano and his parents that I realized I missed out. I know it's not my parents' fault, it's just who they are. "I'm here with Eva and I'm going to book us flights today."

"You are going to book flights?" Stefano says, chuckling. "The last time you booked yourself a flight you ended up going to another airport in a propeller plane."

"How was I supposed to know they had two airports in Toronto?" I shout. "It said Toronto City, you can't blame me for that."

"You thought you were going to die." He can't stop laughing as he retells the story.

"What was I supposed to think? The plane kept getting closer and closer to the water," I defend and Eva snatches the phone from me.

"Okay, I have things to do and you have things to do. I will send you the details. Give my love to Addison and Avery," Eva declares, and she's about to hang up when Stefano quickly chimes into the conversation.

"My parents are here. I'll tell them you are coming." I close my eyes and shake my head.

"Great." Eva forces a smile on her face. "Can't wait to see everyone." She quickly hangs up and tosses the phone at me before grabbing her own cell phone.

"What are you doing?" I ask as she moves her fingers fast.

"I'm booking us on a flight. See, I'm already doing amazing as a wife."

I roll my eyes and pull away from the building. "His parents are going to be there." She looks over at me. "It's one thing when it's just you and me," I continue, "but now your whole family will be there."

"I know." I hear her take a deep breath.

"Are you sure this is what you want to do?" I ask again when I pull up to her house.

"I have to do this, Levi," she says, her voice going soft. "There is a little girl at stake." She unbuckles her seat belt. "And I'm never going to not do what I can for her. If I have to get fake married to someone and pretend for a year so she's with me forever, then that is what I'm going to do."

"Fine," I agree with her when she reaches for the door handle and opens the door.

"You should call Bridget." She mentions another one of the girls I hook up with more frequently than the others.

"Why?" I ask, my eyebrows pinching together.

She smirks at me. "You'll be less stressed." She can't even hide the smile. "And hopefully in a much better mood."

"I'm fine," I hiss at her.

"Are you sure?" she asks as she puts one foot out. "You don't look fine." She gets out of the car and bends down to finish. "And you're even walking sluggish."

I glare at her. "No, I'm not," I retort.

"Okay, fine, you aren't, but we should really sit down and talk about what the lawyer said."

"We will have to talk about all the things," I admit, "but let's get this one thing out of the way and we can talk about the rest."

"Okay," she agrees. "We will talk tomorrow after we speak to Stefano. He's usually good at this sort of thing."

"What sort of thing?" I ask, confused now.

"Being a parent." She chuckles. "He's going to lay it out for us."

"Is that what you think he's going to do?" I turn toward her. "Two things are going to happen, either…" I hold up my finger. "One, he kicks my ass for even agreeing to this." I swallow down that thought, knowing he wouldn't kick my ass, but he would threaten to do it. Along with that goes his family of a million to come after me. "Or two, he will tell us we are both insane and come up with an even bigger plan than the one we have."

"Fifty-fifty, then." She smiles. "Go get the balls drained, and I'll send you the flight details." She doesn't even wait for me to respond; she closes the door. I press the button to roll the window down.

"Are you going to call Juan?" I mention the last guy I know she hooked up with, she even dragged out the beginning of his name. She turns to look at me, walking backward, the smile on her face from ear to ear. Even with all the shit she has going on, the one thing you can count on her to do is to smile. "You should, you are walking a little to the side."

Seven

Eva

The alarm rings on my phone but I'm already up. I've been up most of the night, again going down the rabbit hole that is Google. I was so far down the hole I texted Alice in the middle of the night and asked her if it would be possible to get updates on Cici daily.

She replied right away.

Alice: *She's sleeping like you should be. Will follow up in the morning.*

When I got home yesterday, I pulled up flights. I got us both booked on the second earliest because no one should legally be allowed to enter an airport at 4:00 a.m. for a 6:00 a.m. flight if you aren't going to be sipping pineapple drinks by the beach four hours later. Once I texted Levi the confirmation, I then went about canceling and rescheduling all my appointments the following week. Even though I went to work the day, and pretended I was fine, I knew deep down I wasn't fine. I also knew deep down I would have a breakdown eventually, and I wouldn't want to do it in front of anyone. I knew I wouldn't be able to do anything the following week. I knew once everything was settled, more or less, and I gave myself time to think about it, it would be a very hard day.

Going over to my closet to get dressed, I stare at my clothes. "What does one wear when they are getting married?" I ask myself as I go through the hangers in my closet. "Should I do floral?" I look at the floral dresses I have. "I'm going to do…." I go on, walking over to the white pants I have, sliding them on. They sit tight on the hips but then flare off all the way down to the floor. I walk over to the drawer, taking out a lilac lace bra before my hand grabs the lilac silk top that is classy and elegant. If we take pictures, it will look great. I put one arm in and then the other, before I crisscross the front and fasten the buttons on the side and knotting the sash on the side. Turning I grab a pair of white high-heeled sandals before I walk out and to the bathroom.

I try to cover the puffiness in my eyes as much as I can. My hair also has a mind of its own, so again, I wear it pinned away from my face. Instead of a ponytail, I decide to wear it in a bun at the nape of my neck. I'm putting in the last bobby pin when my phone rings from my bedroom.

I snatch it up from the side table when I see it's Levi. "Hello, dear," I answer, pretending I'm happy.

"I'll be there in fifteen minutes," he says to me. "Are you bringing a bag?"

"No." I walk out of the room with the shoes in my hands. "Why would I bring a bag? We are in and out."

"I don't know how these things work. I brought an in-case bag."

"Ugh." I put my head back. "Should I bring an in-case bag?"

"I would," he advises. "Be there in ten."

"Goodbye." I hang up, dropping the shoes on the stairs and rushing back to my bedroom. Pulling the stool out of the corner of the room, I grab my carry-on bag. I throw in a couple of outfits that would look good in pictures, before rushing to the bathroom and taking out my makeup bag. Shoving a bunch of shit into it, I toss it in the carry-on bag along with a pair of flat shoes.

In five minutes, I'm ready again, this time with an in-case bag. Dumping the bag on the stairs, I sit down and slide my feet into the white, high-heeled sandals and tie them around my ankle. I walk back to the kitchen, where I take out two to-go cups and fill them with coffee and milk. I'm slipping the covers on when the front door opens, and Levi steps in. He doesn't even see me in the kitchen; instead, he shouts my name up the stairs, "Eva!"

"In here," I call to the doorway where he stands. His eyes look from the stairs to me. "I made you coffee," I say, holding up the to-go mugs. "See, I'm already starting with my wife duties." I smile at him as he laughs at my joke.

"Where is your bag?" he asks, and I motion with my chin toward the bag on the steps.

"See, you are also starting with your husband duties." I wink at him and all he does is shake his head.

"After you," he mumbles and I walk out of the front door, hearing it slam shut after him.

"I see we are still grouchy," I observe as I walk toward the car. "You could have taken care of the problem yourself." I juggle the cups in my hand, opening the door and getting into the car. I place the cups in the cupholder before I buckle my seat belt.

He gets in and starts the car. "Are you nervous?" I ask as he pulls out of the driveway.

"Not really," he replies, looking over at me. "You?" His hair looks like he ran his hand through it a million times.

"Yes," I answer him honestly. "I spent all night thinking of things."

"So, no Juan?" He snickers, grabbing one of the cups of coffee.

"Good one." I grab my own cup as he makes his way to the airport.

"Who has to-go cups in their house?" He looks over at me as he takes a sip of the coffee.

"A good wife does." I try to hide my smile, but when he glares at me, I can't help but chuckle.

We get checked in and I'm not shocked at all when he upgrades us to first class. "It's a one-hour flight," I mention to him as we walk away from the girl. "You go up and you come down." I motion with my hand.

"You know what else goes up and comes down?" he says as we walk toward security.

"You mean your little friend?" I tilt my head to the side.

"Um, unless you've seen it, you can't call it little because it's not," he defends with clenched teeth. "I was talking about the sun."

"No, you were not." I shake my head at him as he tries to hide the smile.

"No, I wasn't, but just for the record, it's huge," he boasts.

"Of course it is," I humor him as we walk to the gate, getting there at the same time they are boarding.

We walk in and sit in the big seats. "This is nice," I note, looking at all the extra room. The flight attendant comes over and asks if we want something to drink. I wait for us to take off and be in the air before I ask him, "Did you make a list?"

"I did." He reaches for his phone. "You ready?" he asks and I nod my head.

"As ready as I'm going to be," I reply nervously. It's only when I look back at him does my stomach decide it's time to turn at the same time my chest feels a sudden tightness in it, making it a touch harder to breathe. It feels like my heart is doing flutters.

"So we get married." I don't know if he's asking me or telling me, so I don't say anything.

"Prenup?"

My eyebrows press together. "Damn fucking straight,

I didn't bust my ass for my 'husband' to take my shit away from me."

His eyes go big as he stares at me. "Well, at least we agree on that. Not that I would take shit away from you. I would never, by the way."

"And I would?" I retort, insulted he would think this and forgetting I'm the one who insinuated he would do it to me.

"Better safe than sorry," he says to me, looking down at his list.

"Obviously, we have to get papers drawn up for me to get custody of the baby after the divorce," I remind him, "just to be sure."

"That sounds like a good idea. Where do we live?"

"My house," I say like it's the obvious answer because it is.

"Why?" he asks, all shocked and offended.

"Because it's home." I turn in my chair to look at him.

"But I have a home." He points at himself.

"Do you?" I quiz him with all the sarcasm I have in my body. "How many women have been in that home?" He just glares at me. "Let's say in the past seven days."

"One." He puts one of his fingers up. "You. Ha ha." He chuckles as if he just won the debate.

"Slow week." I roll my eyes at him.

He shrugs. "Full moon maybe."

"Okay, honestly," I declare to him, "we can't live in your house." He just stares at me, his body turning to mimic mine. "Imagine CPS is there and one of your girls shows up looking for Mr. Big." I point down to his crotch and he immediately covers himself.

"Okay, one, you didn't even sound like you were convinced about me being big," he reminds me, and all I can do is stare at him with my mouth hanging open. "And two, why does that make me sound like a pimp?"

"It is what it is." I lean over and put my hand on his arm that is still covering his dick area. "It's okay. I still love you." He smirks at me, as if his house is still an option. "But seriously, the baby should be living in my house so when we divorce, she isn't thrown for a loop again."

He moves his head side to side as he thinks about what I just said, finally giving in. "Fine," he pouts and looks back down at his phone. "Now, what about dating?"

"What about it?" I ask, confused about this question.

"Well, I date." He points at himself and I can't help the laugh that escapes me and fills the airplane.

"No, you don't." I shake my head, still laughing. "You spend four hours with someone naked." I wait for him to tell me I'm lying.

Instead, all he says is, "Sometimes longer." I throw my hands up.

"Sometimes shorter, I'm guesstimating and giving you the benefit of the doubt." I smile sarcastically at him.

"What if I want to sleep out?" he asks as if I'm his mother.

"So sleep out," I tell him. "Levi, the only thing that is going to change between us is you and me seeing each other more than we did before." I squeeze his arm with my hand. "If you want to bring a girl home, you take her back to your lair and do your thing." He looks at me as he processes what I just said. "The only thing I ask is that you just wash your hands when you get home before touching the baby." Now his laughter is the one filling up the plane, and the pain in my chest loosens up just a bit and my stomach is starting to settle.

"Okay," he says, putting away his phone before turning to me. "Now let's break it to your cousin"—I tilt my head to the side—"and my best friend."

"Don't worry," I reassure him, "I've got your back." I smile at him as he just rolls his eyes, so I lean over and kiss his cheek. "I always have your back."

Eight

Levi

I listen to her tell me she has my back and something in my stomach is unsettled. "Okay, can we go back to the dating question again?" I look at her, her back is to the plane wall. Her hair is pulled back again and tied at the base of her neck.

"I'm pretty sure I left that wide open for you." She chuckles and I put my ankle from my right foot on my left knee, folding my hands together on my stomach. "You can bang anyone you want until your heart's content." She smiles and scrunches her nose. "Until you have drained all the liquids from your body if you need to. Especially if it makes you less this." She picks up her hand and does a circle in the air toward me. The sleeves from her silky top move back and forth while she does it. The silver Tiffany bracelet I bought her for her birthday with the little blue heart on her left wrist jangles.

"No one is talking about me. We already got that settled." I ignore what she just said. "I was talking about you."

"What about me?" Her eyebrows pinch together as she just stares at me. Her blue eyes go to a light yellow with the sun coming in from the window beside her.

"What if you want to date?" I ask, my foot moving up and down now with nerves. I'm not sure why my foot is even moving up and down. It suddenly gets hot in the plane and I reach up to turn the gray nozzle over my head, hoping to relieve it.

"Levi," she says my name. "I'm going to be raising a nine-month-old child. When do you think I'm going to have time to date?" She tilts her head to the side. "Let alone the energy to date."

I lean into her and whisper as quietly as I can, "So you aren't going to have sex for a year?"

"I don't know." She shrugs. "Maybe I'll get a friend with benefits if I have to. I have a whole treasure chest of delights at home." My eyes go big. "Oh, please, like you've never ordered yourself one of those silicone vaginas." She snaps her fingers. "What are they called again?" She looks up trying to think of the name of it. "Flashlight." She shakes her head. "No, that's not right." I just stare at her as she tries to remember what it's called.

"It's called a flesh something," I tell her and her eyes go big that I even know this. I hold up my hands. "Not that I ever ordered it, but someone ordered it for Daniel as a gag gift for his bachelor party." She looks at me and nods as she gives me a face that says she doesn't believe a word I just said. "This may be shocking to you, but I've never had to order myself one." She rolls her eyes at me. "I have no problem getting it or not getting it."

"Really?" She crosses her legs and puts one hand on her knee before leaning in. "What's the longest that you've ever gone without?"

"Sixteen years," I counter her and she rolls her eyes. "I don't know, I have never counted."

"Think about it," she asks me, "a week?"

"I've gone longer than a week, even a month," I reply, proud of myself.

"Wow, a whole month," she says and claps her hands. "You should get a sticker for that." I glare at her. "Anyway, as much fun as this conversation is about the fact you can't go long without sex—"

"The conversation was about you and dating." My foot moves again up and down as I repeat my question, "Are you going to just bring the guy home?"

"Are you insane?" She gasps. "I don't even bring the guys home now and no one lives with me."

This declaration shocks me.

"What are you talking about? I've been at your place and—"

She holds up her finger. "You've been at my apartment and, yes, I had my friends over."

I can't help but laugh at the "friends" word. "Is that what you are calling them?"

"Yes." She nods. "Anyway, my apartment wasn't my home. This is my home and I'm not going to bring anyone who I'm not serious about into said home. I'm not going to have my home defaced for a quick *wham, bam, thank you, ma'am.*"

"If it's a *wham, bam, thank you, ma'am…*" I lean into her. "…he's doing it wrong."

All she does is glare at me while she grumbles between clenched teeth, "I mean, look at you. If your walls could talk, what do you think they would say?"

"Are my walls male or female?" I ask.

"Does it matter?" She swings her legs in front of her.

"Well, if the walls were female, they would most definitely call me a pig." I smile at her. "But if my walls were male, they would most definitely give me a high-five."

"You're a pig," she spits out at the same time the captain comes on and tells us we are preparing for landing.

"Buckle up," I warn her and she makes sure her seat belt is on. I fold my hands on my lap, putting my head back, and closing my eyes. The past couple of days have been a whirlwind for me, I can't even imagine what it's been for her.

We don't say anything to each other until we both stand up when we hear the ping for the seat belt sign. I stand, opening the overhead bin to grab my backpack and her purse before I step out into the aisle and wait for her to walk in front of me before we exit the plane.

We walk through the airport, following the signs to

go to baggage claim and the exit. "I'm getting really nervous," she admits softly, putting her hands on her stomach as we walk out of the glass doors that say exit only.

"It's going to be fine." I grab her hand that is beside me. She looks up at me and smiles, but it's fake. I know it's fake because her eyes don't light up. If you know her long enough, you can see when she is fake and when she isn't, and this right here is as fake as it gets. When it's the real smile, her eyes almost squint together and they look bright like the sun.

Still holding her hand, we step onto the escalator going down to baggage claim and the exit. As we get closer to the bottom, I look around and spot Stefano before Eva does. He's standing right in front of the escalator, his phone in his hand, and his fingers look like they are going a mile a minute as he types. He must feel me staring at him because his fingers stop moving and he looks up. I release Eva's hand to hold up my hand toward him. Eva looks over and he smiles at her. I look over and see Eva raises her hand also to say hello to him as we move down.

He walks closer to us, and when we step off the escalator, he goes to Eva first. "Hey," he greets, giving her a sad smile.

"Hey," she replies softly as he takes her in his arms and gives her a hug. I suddenly get nervous about telling him our plan. I mean, he knows I would do anything for Eva. He also knows she would do anything for me. What's the worst that can happen? He takes me outside and kicks my ass. That would be worst case, the other would be probably his father helping him to kick my ass. Then let's not even think about the number of cousins and cousins' cousins that he has.

"You didn't have to meet us," Eva says softly once he lets her go.

"Of course I did," he says to her, holding her arms in his hands. "Can you imagine what my mother and father would have done to me if I didn't come to meet you?" he deadpans to her, making her laugh. "Besides, if I hadn't come, they would have, and I don't think you are ready for all of that."

"You are right on that," she mumbles to him.

"I'm so, so sorry about Lisa," he consoles her and she looks down at her feet. I see her mouth exhale before she blinks away the tears.

She lifts her head and gives him a sad smile. "Thank you."

"My dad said he reached out to you also," he tells her at the same time he reaches out to take her luggage from her.

"I know," she says as we make are way out of the airport. "It's been a busy couple of days. Every single time I said I would get back to him, I remembered I had to do something else."

"I can't even imagine," he soothes, putting his arm around her shoulders. "Well, whatever help you need, we are here for you." She just nods, and the only thing I can think is, *you may change your mind once you find out what she needs from you.*

"Shall we go?" Stefano suggests, ushering us out the door and toward his car.

"Shall we go and have something to eat?" He looks over at us as we walk to the underground parking garage and to his car.

"Where is the wife?" I ask, knowing Eva is probably too nervous to ask him.

"The wife," he says, smiling, "is at work."

Eva looks at me with big eyes that sparkle. "Oh, let's go there." She looks at Stefano. "We should definitely go there." We stop when he gets to his car.

"What?" he asks, confused by this as he looks at me and at Eva. "She's working." He takes his keys out and pops the trunk for me to put the luggage in. I walk over and place the bags in the trunk before taking off my backpack, adding it to the mix.

"Oh, great," Eva says and she wrings her hands nervously in front of her. "I would love to see where she works."

I put my hands in my pockets. "Maybe we should do lunch first." I look over at Eva. "Then perhaps break the news to him." It's with that sentence you can see the patience Stefano had is gone. "Or we can just rip it off like a Band-Aid."

"Okay, you two," he starts, his eyes moving between me and Eva. "What the fuck is going on right now?"

"Well." Eva takes a step toward him. "You see, we came here really because we need to speak to Addison."

His eyebrows pinch together. "Why?"

Oh, boy, I think in my head. My hands get a touch

clammy and I look down nervously, not knowing what to say. I turn my head to look at Eva, who is also wondering what to say at this point. "Well," she struggles, shrugging her shoulders and smiling big. "There is something we need her to do for us."

"For us?" Stefano repeats, his eyes shooting to me. "There is an us?"

"Not really," I admit because it's the truth, more or less. "But." I look up. "How do I say this?"

"Like a Band-Aid," Eva reminds me and I look over at her. "We need to talk to her because..." Her voice trails off and she takes a deep inhale and exhales just as fast. "We need her to plan our wedding."

Nine

Eva

"*I*'m sorry?" Stefano questions as soon as the words "we need her to plan our wedding" come out of my mouth. He laughs and claps. "Jesus." He chuckles. "I thought you said you needed her to plan your wedding." He points at Levi, then at me, the laughter on his face fading away as he takes in my face and looks over at Levi, seeing him avoiding his eyes.

"Um." I start to hum as I move my head back and forth. "It's a kind-of, sort-of kind of thing." At this point I'm just putting words that don't make sense together. I'm trying my best to calm down the situation because I can feel the temperature rising and it's not from the sun.

"I'm sorry." Stefano glares first at me, then at Levi,

who just stares at him. "What?" he hisses out.

"How about…" I step closer to Stefano and almost in front of Levi. "…we go and see Addison." I move in front of him to stop him from glaring at Levi and focus on me. I also realize that I've stepped in front of Levi to make sure he doesn't hit him. "Then we can fill you guys both in."

"Fill us in." His voice comes out louder than I think he even knows, and with the emptiness of the parking garage, his voice booms and echoes.

"Are you crazy?" He looks at both of us. Levi and I just side-eye each other. "You can't marry him." He points at Levi. "He's—" he says, then he looks back at Levi. This time, Levi's eyebrows shoot up, waiting to hear what his friend has to say. "He's—"

"He's," Levi says, holding up his hand. "He's right here." They share a stare down before Levi puts his hands on his hips. "Also a little bit offended, what's wrong with me?"

"What's wrong with you?" Stefano repeats the question, throwing up his hand in the air. "What is wrong with you?" The question is now more shouting than anything else. Levi takes a step forward and I can tell he's getting pissed, something that isn't going to help anyone if he does.

I put my hands up toward Stefano to stop him from talking and turn back to Levi to stop him from advancing closer. "Okay, you two." I try to calm the situation down. "So much for ripping it off like a Band-Aid," I mumble to myself more than anyone else. "We really don't have that much time." Stefano just looks at me. "We have two maybe three days, max." I look up as I try to remember what freaking day it is. "Maybe four." Stefano just stares at Levi. "So can we get this show on the road?" I ask and turn to Levi, tapping his chest with my hand. "Shall we?" I slide my hand in his, pulling him to the side of the car. "I'll sit up front," I tell him as he reaches for the handle of the door. "Just to make sure." I try to make a joke. "Stefano," I call to him as Levi gets in the back seat, "we need to get the show on the road, which means you need to get in the car and move us along."

He puts his hands on his hips. "Oh, I can't wait to fucking hear this," he grits out between clenched teeth, walking toward the driver's side of the car. Once I see him open the door and get in, I follow his lead.

Pretending to look around his car, I try to cut the tension. "This is a nice car."

"Save it," Stefano grumbles to me and I can't help but chuckle. "It's the same car Levi has." I roll my lips trying not to laugh out loud.

I don't say anything as he pulls out of the parking garage and heads straight to Addison's work. The drive takes five minutes but no one says anything. He pulls into the parking lot and I stare at the house ahead of us. The little bungalow in front is white and looks so inviting. "I love it," I say, looking at the house. Once the car is stopped, I open the door and get out.

I take a second to look at the side where it looks like a huge barn is. The barn Addison and Stefano got married in not long ago. You can't tell from the outside how amazing the inside is. It's rustic with wooden floors and exposed beams that can be dressed up or dressed down. It doesn't look like it but it's huge, and I'm sure can fit five hundred people. I know that right behind the barn is a kitchen where the caterers can set up. I accidentally walked into the kitchen while looking for the bathroom.

I also spot a couple of other buildings behind it that I didn't notice during the wedding. I'm even more intrigued than I was at the wedding. I hear two car doors shut and look back to see both of the men out of the car but on their side of the car. "Okay, you two," I say to them, "you both need to stop pouting." I turn before walking up the five steps and pulling open the door.

I take a step in and gasp at how nice it is. There is a desk in the middle of the room that is empty and I look over to where the living room and dining room would be, but instead it's a waiting room area. It's filled with cream-colored couches with a glass table in front of them holding a huge bouquet of white and cream roses. The walls are filled with pictures from the past events they've done. I step deeper into the room. Walking over to the side, my eyes go from one picture to the next. I hear the clicking of heels coming closer to me and look over at the hallway when I see Addison coming toward us. Her face goes into full-smile mode. "Oh my goodness," she says, walking in and seeing us here.

She is followed by four other women and all I can do is gawk at them. "I'm sorry, is this an event planning business or a modeling agency?" I ask them and they all smile at me.

"It's both," one of the girls replies to me as Addison walks over to Stefano, kissing his lips. "What a great surprise." She comes to me, leaning in, and she kisses my cheeks before hugging me. "I'm so sorry I couldn't meet you," she apologizes, hugging me. "I'm so sorry to hear about Lisa," she continues and I just nod at her. I guess I should get used to people telling me that.

"Thank you," I tell her. "So who are these supermodels?"

"These are my bosses," she introduces, looking over at them. "Shelby, Clarabella, Presley, and of course you remember Sofia," she says of the woman who married Stefano's cousin. It was actually at her wedding that Stefano came face-to-face with the daughter he had no idea he had. It was a shock to everyone, but the minute he found out, he was all in. She's also the best kid I've ever met. I mean, I'm not around many kids, but I'm pretty sure she's the best there is out there.

"I have to say, every single time I look at the barn, I fall more and more in love," I tell them as I look around.

"Well, thank you very much," Shelby says, smiling at me.

"What brings you to town?" Clarabella looks at me with a smile.

"Well, funny you should ask that." I look over at Levi who is standing to the side, away from Stefano. I really hate that I've put him in this position with him. I hate I have to drag him in here with me, but I have no other choice. "We need you guys to help us get married." I look over at Levi, ignoring the four sets of shocked gasps that come out. "Today would be a good day."

"Excuse me," Addison says, putting up her hand, "but what?"

"Yeah, that's what I said," Stefano adds before he turns and glares at Levi, who just rolls his eyes at him.

"Would you give her a minute to explain before you come at me guns blazing?" Levi tells him, putting his hands in his pockets.

"My sister passed away." I look at the girls and ignore the stinging and burning that my eyes feel. "And, well." My voice trembles and instead of continuing I take a second to steady myself. Levi walks over to me and puts his arm around my shoulders, trying to give me support. If only he knew how much it means to me. "And now I'm going to be adopting my niece." All the women put their hands to their chests, giving me a sad look. "And the best way for me to do this according to a reputable source"—I use my index finger to wipe the tear that is going to escape from my eyes—"is for me to be married."

"Which is why we are getting married." Levi now looks at Stefano. "She needs help and I'm obviously going to help her."

"Oh, thank God," Stefano exhales, clapping his hands and putting them on his knees. "I thought you lost your mind." He laughs at me, then looks at Levi. "This makes much more sense than you two." He moves his hands from me to Levi. "You know, being together."

"Again." Levi sounds a touch irritated, and I feel the heaviness of his arm around my shoulders. "I'm right here." I reach around his waist, showing him that I'm here for him.

"I'm not saying anything bad," Stefano backtracks. "I'm just—"

"Maybe you should stop talking," Addison mumbles to him.

"Now would be the perfect time for you to, I don't know," Sofia starts talking, "shut up." She picks up her hands to her sides and shrugs.

"I'm just saying he's him," Stefano states, "and she's her."

"I'm looking at a woman and a man who look like they need to get married," Clarabella states.

"Sorry, want to get married."

"Look, I need to do this," I inform them all, "if not for me, then for Cici. So I need to get married." I shake my head. "We need to get married and we would like you guys to work your magic and make it happen."

"Or we can go to Vegas," Levi throws in, and the minute he says the V-word the gasps fill the room again. This time it's not a sad, shocked gasp, it's a *how dare you say that* kind of gasp.

"Did you just use the V-word?" Presley accuses him, putting her hand to her mouth as if he said a bad word.

"And she is not talking about the—" Clarabella says, pointing down at her vagina.

"Everyone needs to just…." Addison picks up her hands. "Just, we are going to do this." She looks at us, and for the first time since all of this started, I feel a sense of relief. As if it's all going to be better.

"So we can be married," Levi asks her, "today?"

"But—" Shelby steps forward, holding up her hand to stop us all from talking. "There are a couple of things you need in order to make this happen, and number one besides obviously having a groom—" She points at Levi.

"Also, can we say you get top props for that?" Clarabella winks at her.

"Not that." Presley slaps her. "You need a dress." She points at me and I shake my head.

"I don't need a dress," I inform her and feel Levi's hand move away from my shoulder.

"Yes, she does." I hear from beside me and I look over at him. "You need a dress," he assures me and all I can do is stare at him.

"I'm wearing white and something old." I point at the shirt. "Something sort of blue." I hold up my arm at the bracelet he gave me for my last birthday. "And someone is going to lend me something." I look around at the women, waiting for them to offer me something.

"You're right," Shelby declares, nodding at me. "We can lend you a dress."

"Well," Clarabella adds, "because we are just awesome, we have a selection of dresses that we actually carry from one of the stores in town as samples. It's good for her and for us, apparently."

"Why don't you go with them?" Levi looks at me. "See if there is anything you might like." I immediately start to shake my head. I am not going to be buying a wedding dress that I don't need. It's another expense I can't take at this time. I'm already dreading the lawyer bill and I don't even know how much it's going to cost me in order to draw up the adoption papers. "You do that and I'm going to go and check out where we are going to exchange our vows."

"Exchange vows?" I repeat his words, suddenly confused by what is going on.

"Well, yeah, this might be my only wedding," he jokes with me, giving me a sly smile. I shake my head, not sure what to say.

"Okay, then it's settled," Clarabella says, clapping her hands happily. "Let's take her to the bridal suite."

"You are going to love it," Addison reassures me, "it's not as pretty as your place. But it'll do. I'm going to get some information from Levi and join you guys in there in a little bit." The girls usher me away from Levi and I look over my shoulder at him, mouthing the words, "Help me."

He just smiles at me and I look over at Stefano and glare at him. "Don't hurt my groom before I marry him," I threaten, right before I'm dragged to the back of the house.

We walk down the back steps. "I can't believe you are going to be getting married," Presley says from beside me. "I mean, I would one thousand million percent do the same thing."

"Without a question, I would marry someone for my niece or nephew," Shelby agrees.

"It's not someone," Presley reminds her, "it's her best friend."

"I married my best friend," Shelby says. "Best decision I ever made."

"Okay, I think we are all getting ahead of ourselves," I say. "You married him because you love him. I'm marrying him to get my niece."

We walk down the path toward the venue, and even when I walk in now seeing that it's really bare, with no decoration, I just love it. *If I ever get married, this is where I'm having the ceremony*, I tell myself as we walk to the rear of the venue, heading out to the bridal suite.

The little white cottage is sitting there with a sign that says bridal suite. Presley opens the door and I walk in. I don't know what I'm expecting but what is there is even better than I had imagined.

Against the side wall are four stations set up with gold vanities and matching gold plush chairs in front of them. Mirrors with big chunky gold frames hang down in front of each chair. White vases of roses fill the room. A rack of dresses is on one side and wedding dresses on the other side of the room. It's so glamorous and I make notes for back home. "I'm not going to lie," I say, spinning in the room, "I'm so going to steal this for my place back home." Thinking maybe we should put in a bridal suite. Where they get ready and head to the ceremony.

"Steal away," Presley encourages, smiling at me.

I look at them. "But seriously." I walk over to the rack of wedding dresses and spot a silky sparkly one. "How fast can we get married?"

Ten

Levi

I watch Eva walk out the door with the four ladies, waiting until the door is closed before I turn and look at Addison and then Stefano. "Okay," I urge, holding up my hand, "let's get it out of the way before she comes back." What I really want to do right now is sit down and just take a second to breathe.

"Let's get it out of the way," Stefano repeats my words.

"Stefano," Addison scolds him softly as she puts her hand on his arm. He turns to look at her. "Would you give him a chance?"

He watches her for a second before he turns to me. "This is…" He looks down at his shoes, shaking his head.

"It's the craziest thing I've ever done," I admit, "but it's also the only thing I can do."

"You are going to get married to her," Stefano reminds me. "That's a big deal."

"It's not that big of a deal," Addison states and he side-eyes her, his glare softer than he would give anyone else because he loves her more than life itself. Something I've never had; also I don't think I've ever really wanted it. I mean, I love Stefano and I know I love Eva, obviously. I just don't think I have it in me to love someone like that. Okay, fine, maybe that isn't true because I would go to the ends of the earth for Eva. "It's a big deal if you make it a big deal. If you were listening to them instead of being all Hulk, you would have heard them say it's for Cici. You can't tell me that you wouldn't do the same thing for anyone in your family."

"Yes," he agrees with her, "but—" I don't wait for him to add more; instead, I speak out.

"Stefano," I say his name and he looks back over at me. "It's Eva, she's the most loyal person I know. She is the most selfless person I know. She is the most genuine person I know. There is no one else in this world I would do this for besides her."

"Wow." He snickers. "What if I needed you to marry me?"

"You'd better be down on one knee and have a big-ass ring for me," I joke with him and my hand comes out to squeeze my neck. "But seriously, I know how important this is to her. I know how important her family is to her. I also know I'm not going to let her down."

"I believe you," Stefano states. "It's just, it's you."

"Yeah, it's me, and you should know I would never do anything to hurt her."

"But what if, like, things get blurry?" he questions and Addison slaps him. "What?"

"It's none of your business," she hisses at him. "Literally not your concern. Remember the other day when Avery got upset because of something that happened that had nothing to do with her. What did you tell her?" She raises her eyebrows. "Not your monkey, not your circus."

"It is my monkey and it's my circus. It's my concern. She's my cousin," he explains, "and he's my best friend."

"And they are two grown-ass adults who can make their own decisions," Addison puts in. "Now what you need to do is ask them what they need."

"Yes," I agree with her. "You need to help me."

"With what?" Stefano gawks.

"Realistically, how fast can we be married?" I ask Addison and she looks at Stefano before turning back to me.

"It's just the two of you?" she asks.

"Yes." I nod, knowing that whether he agrees with us or not, Stefano will also be there. There is no way he wouldn't be. At least I hope he's there.

"You don't want any decorations, right?" She walks over to the desk, leaning over it and grabbing a pad from the top of it and a pen. She turns to look at me, waiting for me to answer.

"Well, yeah." I look at her. "Obviously, let's add

some decoration." Stefano looks at me and I'm not sure what he's thinking. Frankly, I'm not even sure what I'm thinking. "I'm not a savage," I quickly add. "Even if it's fake, I'm not going to the courthouse with her, so I think we should add some decorations. She deserves better than that." At this point, even I'm unsure of what I'm saying or why I'm saying it.

"Okay," Addison says. "I'm assuming since you will be having decoration, you will also be wanting flowers."

"Her favorite flowers are orchids, but I'm not sure how that would be in a bouquet," I tell her. "She also loves roses but the cream or white ones or the light pink ones, not another color." They both look at me shocked. "I bought her purple roses once, and let me tell you, I will not make that mistake ever again. And I don't want one carnation either." I shake my head. "I bought her those once and she asked why I hated her." I laugh thinking back to when I bought that for her. It was at the beginning when we were getting to know each other, and if I have to be honest, I was falling for her. But then I knew if I went there with her, I would lose her friendship, so I put her in the *do not even think about* category since then, and that is where she is going to stay. Forever. I don't have much in my life, relationship-wise. I have parents who I talk to maybe twice a year, Christmas and birthday. Then I have my work friends, who are more like colleagues. It's not like I would tell them my deepest darkest secrets. So besides Stefano, who is my go-to all the time, Eva is my ride or die, and there is no way I'm losing any of that. "What else?"

"Well, food would be my next question." Addison writes down something on the pad. "But it's just the two of you."

"Right," I say, rolling back on my heels, "but you two will come, right?" I look at the both of them and they both nod their heads. "So it'll be four of us, plus Avery." I snap my fingers. "She can be the flower girl, or whatever it's called."

"She would love that, obviously," Addison coos. "She gets to wear a fancy dress and probably a tiara, you might be her favorite person that day."

"My parents are in town," Stefano reminds me.

I close my eyes for just a moment before letting out a huge breath. "Your father is going to kick my ass."

Stefano smirks at me. "Yes." He nods at the same time, his smirk going to a full-blown smile. "But the good news is he's a bit older now, so it'll hurt a touch less."

"Well, that depends," I waffle. "Who else is in town besides your dad and mom? Your family usually travels in packs."

Addison can't help but laugh. "That's a good one." She points her pen at me. "They do travel in packs. When he told his parents about Avery, ten people showed up."

Stefano rolls his eyes. "It wasn't ten, it was six," he corrects. "But you can add my parents."

"Okay," Addison says, writing down on the pad. "So food for twenty?" My eyes go big. "About. I'll get better numbers when I talk to Vivienne."

"Don't talk to my mother," Stefano suggests right

away. "It's going to be a small gathering of one hundred people. Let this guy…" He points at me. "…talk to my father and we will get a better range of how many people are coming."

"I'm going to put twenty as a minimum," she says. "I know this isn't a big deal, but to me it is. What were you thinking about for cake?"

"Red velvet is her favorite," I share, "but with cream cheese frosting and not vanilla."

Addison just looks up at me, shocked maybe that I know so much about her.

"Right," she goes on, "rings?"

I look over at Stefano. "We'll go out later to get something. I'm assuming there is someplace in town that has rings and stuff." There is no way I'm not getting her a ring. I also know she's going to freak out, and I'm going to have to pull out the do-me-a-favor card. But considering that the last favor she asked me I said yes to, I'm thinking she's not going to give me a hard time.

"There is someplace in town that has rings and stuff," Addison repeats what I just said, trying to hide her smile.

"Good." I nod. "So how fast?" I ask. "Professionally speaking, of course."

"We have to get you a marriage license but that doesn't take any time, you can get it immediately. I have to make some calls to make sure I can get the cake on time. The flowers shouldn't be a problem and I'm sure we can snag Luke to do the food, depending on how many people there are coming. So realistically, I can have this ironed out by tomorrow. Which means you can get married the day after." She smiles at me, folding her arms in front of her. "You guys have clothes, right?"

"I told her to pack a couple of things," I tell her, "and she has a bag, but I have no idea."

Addison laughs at me. "I was talking about you, really. You do have a suit, right?"

My eyebrows pinch together. "Um," I start to say, "I didn't pack a suit."

"Lucky for you we also have suits." She shakes her head. "Comes to get married, doesn't bring a suit," she mumbles under her breath, making Stefano laugh. He walks over to her and bends to kiss her lips. "We have someone in town who does last-minute alterations. We are going to see what Eva chooses for a dress and you can choose your suit."

I nod at her. "See, crisis averted," I joke and she glares, "it'll be fine."

"It could be pricey," she awkwardly says.

"Whatever it is, I'll cover it," I tell her, then look over her shoulder to make sure we are alone. "But just don't tell her. She doesn't need the added stress. Even for the dress, don't show her any prices. If she likes it, just get it."

She smiles at me. "Sounds good." She looks over at Stefano, raising her eyebrows. "Now are we, and by we—I mean are you calmer now that you know the full story?"

"I know why he's doing it," Stefano replies, putting his arm around her shoulders. "I just don't want them to, you know, get hurt."

"Stefano, we both know the score." I ignore the tightness in my chest. I don't have a chance to think about it because we hear laughter coming from outside.

The back door opens and she comes into the room, laughing with the sisters. It's been a whirlwind couple of days and anyone else would have been in a puddle of tears. They would have been curled up in a ball, but not Eva. Not Eva, she's like *let me dust myself off and I'll be ready to go in ten minutes*. And she'll do it flawlessly.

"Hey." She looks at me as she comes into the room. "No bloodshed?" She looks around. "I like it, I like it." She looks over at Stefano. "No bruised knuckles?"

"This isn't fight club," he jokes with her.

"Wow." She folds her arms over her chest. "It's like you don't even care he's going to marry me," she states with a straight face and Stefano takes a step forward shocked. "I'm kidding." She laughs. "Now how are the plans going?"

"Good," I answer her. "I think we can get married in two days."

"Ugh, okay, fine I guess." She tilts her head to the side and walks over to me, wrapping her arm around my waist, putting a hand to my chest, smiling up at me. This time her smile hits her eyes a little bit. "Isn't that love?" She rolls her lips and I can see my Eva is coming back. She turns to look at everyone in the room. "He can't wait to marry me."

Eleven

Eva

"Knock, knock, knock." I hear as the door to the bridal suite opens. I'm sitting down in one of the plush chairs, wearing a white satin robe that says Bride on it. The room is filled with vases and vases of roses. The woman behind me is curling my hair, as I'm drinking my second glass of champagne. I'm trying not to think about the fact that my chest feels weird. I'm trying not to think about how my stomach flips and flops when anyone gushes when they come in the room, excited about me getting married. I'm trying not to think about the fact that by the end of the night, I'm going to be married to Levi. "I come with gifts." I look over to see Stefano's mom, Vivienne, come in the room with two bags in her hands.

"What?" I ask as she walks in. She's wearing an ice-blue dress that matches her eyes perfectly. It's satin and tight all the way down to the floor, with little cap sleeves.

"Well, it's your wedding day." I look at her, knowing full well that she knows this isn't a real wedding. I know this because yesterday we sat down with Mark to explain what was going on. We did it at Luke's to make sure everyone kept their voices at a reasonable level. I was more nervous telling Mark than anyone else. He's been like a father figure to me, and I didn't want to let him down. I don't wear my heart on my sleeve. I don't tell people my problems. I deal with it and move on, so having to sit down and tell him what was going on was a lot for me. It really helped that Levi was there holding my hand. He's been holding my hand since I got the call about Lisa. Even when I asked him to marry me and he thought I was joking, in the end I knew he would agree to it.

"It's my fake wedding day," I mumble to her and she just smiles at me.

"Well, whatever it is," she says, her French accent very apparent right then and there. I don't know the whole story, but I know she came here when she was in college from France and fell in love with New York, so she stayed. From the little bits and pieces here and there, I think she's even related to royalty back in Paris. "I wanted you to have a couple of things."

"A couple of things?" I remark, putting down the empty glass of champagne and hoping it gets topped up sooner than later to help me with all the nerves.

"They are just little things," she assures me, handing me the first bag, "so you know we support you."

"I don't know what to say." I put the bag on my lap and pull out the white tissue paper before pulling out a brown box. I place the bag on the floor before opening the box and seeing a silk handkerchief in the middle of it. I take it out, seeing it's got lace on the outside of the silk. In the middle of the silk is Levi & Eva with the date.

"It's to help dab your tears away," she explains. "It will look nicer in pictures than a tissue."

My eyes get suddenly so dry they hurt to blink, or maybe they are filled with tears and I'm ignoring it all. This little secret wedding has turned into a party for thirty. It went from just the two of us with two witnesses to Stefano's parents. Then I couldn't leave the sisters out of it, so I invited them also. Needless to say, it isn't going to be just the four of us. This morning when I woke up in the honeymoon suite I was staying in, I kept thinking to myself we should have just gone to Vegas. "This is so thoughtful," I tell Vivienne, trying not to ruin my makeup with tears.

"It was nothing; I wish I had enough time to do more."

"It's not supposed to be that big of a deal," I remind her as she hands me the next bag.

"This," she says, "is from the Dimitris family."

"Good God." The sting goes from my eyes right to my nose. "This is really too much," I tell her, "like, this is just for show."

"Regardless," she goes on, "it's for you and you can pass it along to Cici when it's her turn." I take the box out of the bag and the little box should tell me I shouldn't take this gift. However, I know if I fight it, they will start to lay on the guilt. "Your father would have wanted you to have this." And there it is—the guilt—as I open the box and see diamond earrings. "They match the outfit perfectly."

"Yes, they do." I don't even fight it because it'll be a losing battle. I also don't have time to fight it because my phone rings. I reach for it, seeing it's Alice.

"Hello." I pick up the phone on the second ring.

"Eva," she greets breathlessly, "good news. Just got off the phone with the lawyer and we have the reading of the will in two days."

"Oh my God," I say, putting my hand to my mouth. "Will I be able to get Cici?"

"CPS is already aware that there is a will in place. They will be meeting with the lawyers tomorrow, so hopefully they have everything they need and you can get Cici."

"I have no words, thank you so much."

"It's my job," she reminds me. "What are you doing?"

"Well," I stall, looking into the mirror at myself, "I'm getting married in about an hour, give or take."

"What?" she huffs. "Today?"

"No time like the present," I tell her and she laughs.

"It's a good thing you both signed the prenup yesterday." It's my turn to laugh, as soon as we filed our paperwork for a marriage license, we got on the phone with Alice to discuss a prenup. It was pretty simple and she emailed over the copy and we just signed it and returned it.

"Thank you for squeezing it in so quickly," I reply and hear another knock on the door.

"I have to go. I'll call you tomorrow, Alice."

"Happy wedding day," she gushes before I hang up on her.

"Can we come in?" Presley sticks her head in the door and I just smile at her.

"Come right in," I invite her and Vivienne looks over at me. I can see she's hiding something.

"We come with gifts," Presley says, walking in followed by Shelby, Clarabella, and Sofia who are carrying wedding dresses.

"What are those?" I point at the dresses they are carrying.

"We have three choices for you to choose from," Presley says. "Now, we know that you chose not to have a wedding dress and to be married in pants and a top, but—" She points over to the pantsuit I picked up in town.

"You are getting married," Sofia reminds me.

"Yes, but—" I put my finger up.

"You have to have a wedding dress, even if it's fake," Clarabella states. "It's like bad karma if you don't."

"Look at JLo," Shelby points out, "she went to Vegas to get married with Ben and she brought her glam squad and a Ralph Lauren gown."

"Well, she's JLo." I laugh nervously. "I am not." I look at the girls. "And if I'm not mistaken, she actually loved Ben."

"How about we save that debate for another time?" Clarabella suggests. "We are still debating if Jake has Taylor's red scarf."

"Ugh," Presley says, "I bet he does."

"Okay, fine." I give in. "I don't care which one as long as we can return it after the wedding."

"Good," Sofia cheers, "I thought you would say that, so we are going with this one." She picks up the dress in her hand and it's absolutely stunning. The top is a sweetheart neckline, but it's full of sparkle. Even the spaghetti straps have sparkles on them. But then white silky material looks like it's draped over from one side to the other, going all the way to the floor. There is a huge slit on the left side, and the same sparkly material from the top is layered under the silk. It's sexy and glamorous, and if I was getting married, it is what I would choose. "Wait until you see the back." She turns it around and it looks like it's sheer all the way to the bottom of my back, where the silk drapes giving you a little train. "It's stunning."

"Isn't it a bit too much for a wedding that, you know, is small?" I ask them.

"We are just following orders," they say, avoiding looking at me.

The hairdresser finishes the beach curls I asked for and pins the hair on the side in the back. I get up and slide the white robe off me and step into the dress. I hold the front to me as they zip up the back. The beads and pearls of the front are so delicate I'm afraid to touch them. "Maybe we should go for the other one." I point over to the plain dress. "It looks like it's less likely to get damaged."

"You can change after," Presley assures me and the door opens and this time Addison steps in wearing a coral silk dress.

She gasps when she sees me. "I knew that was going to be her dress," she boasts, holding a massive bouquet with orchids, white roses, and blush flowers. "I got the flowers."

"Okay, this is getting a bit ridiculous," I say when music starts playing.

"What is that?" I ask them, and everyone avoids looking at me as they pin a veil in the back of my hair. I don't have time to second-guess anything because Addison comes over and places a pair of shoes in front of me and I slide my feet into them.

The door opens and Avery comes jumping in. "Look, I'm a princess." She twirls as she goes to Vivienne, who holds her face and kisses her cheek.

"Okay, we need to go," Addison urges and we walk out of the suite and head toward the reception space.

"We'll go get our seats," the girls say, leaving me with Addison, Avery, and Vivienne.

"Hey." I hear someone say from the side and look over to see Markos coming toward us. "I'm just in time." He smiles at me. "You look so beautiful."

"Thank you," I answer him, as Vivienne goes to him and kisses his lips.

"I took it upon myself to help you down the aisle," Mark says nervously. "You don't have to accept it."

I smile at him, the pain in my chest feeling even more pressure. "Thank you," is all I can say because the lump forms in my throat.

"It's time," Addison announces, and I hear music even louder now.

"Is that music for us?" I ask, but all she does is turn and walk into the venue.

"Shall we?" Mark offers me his arm and I slip my hand in his.

"On a scale of one to ten, how crazy is this plan?" I ask nervously when I hear the music stop.

"One thousand and fifty percent," he jokes as the chords of a harp fill the room. "It's time."

He leads me, and when the doors open, it dawns on me that it's "Here Comes the Bride" I hear. I gasp when I see the room filled with people. "Oh my God, this is not happening," I say, but Mark just leans over.

"Smile, you're on video and there is a photographer." My eyes go big as I look down the aisle to see Levi standing there wearing a beige linen suit. His hands are on top of each other in front of him as he watches me walk down the aisle. I don't even think I'm walking down the aisle, it's more like I'm floating. I must be floating because I don't think my feet are touching the floor. I blink away the tears, suddenly pissed I forgot the handkerchief in the room.

I don't notice all the decorations around us. I can only focus on Levi, who is trying not to laugh at me. I hope he can tell from my stare that I'm about to freak out. When we get to the end of the aisle, he comes forward and shakes Mark's hand before holding out his hand for me. I slide my hand in his and he leans in. "Breathe," he whispers in my ear, right before he kisses me on the cheek. "Ten minutes and this is over."

I look over and I glare at him for being calm, cool, and collected. "Smile for the camera," he mumbles as he stands next to me.

"What the hell is all this?" I hiss at him as the guy in front of me starts talking about gathering today to witness the marriage of Levi and Eva.

"Surprise!" he says to me, his eyes filled with mischief, before looking back at the guy in front of me.

"Levi and Eva," the man starts, "face each other holding hands." I hand the bouquet to Addison, who stands beside me. "And repeat after me."

"This is it," I mumble under my breath, turning to put my hand in Levi's. I don't bother looking at all the people sitting here because I might just run out the back door. Also, I make a mental note to kick the shit out of Stefano for knowing all these people.

"Evangeline." He uses my real name. "Repeat after me, I, Evangeline, take you, Levi, to be my husband."

The lump in my throat grows so big I'm not sure I'm able to say anything. I blink faster and let out a big exhale before I look into his eyes. "I, Evangeline, take you, Levi, to be my husband." My eyes never leave his as I finish repeating what he says, "To have and to hold from this day forward, for better, for worse, for richer, for poorer, in sickness and in health, to love and to cherish, until parted by death."

A lone tear escapes and Levi lets go of one hand to wipe the tear away. I hear the aw coming from somewhere, and if I was in my right mind, I would laugh at them. "Now, Levi," the man says, "please repeat after me."

Levi smirks and then his smirk leaves his face. "I, Levi, take you, Evangeline, to be my wife." He smiles when he says the word, before finishing. "To have and to hold from this day forward, for better, for worse, for richer, for poorer, in sickness and in health, to love and to cherish, until parted by death."

I can't help the smile that fills my face. "Now, do we have the rings?"

I look at Levi, my face filled with horror. "We forgot rings," I tell him and he just shakes his head.

"I got them." He turns to Stefano, who hands him the rings.

"This is why I'm marrying him." I look over at the guy who is officiating the wedding.

He chuckles. "Levi, place the ring on her finger and repeat after me."

My hand shakes in his as he holds the ring he is slipping on my finger. My eyes look down at his hand as he says the words, "I give you this ring as a sign of our love for and commitment to each other." I look back up at him as he continues and the ring reaches the bottom of my finger. "I promise to support you, care for you, and stand alongside you for all of our days."

All I can do is smile at him as he hands me his ring. I hold his hand in mine, and whereas mine was shaking, Levi's is steady. I take the black band and place it on his finger, repeating what he said to me, "I give you this ring as a sign of our love for and commitment to each other. I promise to support you, care for you, and stand alongside you for all of our days." Only when it's at the bottom of his finger do I look up at him. He has his own tears in his eyes, no doubt regretting saying yes to my favor.

"You are lucky you didn't put honor and obey in that." I lean in to make him laugh.

"I thought about it." He laughs. "But I figured I'd be pushing it."

"Good call," I agree while the man is declaring us husband and wife.

"You may now kiss your bride," he invites and Levi steps forward.

"Your lips had better be clean," I say right before he smiles and leans in and kisses my lips.

It's very quick but long enough for the photographer to get the picture. The crowd is on their feet clapping for us.

"Well, husband," I say, reaching up and wiping the gloss off his lips, "only three hundred and sixty-four days to go."

He laughs when I say that, shaking his head and slipping his hand into mine, leaning sideways to me. "But who's counting?" he replies.

Twelve

Levi

"Shall we?" I look down at her hand holding mine as we take our walk down the aisle. Everyone is on their feet. I look over at her and I swear on everything that I have she is the most beautiful bride I've ever seen. When the doors opened and I saw her, my heart stopped in my chest. It felt hard to even breathe. Her eyes looked at all the people there like a deer in headlights. Until she saw me and it was like she calmed down.

When we finally make it into the reception space, there is a server there holding a silver tray with two glasses of champagne on it. I grab them both and hand one to Eva. "Shall we toast to our wedding?"

"You have a lot of explaining to do," she accuses, and

it looks like she's about to say something else when the photographer comes over and starts taking pictures.

"Smile." I put a big smile on my face as she glares at me, but at the same time planning my murder, it's a beautiful sight. She finishes her champagne in four gulps before placing it on the silver tray. I add my empty glass to the tray also when the rest of the guests come out of the ceremony space.

"Congratulations," Stefano says when he walks into the reception space, shaking my hand and then slapping my shoulder. "You pulled it off." He turns toward Eva. "Were you surprised?" he asks as he bends to kiss her cheek.

"That's an understatement," she replies, still holding her bouquet in her hand. "I can't believe we forgot the rings." She puts her hand to her head and I see the ring I bought for her yesterday.

"I can't believe you didn't freak out about it," Stefano states, shaking his head laughing, and it's at that moment she looks down and sees the ring I slid on her finger. I glare at him for bringing it up. I mean, I know eventually she would have seen it, but I was hoping she would have had a couple more drinks in her before she did.

"What the fuck is this?" She looks down at her ring, her eyes huge before she looks up at me. "What is this?" She studies her hand for a second before looking back up at me.

"I think that's what they call an engagement-slash-wedding band." I put my hands in my pockets to stop them from reaching out to grab her hand and study the ring on it.

"This is," she starts and looks around seeing the photographer there, "this is too much."

"I wasn't going to let you get married with a cheap-ass ring," I inform her. "I'm not an asshole."

"Um, you could have gotten me a plain gold band," she suggests. "This is—"

"It's a four-carat, pear-shaped diamond ring with an eternity band," Stefano fills her in. "Even I was impressed."

"Four carats," she repeats, looking at me and then down at her hand. "Can you get a refund when you return it next year?"

"I'm not returning a wedding ring; that's like bad karma," I tell her, nodding at people who are smiling and shouting congratulations as they come into the reception space.

"Can we have the bride and groom pose for pictures, please?" the photographer asks. "If you would come over here." He points at the outside of the barn.

"This discussion isn't over," Eva states between clenched teeth as she walks in front of me and I get a view of the back, or actually the lack of her dress back. She swings her hips right and left, and I blink a couple of times before I look to the side to make sure no one has caught me trying to check her out. We walk outside and the heat hits you right away. "Over there is perfect." He points at the side.

I start walking when Eva stops beside me and quickly slips out of her shoes before walking on the grass. We walk over to the side where there are piles of rocks right before the field starts. He points at the rocks. "Eva, can you climb up there?" I hold out my hand for her as she climbs on the low rock. "Levi." He points for me to stand behind her. I follow his lead, stepping up and standing behind her. "Very nice," he says, taking a test shot. "Levi, put your left hand on her hip so we can see your wedding band." I grab her hip in my hand, pulling her to me at the same time.

"Getting frisky there." She looks up at me and I can't help but laugh at her. "But if you go any lower, I'm going to break that pretty little hand of yours." This really makes me laugh. "You may have paid for the cow but there will be no milk-giving."

"Perfect," the photographer says, capturing the moment. "Eva, hold your bouquet down on one side." She does as she's told. He takes the picture and looks at it. "Nice," he says as the wind picks up and blows her dress to the side, her hair tickling my nose. I move her hair to the side with my spare hand, her neck is now on display. "Okay, bend down and kiss her neck."

"Um," I start to say, "I think we should just stick to standing side by side." I look at her, waiting for her to say something to him.

"It's one picture," she states, "just pretend."

"How do I pretend to kiss your neck?" I chuckle as I lean down and I get as close as I can. "How's this?" I ask and she giggles and lifts her shoulder.

Her hand comes up to touch my face. "That tickles," she admits to me as I hear the clicking of the camera go off.

"Just a couple more seconds," I say. I close my eyes, trying to focus on anything but the way her hand is on my face. How her hip fits in my hand perfectly, and especially how her ass feels on my cock.

"Perfect," he says and we spring apart as if someone doused us with ice water. I slip my hand in hers as I help her off the rocks.

"You okay?" I ask as we walk toward the reception, our hands still intertwined with each other. The sun has gone down and you can hear the soft hums of crickets in the air.

"Yeah, Alice called before," she says. "CPS is having a meeting with the lawyer tomorrow to go over the will and stuff. The reading of the will is in two days."

"Okay, we can go together," I tell her, our steps going slower than usual.

"You don't have to do that; you've done more than enough."

"I think I should, as your husband." She looks over at me. "Don't you think?"

"I have no idea what to think," she admits, "this is all foreign territory for me." I drop her hand out of mine and put my arm around her shoulders, bringing her to me. She puts her head on my shoulder. "Everything is so real right now." Her voice gets low and I stop walking, knowing she needs a minute.

I turn her and pull her into my arms. She drops the bouquet at her feet as she wraps her arms around my waist, her forehead in the middle of my chest. "It's going to be okay," I reassure her, kissing the top of her head as she looks to the side. My hand rubs her bare arm as she looks out into the distance.

"You promise?" she finally whispers and I can feel wetness on my shirt.

"Yes," I confirm. At this moment, I would promise her the world because there is no one who deserves it more. There is no one who has busted their ass more than Eva to get where she is. There is no one who has put other people before herself. There is no one, and I mean no one, who deserves to finally have smooth sailing more than Eva. "I promise."

She finally looks up at me and I can see the tears in her eyes as she tries to blink them away. She puts a smile on her face. "Thank you," she finally says to me.

I smile down at her. "What's a fake wedding between friends?" She throws her head back and laughs. Filling the empty night with her laughter is like music to my ears.

"It's going to be okay," she finally declares. "Now let's get in there and eat some food. Maybe drink a little and head on home."

"Sounds like a great plan," I tell her as she slips out of my arms. "I, for one, need a nice big drink."

"Wow, married for an hour and I'm already pushing you to drink." I look over at her and she winks at me. "It's starting off very promising."

I don't answer her; instead I walk into the reception space where everyone is sitting down to eat. I walk over and pull out a chair for her as she sits down. For the next three hours, it feels like it's normal. Or at least our brand of normal. Until I'm at the bar getting a bottle of water when Markos slides up to the bar. "What are you drinking?" he asks, leaning on the bar and looking toward the dance floor where the girls are dancing.

"Water." I lean against the bar looking at him. "Do you want anything?"

"No." He shakes his head. "I'm just here to do my duty." My eyebrows pinch together. "Her father was my uncle," he starts, "and it's my place to inform you that if you hurt her, I'll hurt you."

I look at him. "Why would you even think I'm going to hurt her?" I ask. "I would never hurt her."

"Well, I had to make sure you know that if you do, I'll kick your ass."

"Message received," I assure him as the bartender gives me my bottle of water. "Sadly, this isn't the weirdest thing that has happened to me today." I unscrew the top of the bottle and take a sip, looking back at the dance floor, watching Eva throw her head back and laughing. Her hair is now pinned up in a ponytail.

"Something tells me this day is going to change your life," Mark states before pushing off and walking over to his wife. I don't move from the bar; instead I watch Eva dancing around to "Dancing Queen," thinking that maybe Mark isn't wrong.

When the plane touches down the day after, I have to wake her up. "Eva," I say softly to her and she opens her eyes. "We're home." She nods for a second, closing her eyes and getting up. I unbuckle my seat belt, standing up and opening the overhead bin.

The black band on my hand catches my attention. "I can't believe I fell asleep," she says as I hand her her bag. She reaches out and grabs it and her ring catches my attention. "We really did it," I say to myself as she steps out of the row and walks off the plane.

We walk down toward the baggage claim, neither of us saying anything to the other as we wait for our bags to come out. They are the first two out, and when we get into the car, I look over at her, her head buried in her phone.

I pull up to her house. "I have to head home and pack," I tell her and she nods at me, "get things settled there. I'll swing by and get you tomorrow morning."

"Okay." She opens the door and I follow her out to grab the bag for her.

"I'm leaving right after the lawyer's office," I remind her. "I have to head out, it was scheduled before all of this."

"You mean before you married me," she jokes with me and I chuckle.

"Have fun, husband." She grabs her bag from me. "Be safe." She turns to walk away, looking over her shoulder. "The last thing I want is another kid in the house and a baby momma." I can't help but really laugh now.

"Never imagined my wife telling me to have safe sex with someone else." I put my hand on my hip.

She gasps and turns to look at me. "You imagined yourself with a wife and didn't tell me?" She pffts. "Regardless, I'm the perfect wife." She walks backward.

"I wonder if they give out trophies and stuff." She tries not to laugh at her own joke but fails. "I could put it on the fireplace mantel." She walks up the steps to her front door.

"You're a nut!" I shout at her as she steps into her front door.

"I've been called worse!" she hollers, lifting her hand to say goodbye before closing the door. I don't move from my spot, and for the life of me I don't know why. It's almost as if I don't want to leave her, but I know it's silly.

"She'll call you if she needs anything." I try to talk to myself as I finally turn around and head back to my car. Opening the driver's door, I get in, looking once more at the front door. I don't know if I'm disappointed that she's not there waving or that she didn't ask me to come back to her. I shake my head, trying to clear out all the thoughts I don't want to have. "Snap out of it," I say right before I pull off and head home.

Thirteen

Eva

The phone ringing has me blinking my eyes open. It takes me a minute to realize where I am. The fog from my sleep makes me close my eyes again. But the ringing makes me open them again. I reach out from under the warm cocoon of my blankets to grab it. "Hello," I mumble, putting it to my ear and pressing it into the pillow.

"Are you still sleeping?" I hear Levi whisper, and I moan as I snuggle deeper into the bed.

"Couldn't sleep last night," I mumble to him, my eyelids feeling like they weigh a hundred pounds. "I think I fell asleep at four in the morning."

"I hate to say this but," he talks, and my eyes open,

suddenly afraid at what he has to say, "it's, like, nine o'clock."

I go from lying down to sitting in the matter of a second. "What?" I shriek, taking the phone from my ear. Checking the clock on the phone at the same time, I turn my wrist around to see if perhaps it's a different time. "I set an alarm," I snarl.

"Did you do it for a.m. or p.m.?" He chuckles and I glare at the phone, but I don't say anything when I go and check and see that I did, in fact, set it for p.m.

"You're my husband one day and already you are getting on my nerves," I warn him, without telling him he was right.

"Actually, it's been two days." I look down at the phone. "And because I'm such a good husband, I'm going to let you go get dressed and I'll pick up coffee on my way there."

"Now this is what I'm talking about," I say, throwing the covers off me, "music to my ears." I toss the phone to the side before rushing to the bathroom. I quickly wash my face and brush my teeth. I comb through my hair, deciding to leave it loose today. Reaching for my makeup bag, I quickly add a layer of mascara before going into my walk-in closet. "What does one wear to a reading of her sister's will?" I ask the hangers, trying not to think about the fact that I'll never be able to call her again. I will never, ever be able to ask her advice. We met each other later in life, when our teenage years were behind us, but she was still my older sister. There were times when she would give me advice. Times where she would just listen to me talk. And there were times when she was my biggest cheerleader. I ignore the tightness of my chest. I also ignore the way my chest is heaving when I pull a pair of black pants off the hanger. I put one foot in and then the other, and the tear falls on my hand. I sniff back the tears, ignoring that the tears are not coming one at a time, no, not this time. The tears are raining down my face, and every single time I blink my eyes shut, I see Lisa's smile. She didn't have the best life, but she made the best of what she had of it. Her biggest wish was to be a mother, and it took three IVF tries before she called me screaming at the top of her lungs, right before she sobbed, "I'm going to be a mama." Moving toward another hanger, I slip the black short-sleeved silk top off and now the memory of painting the nursery with her snowballs its way out. Out of the box I locked away to get through the past couple of days. The box I refused to open because no one had time to break down. There were things to be done. I had to make sure I did what I needed to do to ensure I would make Lisa proud; things to do to make sure Cici ended up with me. The little girl with the same blue eyes as Lisa and me. The same blue eyes our mother had. Whatever I was going to do was going to be better than what we had. Anything was better than what we had.

I button up the silk top and that is when it happens. That is when the walls come crashing down and the sob escapes me. I put my hand to my mouth to stop the sob, but it roars out of me at the same time my knees go weak and I crumble there in my walk-in closet. My eyes close,

I was with Lisa in the delivery room when Cici was born. The minute they laid Cici on her chest, there was this overwhelming sense of love that came to her. She sobbed the whole time and all I could do is hold her and cry with her. "Hi, baby," she kept saying the whole time. The whole time she repeated how much she loved her over and over again. It was a memory I was now never going to forget. It was a memory I would spend the rest of my life repeating to Cici every day if she wanted me to.

My head hangs down in front of me, my hair falling in front of my face. I don't hear the front door open. I don't hear him come in the room. I don't hear his voice speak to me. All I know is he's squatting down in front of me. "Hey," he says softly, putting his finger under my chin and raising it. I look into his eyes and all I can do is sob. He sits on the floor in my closet and pulls me into his lap. Pressing my head to his chest, the warmth of his arms chases off the coldness that was filling my bones. "It's okay," he soothes me as I let out the tears that I've been holding back since I got the phone call. "It's going to be okay," is all he says over and over again as I let it all out. I don't know how long I stay like that, once the tears leave me, all I can do is stare at the blank white wall.

"The only thing she ever wanted was to be a mom." My words come out low, my voice still trembling. "Over and over again, every birthday when she blew out the candles, that was her wish." I smile. "I mean, you aren't supposed to tell people your wish but she didn't believe in that, so she told anyone who was within listening range." Levi kisses my head at the same time his arms tighten around me. "I promised her that I would take care of Cici," I say softly before pushing off Levi's chest. "It's silly she even had to ask me. I even thought it was silly when she sat me down, nervous to ask me, so nervous her hands were shaking. I laughed at her because she was the strongest woman I know."

"Second strongest," Levi corrects, pushing my hair away from my face and behind my shoulder. "She's the second-strongest woman I know."

I smile at him. "You're only saying that because I'm your wife and you have to."

He chuckles. "I'm saying that because it's the truth." I put my hands on his chest, feeling his heart beating. "Now, as much fun as this is"—he looks around—"being on the floor of your closet." He raises his hand to look at his watch. "We should be going."

I nod my head and I'm about to get up when I stop. "Thank you." He smirks at me. "You know, in case I haven't told you before."

"I'm keeping track," he teases, pushing the other side of my hair behind my shoulder. "Your payback list is very, very long." I can't help but laugh because I'm sure it's going to be longer by the time we can get divorced.

I get up and he quickly follows me. "Go clean your face," he urges. "The last thing I want them to think is that I did that to you." I gasp as he points a finger at my face.

"Rude." I turn, walking to the bathroom and he follows me in there but stops at the door. I look at my face in the mirror. "My eyes are red and so is my nose.

My sister just died." I throw my hands up, turning to look at him. "Where is my coffee?"

"In the car," he states and I take him in. His black suit with the white button-down shirt fits him like a glove. He always wears clothes like he's on a runway, but his suits, his suits always push him above and beyond. Especially when he crosses his arms over his chest, pulling his sleeves up, letting you see the silver Rolex he wears. There is something about a man and a good-looking watch to make him that much better. "Now, are you ready?"

I take a deep breath in as I turn and look at the mirror one more time, the redness in my eyes is down a bit, but they are still puffy. My nose is still a touch red. "I'm ready." I nod, walking to him. "Let's go," I say, walking past him and toward the stairs. We walk down the front steps and he opens the car door for me.

"Now you want extra brownie points," I joke with him, getting in the car and picking up the white cup of coffee. "Good thing I can scratch coffee off that list." I take a sip. "This is cold."

"I think what you mean to say is thank you," he nudges, right before he slams the car door.

He gets in and I don't drink the coffee because the closer he gets to the lawyer's office, the more my stomach gets tighter and tighter. When he parks the car and I press the button for my seat belt, I mumble to myself as I grab the door handle, pushing it open, "I think I'm going to throw up."

Levi pulls open the door to the office, letting me

walk in before him. I wait for him before I walk into the office. Josephine is there talking to Alice, who just smiles at me. "Sorry we are late, we had a little bit of a meltdown," I admit, looking at Levi, who puts his hand at the base of my back. "I don't know if you've met." I look at Josephine. "This is my husband, Levi." I turn to him. "This is Josephine."

"I think we met already," Josephine says to him and he just nods. "You are married?" She looks at us.

"We are," Levi confirms, slipping his hand in mine.

I don't have time to say anything before a tall man comes out. "Hello." He nods at me. "You must be Evangeline," he says my full name. "I'm Larry." He holds out his hand. "I'm sorry about your loss."

"Thank you," I reply, shaking his hand.

"If you will follow me," he says. And I look at Alice.

"I'll wait here if you need me," she states and I nod at her, not letting go of Levi's hand. We follow him into his office with Josephine following us.

"Please sit." He motions to the chairs that are around the conference table. I pull out one of the chairs and sit down, looking over to see Levi pull out the chair next to me. He pulls my chair as close as it can get to his.

"You okay?" He leans over asking me and I just nod my head.

Josephine sits next to Larry as he opens the folder in front of him. He looks down, starting to read. I look down at my hands and the tears come again. Levi reaches over and puts his arm around me. "It's okay," he whispers in my ear and I just nod.

"To my sister, Evangeline," I hear Larry say, "I leave you my most prized possession. Cici James Crinkle. There is no one who would make a better mother than you," he reads and I put my hand in front of my mouth.

I look over at Josephine, not sure if Larry has anything more to say. "When can I have my niece?"

She smiles at me and gets up from her seat, walking out of the room. "What's going on?" I get up, my legs shaking, my whole body starting to tremble. "Should I get Alice?" "I don't think that is necessary," Larry states and not even a minute later I see Josephine coming back into the room.

The sob rips through me when I see Cici looking around. My feet move before I can even think. "There she is." I put a smile on my face. "Hello, baby girl."

Cici looks at me and gives me a smile before she reaches for me. I hold out my hands and take her in my arms. "I've got you, baby girl." I put my hand on her head, laying it on my chest. "I've got you."

Fourteen

Levi

"Cabin crew, please take your seats for landing." I hear the pilot say and look out the window at the city below us. The flight attendant comes on and tells us we will be landing in a matter of minutes. I lean back in my seat with my hands crossed on my stomach, my eyes looking at the black ring on my wedding finger.

It's been over a week since we've gotten married, and it's been exactly one week since I left Eva at her house with Cici. I didn't think anything about leaving, but the day after, I was itching to return home. I've been on the West Coast and I never thought those three hours mattered, but they really mattered when you woke up at seven and it was ten her time and she was working.

Then when you finish work at eight but then it's eleven her time. So it's been quick phone calls during the week. Texts also have been few and far between.

The wheels hit the runway, and I turn the Airplane Mode off. My finger nervously taps the phone, waiting for it to start beeping with alerts. I look down when it vibrates in my hand showing me emails are coming in. I pull up my text thread with Eva.

Me: *Just landed.*

I look down to see if the gray bubble pops up, showing she's texting me, but nothing comes up. I wait for the ding of the seat belt before I reach under my seat to grab my backpack, then open the overhead bin and grabbing my black carry-on bag. I slide it over my shoulder, while I hold the bag in front of me, waiting for the plane door to open before I walk out. I make my way toward the baggage claim and exit. Passing the baggage claim, I head straight to the parking garage. Fetching the keys out of my bag, I press the unlock button, pulling open the back door and tossing the bag in there, along with my backpack, before sliding into the driver's seat.

I pull out of the parking lot and head straight to my place. In a matter of twenty minutes, I'm walking into my place and tossing my keys at the table by the door, right next to the stack of mail my cleaning lady put there this morning. I dump my bag on the bed, unzipping it as I take out my dirty clothes and toss them in the laundry basket in the closet. The phone rings from inside my suit jacket pocket, pulling it out I see that it's Eva.

"Hello," I greet, putting the phone to my ear and

leaning it against my shoulder.

"Hey." She sounds breathless. "Where are you?"

"I'm home grabbing some clothes." I walk over to the shelf and grab two pairs of jeans along with two jogging shorts. Going back to the bag, I fill it with the clothes in my hands before going back to get some T-shirts.

"Okay, well, Josephine is going to be here in like fifteen minutes," she says, and I hear her running around. "It's their first visit since I got Cici and I'm about to freak the F out." She hisses the last word.

"Okay, I'll be there in ten minutes," I assure her. "Do you need anything?"

"No," she replies, "just get here." She disconnects, and I rush to get to her house.

I pull into her driveway and park next to her car at the same time as a car pulls up to the curb. I get out of the driver's seat and grab my bag from the back of the car. Walking up the front steps, I look over my shoulder to see Josephine coming up the walkway. "Hello," I greet her, opening the front door. Luckily, I know the code to the door. "Come in," I say to her as Eva walks out of the kitchen, baby Cici on her hip. She's dressed in yoga pants and a white shirt that is almost a crop top. Her hair is piled on the top of her head. I can't help the smile that fills my face, and it's strange how nervous I am standing in front of her. She isn't sure what to say to me, but her eyes look behind me at Josephine. "Hi." I smile at her as I walk to her, bending down and kissing her lips. She looks at me shocked, especially when I lean over and kiss Cici's soft cheek. "I'm going to put away my bag in the room," I tell Eva, who just nods. I then turn to Josephine. "Sorry, I was traveling for work and my plane was delayed," I lie to her. "I'll be right back."

"Take your time," Josephine assures me. I nod at her as I take a couple of steps toward the stairs and see the changes that have happened in one week. On top of the mantel is a picture of us from our wedding. I want to walk over to it and pick it up to look at it, but instead I just walk up the steps toward Eva's room.

I place the bag on the floor inside the room. I take off my suit jacket, tossing it on the bed before turning to walk back downstairs. I hear Cici fussing when I get down to the last step. "How have things been going?" Josephine sits with a pen in her hand and a pad, where she is writing notes. She is at the table in front of Eva, with Cici on her lap, but turned toward her.

"It's been good," she states and I know she's lying. The few times I did talk to her, she sounded like she was hanging on by a thread. "Definitely a little bit of a learning curve." She gets up now as Cici lays her head on her shoulder as Eva moves side to side. "I think she misses Lisa."

Josephine just nods at her. I walk into the kitchen and see she has a high chair in the corner. I walk to her. "Do you want some water?" I ask Eva, putting my hand on her lower back.

"Yes," she replies, looking up at me, her look is something from exhausted to scared all in one. "Would you like something?" she asks Josephine, who just shakes her head.

I walk into the kitchen toward the fridge and see bottles in the sink. There is what looks like a coffee machine on the counter next to the real coffee machine, except a bottle is under it. There is also a rack of bottles right beside it. I open the fridge, grabbing her a water bottle before returning to the table. Eva is still standing rocking, but now Cici is lying on her chest. I open the bottle for her and hand it to her. She takes a couple of sips before handing it back to me.

"Well, I think I got everything I need," Josephine says to us. I look over at the living room and see there is now a rocking chair in the corner. Right beside it is a white basket with colorful toys inside it. On the floor is a square carpet thing with toys scattered around it. "I will let you know if we have any other questions." She puts away her pad. I move with Eva toward the door as Josephine leaves. I put my arm around her shoulders as we wave goodbye before walking back into the house.

She steps toward the couch as she sits down. "Where did you get all this?" I ask as I reach down and pick up a toy.

"Lisa's apartment." She grabs one of the little blankets from the side and places it over Cici. "I spent the week going through everything."

I gasp. "Why didn't you wait for me?" I'm pissed I wasn't there for her. "You should have waited for me," I finally say, sitting down on the couch in front of her.

"You weren't here," she responds softly, her voice low. "I worked on it at night." She looks down at Cici. "I got everything done, and finally, this morning, they brought over Cici's things." She rubs Cici's cheek with her finger. "I have to go back and get all the rest of the furniture."

"I'll get a couple of guys from the office," I tell her. "We'll get it all settled next week."

She just nods at me. "I bought beer." She motions with her chin toward the fridge. I get up knowing that was my hint to get her a beer.

I walk over to the fridge, grabbing two bottles of beer. I twist off the two caps, looking over at her. "Do you want a glass?" She just shakes her head.

I hand her one beer before taking a pull of my own. "You look exhausted, by the way." I try to hide the smirk on my face when she glares at me as she takes her own pull of her beer.

"Good," she huffs as she takes another pull. "I feel worse than I look," she admits.

"How are you doing?" I finally ask her, looking at her.

"I've been better. I think Cici is missing Lisa." She looks down at Cici in her arms. "I know they said she wouldn't remember but she misses her. She gets up at night and calls for her." I don't say anything to her. I just listen, happy I'm home. "Even when I get her, she is happy but keeps looking around for her."

"I think I read something that said kids see dead people," I share and she gasps. Cici stirs on her chest.

"Why would you say that?" she hisses at me. "Do you think Lisa is here?" She looks around and I can't help but laugh at her.

"I don't know if she's here now," I say, taking a pull

of my beer. "I'm not really versed in how it works. But from what I read online, people usually cross over."

She looks at me, her mouth hanging open. "What the hell are you reading online?"

I shake my head. "It was something I read a while ago. They did a study."

She's about to tell me something else when Cici stirs in her arms. She looks down at her and smiles as Cici's head bounces up. "Hi, Princess V," she coos to her as she leans forward and puts the bottle of beer on the table in front of her. Cici smiles at her as she rubs her eyes with her hands that are balled up. "Did you have a nice nap?" She kisses her head and Cici buries her face in her chest, rubbing side to side.

"That was a nap?" I look at her strange.

"It was a catnap." She picks her up as she stands. "Did you see any ghosts?" she asks her and I laugh.

"A catnap," I repeat. "It was four minutes."

"You would be surprised what a four-minute catnap will do." She rubs Cici's back. "I'm going to go and start dinner." She walks to me. "Can you hold her?"

I put the bottle of beer down on the table. "Yeah," I say, nervous about this whole thing. If we are being honest, I think I've spent maybe sixty whole minutes in my entire life with a baby. Give or take, and that was when one of the parents would want to take a picture and have me hold them. I get up and rub my hands down the front of my pants, but my hands still stay clammy. "I should wash my hands."

She stands there looking up at me with a tired face,

yet looking more beautiful than I think she's ever looked. A baby with the same eyes as her looks at me, unsure what is going on. Her cheeks looking a bit rosy. "I'm going to wash my hands," I tell Cici, "and then I'll take you."

"Are you nervous?" Eva asks me, her tone sounding like this is entertaining to her. "The big bad Levi who is kick-ass in the boardroom." She looks down at Cici. "The Levi who never lets anyone see him sweat." I roll my eyes. "The same Levi who can skydive by himself?" I exhale. "The same Levi who—"

"Yeah," I cut her off, turning to walk to the kitchen, but not before turning and looking over my shoulder, "that Levi."

Fifteen

Eva

"Big bad wolf Levi." I roll my lips as he walks away from me to the kitchen. "The same Levi who rescued a cat from a tree." I watch him as he walks away from me. His dress pants fit him perfectly, like always, and the white dress shirt is wrinkled in the back, but you can feel that it's soft. I lean my head back on the couch as Cici just stares at him also, a dollop of drool falling from her lower lip. I quickly grab the throw blanket that I now have all over the house for this reason here.

He turns the water on at the sink and looks back at me. "That fucking cat was all the way at the top of the tree." He pushes down on the white soap cap, the foam soap filling his hand as he lathers them. "I almost broke my face."

I can't stop the laugh that roars through me. It's been a crazy week and the last thing I've done all this week was laugh. But with Levi here in the house, Cici looking at me with a smile, and finally us having passed the first inspection of CPS, I finally am able to let go for just a little bit. "It wasn't that tall."

He rinses his hands under the water, glaring at me as he does. "I didn't see you climbing up to help me." He turns the water off, grabbing a dish towel from the side of the sink. "No, not you. You were there filming the whole thing."

I snort and get up. "I was doing it so we could go viral and maybe, just maybe, end up on *Oprah* or maybe even *Ellen*. Also, didn't you get laid for a full six months telling girls that story and then showing them the video? I think what you mean to say is, 'Thank you, Eva, for your amazing cinematography skills.'"

He presses his hips to the counter, his glare on me still strong, but the minute Cici screeches in my arms, he looks over at her and the look is gone. In its place is a warm look, his eyes look like a warm ocean after a sunny day. "Is your aunt a funny one?" he asks Cici when I get closer to him. "Are you sure you want to do this?" His eyes come to me and they stay the same. "How about I try to cook dinner?" He looks around the kitchen.

I chuckle. "You made me Kraft mac and cheese once," I remind him, "and how did that work out for us?"

"I was going by the instructions." He puts his hands on his hips. "It said to boil for seven or eight minutes or until tender."

"And how long did you boil them for?" I tilt my head to the side as both Cici and I look at him.

"Ten minutes," he answers softly.

"And what happened after that?" I roll my lips after his jaw gets tight.

"The noodles fell apart." His teeth clench as he says this. He then grabs one of his buttons at his wrist and unbuttons it, before rolling it up to his elbow. "And then it turned to mush once I added in the milk and cheese." He repeats the action with the second arm until the sleeves are rolled up to his elbows.

"So you still want to attempt to cook for us?" I ask.

"I can order something." He snaps his fingers. "That way you don't have to leave me in charge of the child and we are both happy."

"I've been eating out all week long," I tell him. "I just want a nice home-cooked meal."

"Fine," he agrees, stepping to me, "but the minute I say switch." He grabs her under her arms, bringing her to him awkwardly. "We switch."

"Like in wrestling?" I ask, walking to the sink and washing my own hands. "Are you hungry?" I ask as I walk over to the fridge.

"I haven't eaten since I grabbed a sandwich at the airport," he admits as he holds Cici to his chest, moving side to side, bouncing up and down.

"So how was your week?" I ask as I open the fridge, grabbing a red and yellow pepper, an onion, and the Italian sausage. Placing it on the counter beside the cutting board, I turn to grab a couple of potatoes.

"It was uneventful," he says to me as Cici squirms in his arms. "I think we might have to switch." He looks at me, then down at Cici.

"Why don't you go over there?" I point toward the floor mat. "She likes to play with the square toy." I point at the toy in the middle of the mat. "She doesn't sit up too well on her own, but she can sit in the middle of your legs."

"Okay," he replies, walking over to the mat and trying to decide how he's going to sit down with Cici. I peel the potatoes the whole time, looking over to see Levi.

"We got this," he assures Cici. "Maybe we don't got this," he recants as he gets to his knees, "but we are going to try." I can't help but smile as I dice the potatoes and place them in a pot of water before walking back over to where the peppers and onion are as I slice them. "We did it." I hear Levi say and look over to see him smiling down at Cici as she sits in the middle of his legs. He reaches forward to grab the square activity toy that she loves. She smacks her hands down on the square before reaching out and grabbing the side of one square, as she presses the button. "That's red," he tells her and I can't help but smile. "What's that sound?" he asks gently. "That's a cow."

I turn around and grab a pan, placing it on the stove and then adding olive oil to it. I look over again to make sure he's okay. I see Cici look up at him as he tells her all the colors on the square toy. He could literally be reciting the phone book and she would be interested in him. I turn back, tossing the peppers and onions in the pan before grabbing the knife and slicing the sausage. I'm beyond exhausted, the past week has been crazy almost twenty-hour days. After working at the salon all day long, I would rush over to Lisa's place, and every night I would put Cici in her bed while I would work through packing up her place. Usually she slept the night, but then she would wake up crying and calling out for Mama. I didn't know if sleeping in the house made her think Lisa was going to be there or not. I debated not sleeping there, but I wanted to get it over with.

I know I should have gotten someone to do it. Everyone I know told me the same thing over and over again, but I just felt like I needed to do it. I had to do it for her and for Cici. The hardest thing I ever did was going through her clothes. Packing her stuff, I did put a box aside for Cici for when she got older. It was the outfit she wore when she was christened, knowing that the pictures would be forever in her room. The outfit she would always be in, and the minute I saw it, it took me an hour to pick myself up off the floor. All her jewelry is put aside, waiting for me to find the time to open a safety-deposit box for when Cici wants it. There is no way I can chance losing that.

I thought cleaning out her clothes was hard. It was nothing like cleaning out her bedside night tables. You don't know what you keep in there, but Lisa had pictures of the three of us in there. She even had a picture of our mother. She had so many little books stacked in one drawer, I thought they were books until I picked up one and it fell to the floor. It was as if someone knocked it out of my hand. When I bent over to pick it up, I saw that it was a journal. Lisa's journal, the date entry at the top. My eyes roamed the page for a good couple of minutes before I shut it. There must have been over twenty of them in the drawer and another box full. They were also going in the safety-deposit box for Cici. When she was old enough, I would give her the key and she could do what she wanted with them.

"What is she cooking?" I hear Levi's voice, so I look over at him. "Whatever it is, it sure does smell good." He looks down at Cici. "Are you hungry?"

Cici just babbles back at him. "I know, me, too, girl, me, too." I can't help but laugh as I toss the sausage into the pan and stir everything together before placing the cover half on it.

I move over to the freezer, opening it. "Should we do chicken and carrots with peas?" I ask over my shoulder. "Or broccoli, carrots, and tofu?"

"Eww," Levi says. "Pick A, girl," he whispers in her ear, "pick A."

"If she doesn't eat tofu today, she is going to eat it tomorrow." I laugh at him as I walk over, grabbing another pot to cook her food.

It takes me a good thirty minutes before all the food is done. "Can you put her in her chair?" I ask Levi, who nods at me. He grabs her around her chest with one arm as he pushes himself up.

He walks over to her chair beside the table, the one I unpacked this afternoon. "Um," he ponders, "how do I?" I walk over to him, taking Cici from him.

"You just need to…" I place her in the chair as she slides down on her bum, before I buckle her in. I look over at him and he grimaces.

"I'm never doing that; you can hurt her legs."

"I promise you, I'm not hurting her," I assure him as I put a bib on her.

"I'll do the plates," he states to me, "you feed her." He points at her as he walks over and prepares us two plates. The two of us sit with Cici between us in her chair. He watches my every single move as I feed her.

When she starts to get cranky, I look over and see that it's almost six thirty, Cici is a creature of habit. So I know I have thirty minutes to get her washed and in bed. "I'm going to go and give her a bath," I announce, taking the bib off and placing it on the high chair.

I walk up the steps toward the bathroom and I'm shocked when I feel him right behind me. "What are you doing?" I ask as I turn on the lights.

"I think I should know this, too," he says, putting his hands in his pockets as he leans against the doorjamb. "What if they ask me about this?" I point at the bathtub.

"Well," I start to tell him as I grab the white towel, placing it on the rug before laying her down on it. "The first thing is to put her down." I point at Cici. "And then start the water." I reach for the yellow duck in the corner that tells you the temperature. "Toss this in there to make sure that it's not too hot. Then you add a couple of the other toys." I point at the net that is in the corner drying out the toys from the night before.

He stands up. "Wait," he says, grabbing his phone

from his pocket. "What temp should it be?"

I laugh at him. "Between ninety-five and a hundred." I shrug my shoulder. "You can feel it with your hand, it shouldn't be too hot, then you undress her." I move back over to Cici, who is now kicking her feet and turning over. "Which is easier said than done," I joke, turning her over. Levi comes in and squats down beside her.

"Look at the phone," he tells Cici, handing her the phone, shocking me as she takes it from him and babbles, but it gives me enough time to get her undressed. "Once she's undressed, you just place her in the tub." I grab the phone from her and hand it back to Levi before placing her in the tub.

"Okay, I think I can handle that. I'm going to go clean up the kitchen and I'll be back for after-bath talk." I nod at him, sitting beside the tub washing Cici.

"Wash, wash, wash," I singsong as I wash her. "Scrub, scrub, scrub." Her hands slap the water, making it go everywhere. "Splash, splash, splash."

I take her out of the bath and wrap her in the white towel before entering her bedroom. It was a spare bedroom, but as of this morning, it's now hers.

"Holy crap." I hear from beside me. "Is this all hers?" Levi asks as he walks into the room.

"Yeah." I walk to the changing table. "They picked it up this morning and I spent all day making sure it was just like home," I inform him as I grab the lavender cream. He stands beside me as I get her ready for bed.

Cici starts to get cranky by the time I'm buttoning up her pj's. "Here, rock her while I go get her bottle." I hand her to him and he walks to the corner where the rocking chair sits.

I rush downstairs, seeing the kitchen spotless, all the food put away. I grab a bottle and press the button. The best thing ever invented was this bottle machine. You put in the powdered formula, making you a warm bottle every time. It's a Keurig but for kids. I turn off the lights before walking upstairs. "And then when we met, she fell madly in love with me." He looks up at me, a smile filling his face. "I'm telling her how we met." I can't help but roll my eyes, trying not to smile at him.

"Stop filling her head." I walk over to her and she reaches up for me when she sees her bottle. "Get lost so I can tell her the real story."

"Good night, girl," he says, kissing her cheek. "I'm going to go and get a shower." I just nod, sitting down in the chair.

"Are you ready for bed?" I ask Cici, laying her on her side. "I'm going to let you in on a little secret," I tell her as I give her the bottle. "That Levi, he's a charmer, the key is not to fall for it." I rub her cheek as I rock her. Her eyes close as soon as she finishes her bottle. I get up and place her in her crib. "Good night, baby girl," I whisper, turning on the white noise machine before walking out.

I walk into my bedroom, collapsing on my bed. My body feels like it hasn't slept in over five years. I literally can't move, even if I tried. I'm about to slip out of my pants when the door to the bathroom opens and Levi comes out dressed in shorts. "She down?" he asks and I nod at him, my mouth suddenly dry. I must really be fucking tired if the only thing I can do is stare at his chest. Also, when did he start working out like this?

All I do is watch him walk around the bed to the other side, tossing the throw pillows to the floor. "Um," is the only thing that comes out of my mouth. My heart beats really fast as I sit up.

He throws the covers back and then slides into bed. "I'm exhausted," he says.

I jump out of bed as if someone told me that it was on fire, or you threw ice water on me. "What the hell are you doing?"

"Going to bed." He fixes the pillows under his head.

"In here?" I point at the floor as my voice goes really, really high.

Levi sits up in the bed. "Where else would I sleep?"

"I don't know?" I throw up my arms. "On the couch?" I point at the door toward where the couch is.

"For a year?" He is the one who is hollering now and all I can do is roll my eyes at him.

"We can also get you a blow-up bed." I try to think of where we would put this blow-up bed.

"For a year?" Again, he yells. "A year! You want me to sleep on a couch or a blow-up bed. I will remind you that—"

I hold up my hand. "Fine," I relent, huffing out, "but no fishy stuff." I point at him, walking back to the bed.

"Do you want to put a pillow between us?" he asks once I get into bed next to him.

"Obviously." I grab one of the throw pillows and place it between us.

"This bed is so small."

"It's a queen size," I tell him, fixing my own pillows, feeling suddenly like I'm going to crawl out of my skin.

"We should upgrade it to a king size," he suggests and all I can do is look at him.

"We should, shouldn't we?" I say sarcastically.

"Okay, fine, I'll upgrade it." He lifts the covers and then tries to make himself comfy.

"Well then, I want a memory foam one." I look at him as he chuffs.

"This isn't even memory foam." He stops moving to look at me.

"Well, if we're upgrading, might as well go big, no?" I try not to laugh as I turn the light off in the room. I lie on my side, looking away from him as he huffs and puffs from his side of the bed. "I'm happy you're home, honey." Secretly laughing, but the bed moves.

I look over my shoulder at him as he turns his back on me. "Yeah, whatever," he mumbles.

Sixteen

Levi

$\mathcal{M}$y eyes blink open for a second, seeing the blackness of the room before closing again. A weird sound fills my ears, *maybe it's my imagination,* I think to myself, *or a dream.* It sort of sounds like grunts but then the sound of screeching fills my ears. "What is that noise?" I mumble, asking myself as I turn to my side. My arm flies out beside me, falling onto a warm body. My eyes suddenly fly open, looking around I realize I'm not home. My eyes get used to the darkness of the room to see Eva lying on her back. My eyes go from her to my hand draped over the pillow that is acting as a barrier between us and toward her stomach where my hand has landed.

"It's the baby," she murmurs, moving her head from

side to side, no doubt trying to wake up from sleep. It takes her about five seconds before she goes from lying down to sitting up in the bed, then she turns and swings her legs to the side, standing up. My hand moves slowly off her and falls onto the bed with a thud.

I get up on my elbow as she stands right next to the bed, my eyes go straight to her ass. She must have changed from when she got into bed before, because she is now wearing booty shorts. When did she change out of her pants? Also, when did her ass get so—umm sexy? I blink a couple more times to clear my head. Maybe I'm delirious from the lack of sleep? Or maybe I'm delirious because my life has been flipped upside down in the past two weeks? Maybe also I'm delirious because it's been a month since I've had sex with someone? "Why is she crying?" I sit up in bed, listening to the crying becoming louder and louder.

"How am I supposed to know? I'll have to get my magic ball out to see what it says." She rubs her eye with the palm of her hand before she walks out of the room. The crying gets louder and louder. I look over at the bedside table where the white monitor sits and I see the green lights fill it to the top. The lights go down when she takes a second to breathe while wailing. It takes less than a second to hear Eva's voice coming through from the monitor. "What's up, baby girl?" Eva's voice comes out soft. "Are you hungry? Come here, baby girl." I hear her lift the baby as I toss the covers off me, getting up and making my way toward Cici's bedroom. "What's all the tears for?"

My feet sink into the carpet as I walk into the room seeing Eva holding Cici to her chest, right in front of the crib where she picked her up from. "Should I do something?" I ask and she turns around to look at me.

"Can you get her a bottle?" she asks as Cici buries her face in Eva's neck, looking over at me, not sure if she should cry or not.

"Um," I say, looking at her and then at Cici, "is the bottle ready? Like how does one make a bottle? Do I grab it from the fridge, twist the top open? Do I put it under hot water? Do I boil the water?" I put my hands on my hips, suddenly petrified she is going to tell me what to do and then I'm going to go downstairs and, of course, fuck it up, because chances are I'm going to fuck it up.

Eva walks over to me. "Okay, fine." She hands Cici to me. "Hold her and I'll go make a bottle." The minute Cici is in my arms, she starts screaming. I'm expecting Eva to rush back in here and save both of us, but she just looks over her shoulder at us. "Walk her," she orders me as she heads toward the stairs, leaving me with a wailing Cici.

I put my hand on Cici's back as her eyes stare at the door for Eva to come back. "I feel you," I mumble. "It's okay." My voice comes out softly, making her turn to look at me. She stops crying for a second before she shudders as she looks at me, her lips going into a pout. "I know the last person you want is me." I take Eva's advice and start to walk toward her bed before turning back to walk toward the door. "But she's going to go and get you food. The good stuff." She looks at me, taking her little chubby hand in a fist and rubbing her eyes. I'm a forensic accountant, who literally takes down million-dollar companies for fraud and embezzlement. I sometimes make grown men cry, I'm a beast in some people's eyes, especially most of them trying to hide shit that I will eventually find. Yet, here, this little girl, not weighing more than twenty pounds, terrifies the fuck out of me. She takes a big inhale. "I'm just the middleman." I walk back and forth. "I promise not to keep you longer than I need to." I put my hand on the back of her head, rubbing her softly. "It's just that I don't know how to make a bottle. But I promise to rectify that in the morning." She just looks at me. "Or I'll YouTube it as soon as you fall asleep, just in case you need another bottle before morning." She lets out a soft cry. "She just has to get the goods and then she is going to come and get you." She looks over at the door as footsteps come up the stairs. "I think she got it. I think she is almost here." Cici looks up at me, her eyes filled with water, not sure if she wants to cry or not. Her little bottom lip quivers as she puts her two balled-up little fists against my bare chest, and I can't help but fall in love with this little girl. My eyes go toward the door. "There she is." I kiss her head as Eva comes into the room. "That was fast." I see Eva with sleep still in her eyes, but a smile on her face when she sees Cici has stopped crying.

"Yeah." She walks to us. "There is this bottle-making machine. You put powder on one side and water on the other. You put the bottle underneath it, press a button and boom, formula comes out. It's like a Keurig but with baby formula." She smiles at me, then looks at Cici. "Look what I got." She holds up the bottle at her, shaking it back and forth. She holds out her hands to Cici and she immediately lunges forward. Her hands grab the bottle before lifting it to her mouth.

"Wow," I say, putting a hand on my chest, "cutthroat. Forgotten in a nanosecond."

Eva chuckles as she walks over to the rocking chair. "If it makes you feel any better." She places Cici on her chest sideways. "It's only because I was holding the bottle. Isn't that right, baby girl?"

"Nah." I shake my head, looking at the both of them. "She loves you."

Eva looks down at Cici as she drinks her bottle. She grabs Cici's hand and she wraps her whole fist around Eva's index finger. "She can't love me more than I love her," she declares, bringing her finger to her lips and kissing it. "Go back to bed," she says as she rocks her back and forth, the sound of Cici drinking as if she hasn't had anything to drink in five days.

"Does she wake up often?" I ask, my feet feeling like they are stuck in quicksand, not being able to move. My eyes are also stuck on the both of them.

"The first two nights no, I guess she felt better being in her own bed," she shares softly, "but after that, she has been getting up a couple of times a night."

I take a step toward them, my heart speeding up with worry. "Did you call the doctor?"

She leans her head back on the rocking chair, as her foot pushes up and down to move the chair. "Twice," she admits.

"And?" I wait to hear what the doctor said.

"He didn't really say much, just that she's probably teething." She shrugs.

"Well, he sounds like he doesn't know what he's talking about," I huff and fold my arms over my chest. "We need to get a second opinion. Maybe we can google best pediatrician in the area."

She chuckles at me. "I'll add that on my list of things to do." She smiles at me. "I've got her, go to bed." I nod at her, moving toward them.

"Good night, baby girl," I whisper, kissing Cici's head softly. She stops sucking on her bottle before giving me a smile but then quickly starts drinking again. "Good night." I look up at Eva before turning to walk out of the room. I take one look over my shoulder, seeing Eva's eyes are now closed as she rocks her.

Go to bed, my head screams at me the same time I look at Eva move her head to the side, leaving her neck exposed. My finger moves at my side in the same way it would if I was touching her. I shake my head to get rid of the vision of her sitting on top of me, my cock buried inside her, with my arms wrapped around her as I lean forward and bite her neck.

"What the fuck is wrong with you?" I mumble to myself as I walk back to the bedroom. My cock is now rock hard. "Are you insane?" I look down at said cock straining to get out of my shorts. "You need to shut that shit down. It's Eva. If she even thought you were looking at her in any other way but as a friend, she would knee you and then you would be out of commission for a good week. Is that what you want?"

I get back into the bed, covering myself with the blanket up to my waist, looking up at the ceiling. I put my hands on my chest as I hear soft murmurs coming from the baby monitor. "Good night, sweet girl," Eva coos as she kisses her and places her down in her crib.

I look over at the bedroom door, seeing Eva appear and come straight to the bed. She slides into the bed beside me. "Is she asleep?" I ask as she lies on her back, her position mimics mine.

"Not really." She looks over at me. "But Lisa used to feed her and put her down to sleep. It's called self-soothing."

"It sounds horrible." The words come out of my mouth before I can stop them.

"You don't self-soothe?" She smirks at me. "I'm sure you self-soothe at least once a week, maybe even once a day."

"That isn't what I was saying." I smile at her in the dark and she sits up in the bed. I follow her lead and look over at the door. "What's the matter?" Both of us sit up in bed on our respective sides. I look at Eva and then back to the door, and again back at her, waiting for her to say something—anything.

"I don't know," she says in a whisper, looking at the door and then the baby monitor. "I feel so guilty."

"Why?" I ask, confused about what is actually going on.

"Because I just left her in there alone and awake," she

states and her hand comes up to wipe away a tear.

"She's not crying." I try to make her feel better. "So I'm assuming she's okay with it."

She takes the cover and tosses it off herself, getting up out of bed. Standing there beside it, I lean across the mattress, snatching her hand and pulling her back into the bed. "Go to sleep."

"Fine," she huffs at the same time I go back to my side of the bed and lie with my head back on the pillow. I close my eyes but can feel the nervous energy coming from her side of the bed. I open my eyes, looking over at her, seeing her with her hands on her stomach, her index finger tapping the other.

"You aren't going to go to sleep, are you?"

"No." She shakes her head. "I'll just wait a bit," she says, looking over at the monitor, seeing that there is no green light on.

"Okay." I look up at the ceiling, my eyes getting heavier and heavier. I look over at Eva right before my eyes close for good. She also has her eyes closed, and we fall asleep while listening to Cici snore.

Seventeen

Eva

"Here we go," I say to Cici as I unbuckle her seat belt. "Are you ready for daycare?" I ask as I carefully take her out of her seat. "Where is your bow?" I ask of the little bow I put in her hair this morning. After dressing her in a pink romper, I thought it would be cute to add a little bow, Cici did not, apparently. "I can see we don't like anything in your hair," I mumble to her as I place her on my hip before grabbing her diaper bag. "Is today going to be a good day?" I ask as she looks around. "I think it's going to be a good day."

My shoes click on the concrete as I walk toward the glass door. The bangles on my left hand clink together as I reach up and pull open the door. Stepping inside the daycare, I'm faced with another door, this one with a code to get into the center. I enter the code before turning the handle and pulling it open. I'm about to call out when I see a hand on top of my hand. "I've got it," a male voice assures from behind me.

Looking over my shoulder, I see a dad who is dressed in a suit, holding the hand of a little girl who must be three years old. "Thank you." I smile back at him and he just gives me a chin up.

"Good morning, Eva," Melanie, the owner of the daycare, says from behind her desk at the front door. "Good morning, Caine." I look over at the man who is still standing behind me.

"Morning." I smile at Melanie before walking down the carpeted hallway. Wooden cubbies line the right side of the wall with hooks under them, some with jackets already hanging, and a long wooden bench.

I pass three rooms before getting to Cici's room called the Ladybugs. "Good morning," Sylvia, Cici's teacher, says to us as we stand at the door of the room. The bottom part is closed; the top part open. "How are we doing today?"

"We are in tip-top shape." I look down at Cici. "Aren't we, baby girl?"

"How was her night?" Sylvia asks me and I smile at her. She's been Cici's teacher since she was six weeks old and Lisa had to return to work. If anyone knows her better than me, it's Sylvia. "Did she sleep?"

"Nope," I reply, bouncing her, "we have decided that nights are overrated and we need to drink at least two bottles." I kiss her cheek.

"Well, if you look this good after not sleeping all night, I wonder how you would look with sleep," she jokes with me as I look down at my outfit. I don't even remember what I'm wearing, that is how exhausted I am. My bubble-gum-pink pants go down to my ankles, a classic button-up, white cotton shirt is tucked in with the top three buttons opened. I don't even know if the nude high-heeled sandals go with the outfit but that's what I'm working with.

"Go see Sylvia and I'll be back to get you," I tell my niece as Sylvia opens her arms for Cici, who lays her head on my shoulder, not ready to let me go. I place my head down on hers for a second. "Are we extra cuddly this morning?"

"I have some fruit," Sylvia bribes, "you want some berries?" She claps her hands and Cici leans out of my arms and into Sylvia.

"Good to know she'll drop me for berries." I laugh. "Here is her bag." I place the bag on the door. "Call me if anything comes up," I say and then put my hand to my mouth and blow her a kiss. "Love you."

"Blow a kiss to Auntie," Sylvia urges and Cici smiles her gummy smile at me and blows me a kiss. "What a good girl." She kisses her cheek and quickly turns away. I watch for a few seconds before turning and walking back toward the door. I have my head down as I walk out, obviously not paying attention to where I'm going when I run into someone. His musky smell hits me right away. Looking up, I see the same man who held the door open for me.

"I'm so sorry." I embarrassedly laugh at myself. "I was on the moon."

"No worries." His voice comes out gruff as I look up into his brown eyes. He holds out his hand for me to walk in front of him.

"Thank you," I tell him as I walk, trying not to look over my shoulder to see if he's checking me out. I push open the door, holding it for him with my left hand. My ring is hitting the sun at the same time as I look at the man, who is right behind me.

"Thank you," he says to me and I just nod at him, feeling really guilty for even talking to him.

I get in my car, ignoring that I feel guilty and chalking it up to me being exhausted.

It's just been a really weird couple of days. Moving Cici's things into my home for good. Then Levi coming home and us starting to live together in my space. Him waking with me last night, and then him crawling into bed with me. It was dumb, we've been friends for a long time. We've even slept in the same bed once when we were drunk on vacation. But that is only because neither of us could get up without falling over, so sleeping next to each other seemed like the safest thing to do. I was chalking it up to being sleep deprived for feeling so out of whack. Even this morning when he came upstairs with a coffee for me while I was in the bathroom. Grabbing Cici from me so I could get dressed and then walking out of the closet wearing a suit. The fact that our clothes are now mixed with each other's is again throwing me off. It has been a very unsettling couple of days. I need a good night's rest and I will be back to normal.

Getting to work, I put on my smile as I walk in, making sure no one knows that anything is wrong. This is my workplace, and if I expect everyone to leave their problems at the door, I can't very well drag my ass into work and wallow. Nope, no one has time for that. "Good morning," I greet, walking back toward my office, saying hello to a couple of people along the way. I put my purse in the chair in front of my desk before walking around it toward my office chair.

The knock on the door has me pausing as I sit down. Raquel comes in with a binder in her hand. "Are you ready?"

"I forgot that I was off today," I say to her. "I mean not off, but I wasn't going to be with clients but instead going over admin work." I clap my hands. "Love this time of the month."

"No, you don't," Raquel reminds me, "the last time, you booked clients that day just to be rid of this duty."

"Well, good news," I tell her, leaning back in my chair, "no clients today."

She nods at me as she opens her binder. "Good, because we have two months to get through." She smiles at me. "Also, it's wedding season soon."

The day flies by faster than I thought it would. There were a couple of minor issues we had to deal with. At four o'clock we are wrapping up our meeting and I'm about to grab my purse and leave when my phone beeps with a text.

Levi: Be home at five and will help with dinner.

I smile at that, then text him back.

Me: So domesticated. What do you want to have for dinner?

Levi: If you want something I can throw on the grill, then I can cook.

Me: Oh, steak sounds good.

Levi: I'll leave work now and head over to the butcher. Let me know if you think of anything else.

I ignore the way my heart speeds up and the way my stomach knots.

Me: Will do.

I carry my phone to my purse, grabbing it and walking out of the office. I stop by every room and station before heading out to make sure everything is okay. I drive with the windows open all the way to the daycare, walking in without bumping into anyone. When I walk over to Cici's class, she is sitting on the floor clapping her hands as Sylvia sings a song. I smile at the sight and she must sense me because she looks at me, and gone is the smile on her face and in its place is her crying. "Oh, that's a faker right there," I say as Sylvia gets her and brings her over to me. "Hey there, baby girl," I greet, kissing her neck. "How was her day?"

"Rough." She is honest with me. "She wanted to be in my arms more than not." I don't know what to say. "It's okay, she'll readjust."

"Fingers crossed," I reply as she hands me her diaper bag. "See you tomorrow."

"Are you ready to go home?" I ask as I walk down

the hallway. The door opens and in comes the man from this morning.

"Hey," he says, his suit jacket off, his cuffs rolled up to his elbows, "we have to stop meeting like this." He laughs, putting his hands in his pockets. Leaving me speechless and, luckily, I don't have to say anything to him when a little girl yells, "Daddy!" I look over at the girl running to her father.

"Have a great night," I say as he squats down to grab his daughter in his arms.

"You, too, Eva," he says my name as I walk out of the daycare.

"That was weird, right?" I ask Cici, who slaps my chest and babbles to me. "Yeah, I thought so, too. He is hot, though." I look back, seeing him walking out with his daughter toward a black Range Rover. "There must be something in the water," I say as I buckle her into her car seat.

It doesn't take us long to get home, pulling into the driveway I'm shocked that Levi is already here. I grab her bag and her and walk up the stairs. "Hello," I call as I shut the door behind me. Levi stands in the kitchen, his suit still on, the bags from the grocery store on the counter in front of him.

"Hey," he says, looking up from his phone. Then he looks at Cici and smiles. "Well, hello, you." He smiles at her and she squeals. "I like to hear that better than you crying."

I put the bag down on the kitchen table, looking at the big box on the table. "What is this?" I ask, trying to remember if I ordered anything lately. I've been known in the past to order things in the middle of the night.

"Oh, that's something I bought for you." He walks over to me. "Nothing big. I was hoping to have it installed before you got here, but I had a work call."

"What is it?" I ask, looking at the box.

"It's a baby monitor, but it's a camera one. So you put a camera over her bed or facing her bed," he explains, opening the box, "and then you can watch her."

"What?" I whisper, sitting down on the chair because I feel like my legs will give out.

"Yeah, it's so you can see if she's sleeping when you put her down." He's totally not reading the room. I don't even know I'm crying until I feel the wetness on my cheek.

"That's so thoughtful." I look at him and see his eyes get soft. He walks over to where I'm sitting and squats down in front of me.

"Why are you crying?" His hand comes out and his fingers wipe away a tear.

"I don't know," I admit, "I must be sleep deprived."

He smirks at me, his smile so soft. "Why don't you go and take a shower, and I'll watch the baby?"

I can't help but laugh through my tears. "Do you even know what to do with her?" I ask as he takes her out of my arms.

I wait for her to cry but she doesn't, he leans in and kisses her cheek. "Not even a bit, but I think I can wing it." He smiles at her and she babbles back at him. A big gob of drool comes out and falls on his jacket. "Go and take a shower." He motions with his head toward the stairs.

"If you need anything." I get up. "Come and get me."

"You want me to barge in on you naked in the shower?" he teases me, just like he's done many times before, but this time it feels different. This time I picture him coming into the shower with me, naked as well. "You okay?" he asks and I avoid looking at him, feeling my cheeks start to burn.

"I'll be back." I don't even check to see if Cici is okay before running up the steps and away from Levi. "Good God." I close the bathroom door behind me. "Can you imagine if he knew you pictured him in the shower with you?" I mumble to myself. "He'd probably barf." I push off from the door. "You need a cold shower." I turn the water on. "Ice cold at this point."

I don't spend long in the shower, and instead of relaxing, I'm more tense than I was before the shower. Putting on a pair of shorts and a tank top, I pin the hair on top of my head and walk down the stairs. As soon as I get to the last step, he turns from the kitchen sink and I see he's wearing the BabyBjörn. "Hey," he says to me as if he doesn't have a child strapped to his chest. His suit jacket hangs on one of the chairs, his shirt rolled up at the wrists. I don't even know what to do with the sight of him. Cici looks at me, her arms punching the air and her legs kicking. I put my hand to my chest, feeling like I have a heart murmur or like I feel there is something in my throat. I even clear it, wondering if the pressure will go away.

"What are you wearing?" I ask, wondering if someone can be delusional if they are sleep deprived. I make a mental note to google that when I'm putting Cici to sleep.

"She didn't like being in my arms," he replies, looking down at Cici. "But the minute I put this contraption on, she was fine." Cici looks up at him as if she knows he's talking about her. "Not facing me, nope, she has to look out."

"She's curious." I finally take the last step and walk toward the two of them.

"Also, she hates baby talk," he informs me and I can't help the laugh that comes out of me.

"How long did it take you to put that on?" I point at his chest.

"Two YouTube videos." He holds up two fingers. "And she was not a happy person waiting." He smiles. "I'm surprised you didn't hear her."

"I owe you big-time," I say softly to him.

"What do you mean?" His voice is as soft as mine, almost a whisper.

"I mean this." I point at the baby strapped to his chest. "This whole this." I point at the bags that were on the counter but are now not on there. I look around, wondering if he put them away. "We," I say and then correct myself, "I obviously didn't think this through."

"Hey," he comforts, putting his arm around my shoulders. "It's just another eleven months and two weeks."

Eighteen

Levi

"Good morning, everyone," I greet, walking into the conference room with my notepad in one hand and my coffee in the other. I take a look around and see there is no one here but me. Turning my hand holding the notepad to check the time on my watch, I see that it's almost ten. Am I early for this meeting? I don't have a chance to answer myself because I hear the television on the wall turn on.

"Good morning, buttercup," Stefano announces from the screen, "you are looking good." Ever since he found out that Avery was his daughter, he has cut back on traveling altogether. He may travel but whereas he would go for weeks before, now it's a turnaround of twenty-four hours. I didn't understand it when he suddenly changed, but I get it now.

"Well, considering I only woke up once last night, I feel like a rock star." I put my coffee down and then my notepad. "It's almost the best thing that has ever happened." I pull the chair out and sit in it.

"How is my cousin?" he asks and I smirk at him, trying to play it off as cool. Playing it off as cool because I'm not ready for all the stuff to come up. All the questions that will follow. I just don't know how to explain it to him, without a lot of other shit coming up. Stuff I'm not sure I'm ready to talk about. Stuff even I'm shocked about. Stuff, meaning Eva and her being on my mind for the past two fucking weeks. Every single time I look over at her, it's like there is something new I see that I haven't seen before. Or maybe I have but I just noticed now, which is flipping my head upside down. I tell myself it's just because I'm in her space all the time, but even saying that, my head laughs at me.

"My wife is fine." I point at myself, trying to hold in the laughter when he scowls at me, but I can't help it. "She's fine. Great. Amazing." I clap my hands as his scowl comes to a full-blown glare. It's been two weeks since we've technically moved in with each other, well, since I came back from my business trip. Two weeks since the start of whatever this is.

"How is Cici?" he asks and I lean back in the chair, the smile filling my face so much it hurts my cheeks. I swear I think I even puff out my chest when I think of her.

"Amazing." I rock back and forth in the chair. "Still waking up once a night. But I think she's settling down." With each passing day, I am falling more and more in love with her. I would cut off my limbs for her. The girl can only say one word, which is Mama, and it breaks my heart every single time she says it and she just started waving bye-bye.

"I never thought I would see the day you would be talking about a kid's nighttime routine like it was nothing," Stefano observes. "When do you leave next?"

I avoid looking at his eyes when I pick up a pen and tap it on the notepad, but luckily for me people start coming in the room. "You guys are all late," I joke with them as everyone gets in their seat.

"Okay, shall we start?" Stefano begins. "We have a lot to go through." The meeting gets underway when the big question comes up. Travel. The dreaded subject I was hoping wouldn't be brought up. I've never dreaded this subject before but I know he will ask questions once he gets wind of me not traveling.

"How is everyone's travel schedule?" Stefano asks. We go around the room one by one, as we talk about going away.

My leg moves up and down with nerves when it gets to my turn. "I was supposed to leave next week," I start, "but I pushed it back a couple of days." I canceled the whole thing, but I can start with this, then ease into it. "I have what I need from my end to do the work."

He just stares at me and I can see the questions already in his eyes. He's my best friend, and aside from Eva, I know him better than anyone and vice versa. "Do you have an ETA for your next trip?"

"I have to check." Again, the lie comes out before I can stop it. I don't have to check because I cleared the rest of the month. I wasn't sure I wanted to leave Eva alone with Cici and no help, so I canceled things.

"We can chat on that later," Stefano says to me, and if I read between the lines, he doesn't want to have this conversation in front of the whole staff.

I nod at him at the same time my phone rings. All eyes come to me. "Shit," I swear, looking down and seeing it's the daycare, "it's Cici's daycare." I pick up the phone and walk outside of the meeting. "Hello." I put my phone to my ear.

"Levi." I hear a woman say my name. "This is Melanie from the Small Bumble Bee Daycare." I swear to God I feel like the blood has drained from my whole body.

"Yes," is the only word that can come out.

"I'm calling because Cici has a fever," she says softly. "I've tried to get in touch with Eva for the past twenty minutes, and all I'm getting is her voicemail. You are the next one on the list."

"Okay." I look around, putting the phone to my ear and walking toward my office.

"We have a policy that if the baby is running a fever, you have to come and pick her up," she informs me.

"Of course." I grab my keys from my desk. "I'll be right there," I tell her, "I just have to settle some things."

"That is fine. I'll see you soon," she replies and I hang up on her, walking back into the conference room.

"I have to go. Cici has a fever," I announce to the room.

"Where is Eva?" Stefano asks me and I look down at my phone, pulling up her name and calling her.

It picks up after half a ring. "You've reached Eva."

"Voicemail," I respond, looking down at the phone, expecting it to ring in my hand, but it doesn't. "I have to go." I don't even pick up my shit, I just grab my phone and walk out of the room.

"I'll call you later," Stefano says and I nod at him, turning and practically running out to my car. I get to the daycare in record time. The whole time I've been trying to call Eva but it's going straight to voicemail. My stomach clenches as I walk into the daycare. I enter the code that I've entered only once before when I had to drop her off.

Melanie steps out of her office to greet me. "Sorry about calling you."

"It's fine," I say, looking down toward the hall where I hear crying. "I'll go get her." I don't even wait for her to say anything before walking down the hall.

"It's going to be okay." I hear the woman who is holding Cici say as she cries in her arms.

Once I reach the door, I turn the handle and walk into the room. Looking at the other babies sitting on the floor, I ensure I don't step on anything. "Look who is there," the woman coos and Cici turns her head and spots me.

Her lower lip quivers as she sobs and my heart breaks. That is the only way to describe it. There is a pain in my chest and it feels like someone stabbed me. "Oh, baby girl," I whisper, holding my hands to her as she lunges for me. Her blue eyes look so bright, even though she has been crying. Her little nose is red, along with her cheeks that look so rosy. "What's the matter?" I ask, even though I know she can't answer me. She rubs her face in my chest, along with all of the snot and tears, but I couldn't care less.

"She's been really fussy all day long. She hasn't really eaten much," the woman shares with me, and I look over to see Cici pick up the pacifier that is hanging on her pj's and put it in her mouth.

"It's going to be okay, baby girl." I kiss her head. "Do you need anything from me?" I ask the lady whose name I don't remember as she smiles at me.

"I'll get her diaper bag," she says, walking over to the corner where there is a changing station. She grabs the bag, bringing it to me.

"Thank you." I put the bag over my shoulder before walking out of the room with her. I nod to Melanie as I walk out of the daycare and toward my car. "It's a good thing I got that car seat," I tell her as she looks at me, one of her hands on my shoulder, holding on for dear life. "And Eva said it was silly." I shake my head as I open the back door and place her in the seat. She starts to cry as I buckle her in. "I know you don't want this, but in order to get home we are going to have to do it this way," I explain to her and she whines. "You know, in the fifties or maybe even the sixties I could have driven home with you in my arms." I laugh as she watches me. "I'm sure you understand everything I'm saying."

I get into the driver's seat and look back at her as she lays her head on the side of the car seat. I dial Eva again and it goes straight to voicemail. I don't bother leaving her a message, instead I hang up the phone. When we get home, I dump her bag at the door before kicking off my shoes. "Here we go," I say, putting her down on her mat in the living room. She lets me know as soon as I step away from her that she does not want to be in the middle of the floor. Her wail fills the room as I shrug my jacket off before walking over to her and picking her up.

I put my head on hers and feel that she's really hot. "We should take your temperature," I tell her, walking upstairs to her bedroom. "I know it's in here somewhere." I pull out baskets and find the little handle thing that I've been using daily to make sure her temperature is normal. "Shall we?" I ask, turning it on with a button and pointing it at her forehead. I wait for the beep before looking down and seeing the color red with the temperature. "One hundred and one. Shit," I curse, putting it down. "Okay, time to call Eva." This time I don't dial her phone, I call her work line.

Someone answers the phone right away. "Hey, it's Levi, is Eva working today?"

"She is," she confirms, "she's with a client."

I think about what to do next but I have no idea what to do next. "It's sort of an emergency. Do you think I can speak with her right away?" I declare at the same time that Cici whines in my arms. "Could you just tell her I'm on the phone?"

She takes a long time contemplating and I'm about to

snap at her when she says, "Please hold."

"She told me to hold," I fill Cici in and I swear it feels like a million years before I hear Eva pick up the phone.

"Hello," she says breathlessly.

"Where are you?" I ask, irritated, even though I know she's at work because I just called there. "I've been calling you for the past hour. The daycare called me."

"What?" she shrieks. "Why?"

"Cici has a fever," I tell her. "They said they tried to call you."

"Fuck," she hisses. "My phone was on do not disturb from last night. I must have forgotten to switch it off this morning. I'm coming."

"No," I say, "it's fine. I have her and I'm home."

"What?" Again the shriek comes out of her.

"I said I'm fine, I have her. Her fever is at a hundred and one." I look back at Cici who puts her head on my shoulder. "I'm going to give her Tylenol, I guess, but you have to call her doctor."

"On it," she replies. "Do you know where the Tylenol is?"

"It's in her bathroom, no?" I ask for confirmation, walking toward her bathroom and pulling open the mirrored medicine cabinet. "It's in a white bottle."

"Yes, you have to give her two point five milliliters." I'm about to ask her how the fuck am I supposed to know what two point five is when she continues, "Shake the bottle. Squeeze the top of the bottle and when you pull it out there is a syringe attached to it. Just squeeze it into her mouth slowly."

"Okay, I'm on it."

"I'll be there as soon as I can," she mumbles and I hang up the phone.

"Good news is she is going to be here soon," I tell Cici. "Bad news is you got me." She doesn't smile and her eyes look droopy. "Let's get you some medicine." I walk back into her bedroom and set her on her changing table. She starts to whine. "I know but I need both hands," I explain to her, squeezing the top of the bottle like Eva says and then unscrewing it. "Now I'm going to be honest, I don't know if this tastes good or not." I look at the red liquid. "Let me check." I put a bit on my finger and then taste it. "Not the worst thing I've ever tasted and you did eat tofu the other day, so I'm thinking you can take this. But it's going to make you feel better." I put the tip in her mouth and she sucks on it. "See, my girl is a champ." I praise her as I squeeze it into her mouth. I smile at her. "Now, can I change so we can go and chill on the couch?" I ask after I put the top back in the bottle. "I just need to put on my shorts and a T-shirt."

Picking her up, I walk over to the bedroom, putting her on the closet carpet so she knows I'm not going anywhere. I grab a pair of shorts and a T-shirt and change faster than I ever have in my whole life.

She holds her hands up to me, meaning she's over sitting on the floor as I pick her up. "How are we feeling?" I ask, walking down the stairs and toward the kitchen. "How about we get some water?" I quiz her, grabbing her little pink cup with handles on the sides. She grabs it as soon as I have it in my hand, bringing it to her mouth. I move slowly to the living room. "You know what we should do?" I sit on the couch, grabbing the remote. "Cuddle and watch television."

Turning the television on, I lie on the couch with her on my chest. I kiss the top of her head as I flick through the channels. "It's going to be okay," I soothe her and she looks up at me, drool coming out of her mouth. "I bet you feel like ass right now." She whines as she looks at me, telling me I'm right. "I probably shouldn't say ass." I smile as she lays her head on her arm for a second and then looks back up at me. "I bet you feel like... I can't even say shit," I mumble. "I bet you feel horrible." She doesn't answer me of course, she just rubs her face in my chest with snot all over me. "Wow." I look down at her. "No other woman has ever gotten snot all over me." I smile at her. "You are the first." She smiles at me for a second before laying her head on my chest. I kiss the top of her head. "It's going to be okay." Grabbing one of the linen covers on the couch, I lift her and then put her back down on my chest. "Don't want you lying in snot," I tell her as she lays her head back on my chest. I put my hand on her bum to make sure she doesn't move. I watch television as she rests on my chest and I don't know who falls asleep first, me or Cici.

Nineteen

Eva

I slam the car door shut and rush up the front steps. The guilt has been running through me and eating at me since he called. Fucking phone was on do not disturb, the minute I saw that, I wanted to throw the fucking thing against the wall, I was so pissed at myself. She needed me and I wasn't there, again. I finished my client and then told Raquel to clear the rest of the afternoon. Luckily, I just hired someone new who was starting next week to help me out, so it will be a huge weight off my shoulders.

I open the front door, looking over at the couch. Literally everything in my body stops. The two of them are on the couch sleeping, Levi's legs crossed at his ankles, the television watching the two of them. He has jumped into this whole parenthood thing with me with both feet, not even a look back. Every single day I see him with her, I'm more amazed at how wonderful he is. It also stings just a touch when I think about how good of a father he's going to be to his own children. He may have said he is never having children, but knowing how good he's been with Cici, I have no doubt he's going to change his mind. I push down the bile that wants to come out of me, not ready to fully think about him having a child with someone else. Not willing to think about how this is going to be in a year from now. Not willing to admit to myself just how much I need him.

As quiet as I can, I close the door behind me, turning the knob so it doesn't click. I kick off my heels, placing them right next to Levi's shoes before I tiptoe into the house. Cici is on her stomach on top of his chest with her two hands fisted at her sides, the pacifier hanging loose in her mouth. Her cheeks are red and I reach out to touch her forehead softly. My eyes go from her to Levi, whose eyes now open. "Is she still hot?" he asks quietly and without moving.

"No," I answer him with a soft smile, as he blinks his eyes a couple of times to wake up.

"I gave her Tylenol," he informs me and then his face smiles, "she took it like a champ. I didn't give her a bottle after because I was afraid it was going to upset her stomach. But she did have water, because, well, I thought it was a good idea." The fullness fills in my chest again.

"I would have done the same," I assure him.

"Have you tasted the Tylenol?" he asks and I shake my head. "It's sweet."

"You tasted it?" I ask, shocked. "Why would you taste it?"

"I wanted to know if it tasted bad," he replies and stops moving when Cici stirs on his chest, but she just turns to her side, cuddling more in his chest than anything.

"I'm so sorry, Levi." My voice shakes as I talk to him.

"For what?" he asks and I can see his eyes searching mine.

"You didn't sign up for this." The words come out before I can stop them and a tear also escapes one eye. I tried to be strong the whole time I was driving home. Tried to tell myself that these things happen. Tried not to beat myself up that I fucked up big-time by not taking the daycare's call.

"Hey," he says, "I'm only good with one woman in my life crying at a time." He tries to make a joke out of it. Knowing he is trying to make me laugh, I give it to him. "The doctor said if she still has a fever by tomorrow, to call him back."

I know right away he's pissed. His whole demeanor changes. His eyes go hard, his jaw gets square as he bites down, and the vein in his forehead looks like it's going to explode. "You need a new fucking doctor." He looks down at Cici, making sure he didn't wake her. "What if she has an ear infection?" he asks and I don't have an answer for him. "Or a sore throat?"

"Or it's nothing." It is at this moment when he glares at me that I know I should have not said a word. I hold up my hands sort of like a truce. "I'm just passing along the message."

"I'm going to call him myself," he grounds out between clenched teeth while he whispers.

"When she gets up, I'm going to FaceTime Addison and ask her what she would do. She's the only other person I know who has had a child."

"I approve," he agrees and this time I can't help but laugh out loud, the sound shocking Cici who jumps at the noise. He immediately wraps his arms around her, bringing her even closer to him. "Go away," he whisper-hisses.

I hold up my hand. "I'm going to go see if I can move my appointments tomorrow." I get up.

"I can do it." He looks down at Cici, making sure she is still sleeping. The pacifier now dropping out of her mouth.

"I'm not traveling, so I can stay home with her."

"Are you sure?" I ask as I hold my hands together, and he nods.

"Worst-case scenario." He smirks at me. "Things go bad and I call you." He tilts his head to the side. "That is, if you take off your do not disturb." Now I'm the one glaring at him at the same time I put up my hand and flip him the bird.

His chest moves as he tries not to laugh, but Cici pops her head up and looks at him. His eyes that were glaring at me not even two minutes ago are now filled with softness. "Well, hello, girl." His voice is also soft. "Did you have a nice nap?" She uses his chest to rub her nose back and forth. "I'm going to say that is a yes." He kisses her head and all I can do is watch the two of them. My heart is melting at the sight in front of me, knowing it's going to be a memory I will forever have.

It takes Cici a second to look over at me. "Hello, baby girl." My hand comes out and she smiles so much at me that a whole dollop of drool just comes out of her mouth. "That's a lot of drool." I'm waiting for her to lean toward me but instead she just stays there in Levi's arms, not even bothering to move. She just looks at me as he wraps his arm around her.

"You going to call Addison?" he reminds me and I just nod my head at him because, for some fucking reason, there is a lump in my throat.

I pull up Addison's number and press the FaceTime button. The ringing has Cici stick her head up. "Oh, you wake up for that," I say to her, smiling as the ringing stops and as the white circle goes round and round when it says connecting. Her face fills the screen a couple of seconds later. "Hi." She smiles at me and then looks over to the side. "It's Eva," she tells whoever is beside her.

"Hey," Stefano greets as he sticks his head into the phone, "what happened with Cici?"

I look at the phone, wondering how he heard. "I was in a meeting when the daycare called," Levi informs me and again I look up at the ceiling, trying not to feel guilty but failing miserably.

"She has a fever—" I start to say.

"One hundred and one," Levi cuts in and I stare at him. "I'm just letting her know."

I look at the phone, seeing Addison rolling her lips as her eyes stare at the phone super big, just watching me. "What other symptoms does she have?" she finally asks me.

"Fever and drooling, running nose."

"It sounds like she's teething," Addison assesses. "Teething sadly can last a long time and there really isn't much you can do for them."

"What medical school did she graduate from?" I hear Levi mumble to Cici who just chews on her pacifier, kicking her leg up.

"Did she break through yet?" she asks and my eyebrows pinch together.

"Break through what?" I ask, confused.

"Her gums, can you feel the teeth?" I turn, going to sit on the couch next to Levi and Cici.

"Hi, guys," Levi says, holding up the hand that is cradling Cici, but only for a second.

"You need to feel her gums to see if you can feel teeth," Addison instructs and I just look at Levi.

"I'm not doing that," he retorts, putting his other hand over her face. "Leave her alone." I hear Stefano laugh and see Levi glare at him. "What if I hurt her and she hates me?"

"She's not going to hate you," Stefano and Addison say at the same time.

"Why are you even talking?" Levi yells. "You weren't there when Avery was teething, so you get no say in this. I'll call you when she turns five and wants to borrow a tiara." Stefano can't help but throw his head back and laugh. I try not to focus on him saying he'll call him when she turns five. "You're on the girls' side."

"I'm not on anyone's side." He holds up his hands in a peaceful way.

"Fine, I'll do it." I'm not really sure I want to do it. Because what if Levi is right and it hurts her, what if she hates me for it? "I'm just going to feel your gums," I tell Cici, who just looks at me.

I pull down her lower lip. "Her gums look white," I observe, trying not to freak out, but Levi is the one who is freaking out.

"Is that normal?" he asks, looking like he's going to escape from my touch. "Quick, you need to google."

"I'm on the phone," I remind him as I hold up the phone. "How do you want me to google?" All he can do is glare at me. I ignore him, sticking my finger into her mouth and feeling her bottom gum. My eyes fly to Levi's. "Oh, I think I feel it."

"I want to feel it." He moves his hand up and he's about to put his finger in her mouth, but he stops. "I don't know if I can do it."

"You just saw me do it," I point out to him. "Did she cry? Just touch her bottom gum."

He looks at Cici. "I'm only doing this because she told me and not because I want to." I roll my eyes at him as Addison and Stefano chuckle from their end of the phone. He moves her lower lip down, looking down as he sticks his finger in her mouth, moving it gently on her bottom gum. "I think I feel it," he says to me with shock all over his face. "It feels hard."

"Check and see if it's white," I ask to make sure I saw what I saw.

"No." He shakes his head as he wipes his wet finger in her shirt, not even caring.

"I'll check." I try to show him that it's no big deal. "What is wrong with you?" I look up at him as he glares at me. I move her lip down and I can see two round puffy white marks on her lower gum.

"What helped with Avery," Addison offers, "is teethers." I look at Levi.

"Are you not taking notes?" he asks. "Like get a pen and paper so we can remember."

"That you need a pen and paper to remember teethers is beyond me," I snap at him. "It's like teeth and ers."

"What helps is putting them in the freezer so she can chew on them." Addison tries to break up our little tiff.

"How long does this last?" Levi asks her.

"Avery started drooling at six months old and only broke through the gums at a year."

"Six months!" Levi yells. "That isn't normal." Addison just laughs at him.

"Also, if you wet a facecloth and put it in the freezer for thirty minutes, that will help, too." Addison smiles at me. "Definitely not a fun part of parenting."

"No shit," Levi mumbles, "six months. That's like a lot of days."

"That is like a lot of days," Stefano repeats what he just said, shaking his head. "You're a forensic accountant and don't know how many days are in six months."

Levi just stares at me, his jaw getting tight and the

vein in his forehead really throbbing now. "Hang up on him," he growls between clenched teeth.

If he wasn't so upset right now, I would laugh in his face, but I know he sounds like he is teetering on the ledge, so all I can do is roll my lips and try not to laugh in his face. "Okay, well, thanks for helping," I tell Addison, who is just shaking her head.

"Call me if you need anything." She looks at me and then looks over at Levi. "Have fun, you two."

Twenty

Levi

I lie on the bed with one hand on my chest and the other hand draped over the pillow that sits in the middle of the bed, listening to the footsteps that are coming closer and closer to the bedroom. My eyes burn from being so tired. "Is she down?" I lift my head when Eva walks back into the bedroom.

She drags her feet toward the bed, collapsing on it with a big thud on her stomach, her feet off the side because of the angle. "Yeah," she mumbles. I look past her head toward the monitor screen, seeing Cici is lying on her stomach but isn't moving.

"Was she fussy?" I stop staring at the screen, laying my head back on the pillow, my eyes closing on their own.

The burning only making it worse and I'm wondering why I feel like my body has been hit by a Mack truck.

"A little bit," she relays and I feel the covers moving, so I know she is covering herself up. "I can't move."

My eyes open for a second as I look over and she's turned her head toward me. She's curled under the cover into a ball, her eyes closed with her hands under her cheek. "The light is on."

"Not if you close your eyes it's not," she notes and I toss the cover off me to get up and turn off the light. I walk over to her side of the bed, turning off her lamp. "We should get the clapper thing," she mumbles, her body not moving.

"We put her down at seven." I walk back over to my side of the bed. "And since then she's been up three times." I lean down and touch my phone. "It's now midnight."

"Thanks for the update," she snarks and I look over at her chuckling. "Hopefully, she's down for the night."

I crawl into bed, afraid to move and make noise to wake her up. Since I brought her home from the daycare, she's fevered every four hours. You could tell when the meds would be wearing off. She would get extra cranky and we tried everything. I mean everything. As soon as we got off the phone with Stefano and Addison, I got dressed and headed out to Wal-Mart and Target, where I bought every single teether thing I could get my hands on. I couldn't get over how many different teethers there were. I walked into the house an hour later with three bags full of stuff. I got a giraffe teether. I got a banana toothbrush teether, a pacifier teether, a glove teether, a couple of round teethers you put in the freezer. You name it, I bought it. If it had teether in the title, it came home with me. I don't think I'm asleep for longer than ten minutes before I hear her crying again.

"This can't be happening," Eva huffs and it almost sounds like she's crying in frustration.

"I'll get her," I offer, getting up and walking toward her bedroom. The whine turns into a full-blown wail, then a scream. I walk into the room and she is rolled over from her stomach and is now sitting on her bum. "What's the matter, girl?" I say softly and she holds her hands up for me to pick her up. "What's got you this time?" I ask as I put my lips to her head to see if she's hot, and thankfully she's not. She looks up at me and uses her fist to rub her eyes. "You tired?" I walk over to the rocking chair. "I think it's because you have to sleep in order not to be tired." I grab her pacifier that clips on to her pj's. "Are you having trouble sleeping?" I ask, sticking the pacifier in her mouth. She lays her head on my chest as I start to rock her, putting my head back on the chair, resting my eyes.

"You are going to spoil her," Eva accuses and my eyes flicker open. She's leaning against the doorjamb, her feet crossed at her ankles and her arms folded over her chest. She is wearing another pair of booty shorts with a matching tank top. Her hair is loose around her face, and even though I can only see her silhouette in the semi-darkness, I can picture her face with a smile on it. It feels like someone is sitting on my chest, and it's a lot more than the little girl who is on it.

"It's just until she falls back asleep," I whisper to her, my hand on her back and her bum. "She just needs a little rocking. Go back to bed." She doesn't argue with me, which means she's past the point of tiredness. Usually, she would try to take over this, but not today. She turns and I watch her ass move as she walks back to the bedroom. I don't even think she is trying to strut, but it's happening and I'm full-on gawking at her.

I rock Cici until I hear her snoring softly, getting up as slowly as I can to not wake her. Even putting her in her crib, I try not to move her too much, putting her on her side. She whines a bit as soon as I place her down, but I gently tap her butt. She quickly goes back to sleep as I tiptoe out of the room.

I slide right into bed, my eyes closed even before my head hits the pillow. I hear Eva mumble something from beside me, but at this point I'm not even sure what fucking day it is. I've stayed up in college sometimes for days. I remember going out to party, getting home at six and then rushing to class at eight. Now it feels like I've been awake for over seventy-two hours. I think I mumble something back to her, but I don't even have the energy to open my eyes. It takes me less than ten seconds to fall into a deep sleep.

I don't know how long I sleep, if it's ten minutes or six hours, before wails fill the air again. "This isn't happening." I hear from beside me and I feel something warm on my side, I also feel weight on my legs. I open my eyes not surprised I'm still on my back and haven't moved, since I'm pinned down. Eva's ass is against my hip and her legs are kicked back, intertwined with mine. I don't think she even realizes that she's gone through the pillow barrier, which is now in front of her stomach.

"I'll get her," I offer again, even though I don't move.

"No," she says, moving away from me, my side feels the coldness fall over it. "You got her last time." She turns on the light as she sits on the bed, I guess looking at the monitor to make sure that she's really up and we aren't just deliriously hearing her wail. "She is definitely pissed." She puts the monitor back down on the side table.

I sit up and touch my phone, showing me the time. "It's been two hours," I state, rubbing my face. "She might be fevering again. Fucking teeth." I grab the cover, flipping it off me and tossing it onto Eva's side of the bed. "I don't think I've hated something this much in my whole life." I turn to look at Eva. "I'll get a bottle. She didn't really eat much at dinner, so she might be hungry."

She gets up off the bed, turning to look at me. Her eyes go huge on her face. "What's that?" I look where she is pointing down at my shorts that clearly, without a doubt, shows her my dick.

"That would be my dick," I inform her, too tired to even care at this point. Besides, it was partially her fault for putting her ass on me. How was my dick supposed to know we were both sleeping? How does my dick also not know she's, like, off-limits?

She rolls her lips now. "Do you want to go and take care of it?" She points at the bathroom behind her.

The eyes that were shocked two minutes ago are now twinkling with laughter.

"That isn't how this works." I put my hands on my hips.

"Really?" She cocks her hips to the side and folds her hands under her tits, pushing them up even higher. "So I've been jacking them off this whole time for nothing?" I glare at her. "I just figure once you know, you boom." She uses her hands to emit fireworks. "Then it goes back to sleep."

"It's not my dick's fault that it's awake," I explain to her, "your ass was practically on top of it. How was he supposed to know that you breached the barrier?"

She gasps. "I did not breach the barrier." I tilt my head to the side, walking over to the bed and moving the covers to show her that the pillow is on her side of the bed, at the edge.

"Well, would you look at that?" My voice fills with celebration.

"I moved the pillow when I got up." She throws her hands up, and all I can do is nod at her like, sure you did.

"Are we seriously discussing my dick while Cici is crying?" I ask. "It's fine, it'll go away." I look back at her and my eyes roam from her face down to her tank top, which is loose but is now showing that maybe she isn't that offended by my hard dick. "Stop staring at my dick, it's getting your nipples all hard." I point at said nipples, smirking at her as she looks down at her boob. "Do you want to maybe go take care of that?" I point at the bathroom, trying not to laugh at her.

"I'll get the baby," she huffs and escapes the room, almost as if it's a race.

"I'll get the bottle," I call through the empty doorway, before looking down at my cock. "You are really barking up the wrong tree there, big man."

As I walk toward the stairs. I can hear her talking to Cici.

"Oh my goodness," she coos, "look at those big tears."

"Does she have a fever?" I shout from downstairs.

"I think so!" she yells back and I put my hands on my hips and look up to the ceiling.

"We are taking her to the doctor in the morning!" I holler at her as I walk over to the kitchen and take a bottle from the fake plastic grass that helps dry them. Placing it under the machine, I press a button, and like every single time before, I'm amazed by how quick it's done.

Walking back up the stairs I hear Eva, "You had a full diaper and now you are all clean and dry." She stands her up on her changing table. "There is my happy girl." Cici chews on her pacifier and her eyes finally come to me. She smiles so big her pacifier falls out of her mouth. "See, I told you he was coming with a bottle."

I walk to her with my own smile on my face. "Is my girl hungry?" I ask as I hand Eva the bottle. "Did you give her Tylenol?" I look down at Eva, who nods at me as she walks over to the rocking chair. "I see you took care of your problem." She looks at me and then down at my dick.

I look down at her tank top, folding my arms over my chest, not even trying to hide the smile. "I can say the same for you."

Twenty-One

Eva

"What time is it now?" he mumbles from beside me as I crash into bed on my side. My feet are still off the bed, but I'm pretty sure I can fall asleep on the wooden floor.

"I think a little after four," I reply, not even bothering covering myself up. "How has she been up most of the night and she's not even tired?"

"I think she's overtired," he offers and I look over at him annoyed.

"No one asked you, Levi," I snarl before turning back to my side of the bed. Ever since I woke up with my ass pushed against him and my legs tangled with his, I've been literally stuck to my side of the bed.

I curl into a ball, feeling the bed move from his laughing. "I get it now," he remarks and I groan out.

"What do you get?" I don't even know why I'm talking; I should be saving my energy.

"The movie with Al Pacino in it. *Insomnia.* I didn't get it before, how he went crazy from lack of sleep. But now," he mumbles, "now, I get it. I think I'm getting delirious."

I can't keep from laughing now, my whole body moving as I laugh. "You are also," he declares, and we both hear it at the same time.

The fucking wail makes us both groan. "Is it possible?" I look over at him. "Like should we take her to the ER?"

"No." He gets up. "I may or may not have read online that teething and sleep don't go hand in hand."

"Did you or did you not?" I roll out of bed, looking over at him.

"At this point right here." His eyes are still closed, allowing me to check him out. His chest is bare and very defined. His shorts ride low on one side of his hips, there is just a hint of hair on his stomach that is almost like a flashing arrow leading down to his cock. I've been around him for a long time, seen him pick up girls, but I've never seen his dick as defined as it was a couple of hours ago. "I have no idea."

He shakes his head and I turn and walk out of the bedroom toward her room. "Baby girl," I groan, taking her out of her crib. "There is nothing that I can do for you."

"Bring her to me!" Levi shouts from our bedroom.

"Do you want to come to sleep with us in the bed?" I ask as she sucks her pacifier and she points at the door. "Ugh, don't tell me you've fallen in love with him, too."

I walk back to the bedroom. "Who else is in love with me?" he questions as soon as I clear the doorway.

"Every woman but me falls for the Levi charm." I avoid looking in his eyes, because at this point I'm not sure of anything that is going on. My nipples are getting hard looking at his cock, my ass feels like it's a magnet for his body, and it's just been a very, very long night. I place her in the middle of the bed on her bum. She smiles when she sees Levi and turns toward him and places her head on his chest. "Ugh," I say, getting in bed, "another one bites the dust."

He can't help but laugh. "The only one who has never fallen for my charm is you." He rubs her back. "What's up, baby girl?" He looks down at her, his five o'clock shadow showing, his voice thick with sleep. "You're tired, aren't you?" In one swift movement, he brings her on his chest and moves more into the bed.

"You are smashing the barrier," I tell him as he turns his face toward me.

"Your ass broke that barrier less than four hours ago." He turns his head back and closes his eyes. "Now, why don't you stop talking and let's see how long she sleeps?"

"This is probably why I didn't fall for your charm," I grumble, "you are the most annoying person I know."

"Shh," he says to me, my eyes going to Cici. I see her eyes are getting heavier and heavier.

I move the pillow to the other side of me, against my

back, as I watch the two of them, the soft light coming in from the sun rising outside. Both of them sleeping, his arms protective around her. That is the last thing I see before I fall asleep.

My eyes blink open and I'm in the same position I was when I fell asleep. I blink a couple of times and see the bed next to me is empty. "Levi?" I call his name, turning to look at the bedroom door but it's closed. Getting out of bed, I walk over and pull open the door, going downstairs where I find them.

Cici sits on her foam carpet in front of Levi, who is wearing exactly what he did when he went to bed. His hair looks like he ran his fingers through it, and his back is up against the couch while he holds a cup of coffee in one hand. "This is blue," he says, holding up a blue ball in his hand and rolling it to her.

She squeals as she grabs the ball in her hand. "Blue," he says again. He smiles at her and must feel me staring at him because he looks over at me. "Good afternoon." He smirks, drinking his coffee.

"It's not even," I counter, turning my hand over to see that it's after one in the afternoon. "Oh my God," I huff. "Why did you let me sleep so long?"

"You were out, like out-out. Like drool-coming-out-of-your-mouth out." My hand immediately flies to my cheek to feel if it's wet, making him laugh at me.

"How long have you been up?" I ask, walking over to the coffee machine.

"About an hour, she just finished her bottle."

"An hour?" I ask, looking at him as the smell of coffee

fills the room. "Did she have a fever?"

"No, fever-free." He puts his one hand up in the air. "I also tried to feed her cereal and she was like, not having it."

I carry my cup of coffee over to the couch, sitting on it, watching them. "She looks better," I note, taking her in as she smiles with her pacifier in her mouth. "Oh, now we're happy?" I ask. "If you want to go to sleep, I can watch her."

"Nah." He shakes his head and all I can do is watch it. "I'm up, coffee drank. It's a new day."

I don't answer him because his phone rings from upstairs in our bedroom. "I'll be back." He jumps up and runs to the stairs, and I watch him take them two at a time.

I turn back to look at Cici who is just staring at me, like yeah, I see you staring at him. "Oh, please, you fell asleep on his chest." I get up, going onto the floor with her. "So you can't judge me." I lean over and rub my nose with hers. "He's got a nice body, I never denied that." I take a sip of the coffee. "Now let's talk about why you were up all night and now you didn't eat your cereal." She looks at me, her pacifier dropping out of her mouth as she babbles to me. "Yeah, is that so?" I nod at her. "Let's see if you are hungry now."

Picking her up, I walk her over to her high chair and place her in it, buckling her in. "Do you want some fruit this morning, or actually, this afternoon?" I walk over to the refrigerator and take out some strawberries I know she loves, washing them and then cutting them into tiny pieces. She grabs the pieces in her hand, eating some but then dumping the rest on the floor. "We might have to get a dog." She starts crying from her high chair as I wet a facecloth, walking over and wiping her face. She tries to move away from me. "It's just for a second," I tell her, "there, done." Her soft cries now turn into a high-pitched cry. "Oh my goodness," I coo calmly, picking her up. "What is the matter?" I put my cheek on her head and she's really warm.

"What's going on?" Levi comes down the stairs, looking as if I'm the one making her cry.

"She's warm," I tell him, walking back up to her bedroom where I left the thermometer last night or this morning. "I'm going to check her temperature," I state. As soon as I walk into her bedroom, she projectile vomits all over me. I literally stop mid step as her vomit goes down my shirt.

I close my eyes, thinking this isn't happening. "I guess that is why she's crying?" Levi says from behind me.

"Oh my God," I gag, turning my head to the side, not breathing. "I'm going to throw up."

"Okay," Levi jumps in, "I've got her. I think someone needs a bath." He holds her at arm's length. "Like a full bath and shower." He puts his hand to the side. "I think she also pooped." He gags. "How attached are we to these clothes?" he asks as he turns her and I see that she did poop and it's going up her back. "We are tossing everything, except the kid."

"I'll change and come and get her," I say, walking toward my bedroom.

"Don't worry about me," he throws over his shoulder, "worry about yourself. It's all over your legs."

"Oh, good God," I mumble.

"Throw out those clothes, too," he urges, and all I do is walk into the bathroom, closing the door behind me.

I take one look down and see chunks of white mixed with pieces of berries. "Maybe we should have not done the fruit." I peel the clothes down my body, tossing them into the trash bin, before turning and starting the shower. I place my hand under the warm water stream before getting in.

Putting my head back as the water washes over me, my eyes close and it's immediately visions of Levi. "Fucking hell," I mumble, grabbing the loofah and adding some body wash to it before lifting my leg, starting to lather it from my ankle up. "Looking at my dick is getting your nipples hard." His voice from before plays in my head. I look down seeing the same nipples that were hard when I was looking at his dick. The memory of his dick now plays over and over in my head. I place the loofah at my neck, my nipples getting tight as the soap suds wash down. I rub my nipples with the loofah and my breath hitches. "Fuck," I whisper when I close my eyes and I picture him here with me, naked in the shower. The loofah falls from my hands as my fingers move down my stomach and toward my pussy. I slide a finger inside me as I picture him getting on his knees, his eyes looking up at me as his mouth devours me. His blue eyes turning a dark emerald color as his tongue licks me from my clit to my opening before sliding it in there. "Yes," I hiss, slipping in another finger as my thumb plays with my clit, the sensation making me moan. My eyes close, picturing they're his fingers, his tongue, his teeth. "Oh, God," I moan so loud it echoes.

"You okay in there?" I hear him knocking on the door, and my hands drop away from me.

My heart speeds up as I try not to stutter. "Um, yeah," I call back, closing my eyes and almost banging my head on the tiled wall.

"Are you sure?" I look at the closed door, turning off the water and grabbing a towel.

"Of course I'm sure," I tell him, waiting for him to say something else. "Nice," I scold myself, picking up the loofah and hanging it on the handle before stepping out. "Smooth." I dry myself off, grabbing a pair of shorts and another tank top from the clean clothes basket I haven't put away yet. Getting dressed and pulling open the door, the last thing I expect is to walk out and see him lying on the bed. "Where is Cici?"

"She's in bed napping." He looks over at me. "Gave her a bath and she was practically sleeping when I was dressing her."

"Oh, good." I walk over to the monitor and see her in the middle of her crib on her back, sleeping.

"How was the shower?" My eyes fly back to his and I can see the twinkle in them.

"Fine, why?" I try not to let it show on my face what I was doing in there. Unless he put up a camera in there, he knows nothing.

"I don't know, I think I heard you moaning." His eyes

never leave mine.

"Well, you didn't because I wasn't." My head screams at me to deny until the end.

"Oh, baby," he says and just the way he says baby my pussy contracts and my nipples get hard. *Motherfucking traitors,* I yell internally at them both. "You were moaning."

I roll my eyes at him. "No, I wasn't." I try to sound annoyed but he gets up, standing in front of me. The basketball shorts hang low on his hips and I've decided that I hate them. I hate them all. I also am ninety-nine percent sure he's not wearing anything under them.

"Trust me." He points at me as he walks to the front of the bed. "I don't know a lot of things, but moaning—" He chuckles. "That I know."

I glare at him. "I bet you do." I fold my arms over my chest to hide the fact that my nipples also know what he knows.

"I'm just saying, if you need a little help." He puts his hands on his hips and cocks one of them.

I clap my hands and laugh. "You are going to help me?"

"Hey, as a friend." He puts his hand on his chest and I wonder if it feels as hard as it looks. It must be a little soft if Cici wants to sleep on it all the time. "I'm just trying to be helpful." I glare at him for two reasons. One, because he's right, and two, because I'm almost tempted to just take him up on his offer. My stomach gets tight, my nipples tingle, and I swear I'm getting wet just standing here in front of him.

"I'm going to take a shower." My eyes betray me and roam down his chest and to his dick. Showing me he's hard again.

"If anyone needs help"—I point down at his dick—"that would be you."

"You offering to help me?" His voice comes out thick with lust, so I think my mouth almost blurts out yes.

I don't think it's ever been this hard to say this word before. "No." I shake my head. "I'm going to go check on Cici." Turning to walk out of the room, my whole face feels like it's on fire.

"Pink looks good on you," he teases, right before I step out of the bedroom.

I look down at my black shorts and top. "I'm not wearing pink!"

He smirks and chuckles walking to the bathroom, and right before he closes the door, he says, "I meant your cheeks, baby."

Twenty-Two

Levi

I close the door behind me before I do something I am not sure of, or before I say something I can't take back, like *let me taste you* or *come and sit on my face*. I close my eyes before I look down at my dick, who wants me to do both of those. "Sorry, buddy," I tell him once I pull off my shorts, "it's just you and me." I don't know why but I swear I hear him groan and then weep. "Yeah, I know, buddy." I turn on the water. "Trust me, I know."

I think about taking care of myself in the shower, but to be honest, I'm dead on my feet. I'm even surprised my dick can get up at this point. I turn off the water, wrapping a towel around my waist before walking out and seeing that Eva isn't in bed. Making my way to the walk-in closet, I grab another pair of shorts and a white T-shirt before I head downstairs.

Eva is in the kitchen cleaning. "Is she still sleeping?" I watch her put things in the dishwasher and see that she's not in her black booty shorts. Now she's wearing gray pants that look like they are soft as fuck, with a matching shirt that goes into a V in the front, showing off a touch of her chest. It falls off one of her shoulders and I see a peach strap I know I would snap right off.

"Yeah," she replies breathlessly, looking up at me. "Why don't you go and take a nap?" She laughs. "It might be another wild and crazy night."

"These days wild and crazy nights mean something totally different. I'm going to go catch up on some work," I tell her. "Then I think I'm going to take her for a walk when she wakes up. Get some fresh air."

Her eyebrows pinch together. "Get some fresh air," she repeats to me as she turns on the water at the sink and wets the rag in her hand, before wiping down the counter beside her. "Who are you?"

I can't help but laugh at her, because she is totally right, who am I? I remember not seeing the light once for ten days. I would go to work in the dark and leave in the dark, but things are different now. When they became different, I can't say, well, I can, I just don't want to admit it. "If you're lucky, we might even invite you."

"If I'm lucky," she mocks my words. "I could be so lucky."

I smirk at her as I walk back upstairs and grab my laptop. I swear, I must be working maybe a full five minutes when I hear a soft cry. I look over at the monitor on the side table and see Cici is sitting up. "Shh," I hear Eva say, "Levi is working, and if he hears you, he's going to come running." I can't help the smile that forms on my face. I put my laptop to the side of the bed, getting up and going toward them.

I come face-to-face with them when she walks out of the room. "Well, there she is," I say, earning me a smile from Cici, her one cheek still red from lying on it. "Did you have a good nap?" She lifts her hand and slaps it down right away. "I'm going to go to work and then we can go for a walk." She just squeals at me. "If Eva plays her cards right, she might come."

"Go away," Eva retorts, walking past me. "I might just take her for a walk now."

"No, you won't," I reply and she ignores me, walking down the steps. "Don't you dare."

"I guess we'll find out," she tosses back, looking over at me.

"Baby, if you want to play some games—" I start to say, and the minute I say baby, her cheeks instantly light up. "We can play some games."

"Don't call me that." She glares at me. "I've been around long enough to know you call your women that when you don't remember their names." She tries to pretend it doesn't bother her, but I can feel it does. "I'm not playing games with you. This isn't a game."

I take a step toward the top of the stairs, staring down at both of them. "I don't think you've been paying attention." I try not to lose my shit. "I call the women whose names I don't remember sweetheart." I can see that she remembers. "I've never called anyone baby." I don't wait for her to answer. "I'll be down soon." I turn to walk away from her before walking back to her, taking Cici out of her arms, and kissing the shit out of her for pissing me off.

I walk back into the bedroom and close the door, and I don't know why because it's not like I'm working. No, not me, I'm in the middle of her bedroom pacing back and forth, trying to tell myself this isn't happening. Trying to tell myself she's my best friend and me acting on whatever this is isn't the smart thing to do. Trying to tell myself if I do this, I risk losing her and Cici. Trying to tell myself if I don't do this, I'll regret it for the rest of my life. I look at the bed and then I look at the closed door. Instead of storming downstairs and probably ruining the best thing I have, I walk back to the bed. Sitting in it and grabbing my laptop, I'm not even working. I'm just staring at the screen, biding my time.

When it's almost four I close my laptop, putting it on my bedside table before I walk toward the bedroom door. "And then the itsy-bitsy spider went up the spout again," Eva sings to her and then I watch Cici clap her hands and then flap them excitedly. Eva's eyes look up to mine. "Oh, no," she says, "the big bad wolf is here." She smirks at me before turning back to Cici.

"Wow, one fight and I'm a wolf," I retort and Cici's eyes shoot my way and her smile goes even bigger. She forgets she's happy and then pouts and whines.

"If that isn't a faker, I don't know what is," Eva notes,

picking her up. "You were fine two seconds ago."

"Come here." I grab her out of Eva's arms and bury my face in her neck. "I missed you."

"Oh, please, it's been two hours," she chides, shaking her head. "Are you going for a walk?"

I nod my head. "We just have to figure out if we are taking a stroller or she's going to go strapped to my chest."

"Why don't we use the stroller?" she suggests and I raise my eyebrows at her. "What?"

"What?" I cock my hip. "You're supposed to say, 'I'm sorry, Levi, for snapping at you.'" She folds her arms. "I forgive you." I look down at Cici. "That's how you say you're sorry."

"Fine, go on the walk without me," she pouts, not looking at me.

"And that, Cici, is what you call her being wrong and not admitting it." I look at Cici, who is babbling to me. "She's saying you are right, Levi."

"Is she now?" Eva smiles.

"Let's go for a walk." I smile back at her. It takes us five minutes to grab stuff to go for a walk. We forgot the diaper bag at first, and then have a debate if we should bring it. We have a discussion if we should bring water or milk and water. There is another debate on should she sit facing out or should she sit facing us. In the end, we go with water and facing out. She kept pointing at things as we pushed her down the street, pointing out things to her. For the most part, she likes it, but she gets cranky when we are ten minutes from home, so I carry her the rest of the way. As soon as we get back in the house, Eva goes into the kitchen to prepare her food while I order us a pizza.

I crack open a bottle of beer. "What's she eating today?"

"Today," Eva replies, "she is eating shepherd's pie, with some peas."

"Yum," I say, watching her eat it like a champ. "I guess your stomach feels better?"

She's full of laughing and giggles until it gets to six thirty and then she's just cranky. "I'll clean up," I tell Eva, "and get her bottle ready." She just nods at me, walking up with Cici. It takes me about twenty minutes to get everything clean and have a bottle going. I hear Cici whining by the time I walk upstairs.

"Someone is tired," Eva states, as she stands her up on her changing table as she rubs her eyes.

"I have a bottle." I shake it side to side. Cici reaches for me as I take her. "Go relax, I'll put her to bed."

"Don't rock her until she falls asleep," Eva instructs me as I walk over to the rocking chair and Cici holds the bottle in her hand, bringing it to her mouth. "Good night, baby girl. Can we try to sleep tonight?"

I rock her until her eyes close and the bottle is empty and falls out of her mouth. Placing her down in the middle of the bed on her side, she doesn't wake up and I walk back to the bedroom. "I feel like I did the marathon of my life, along with five people on my back," I remark to Eva when I walk in the room. She walks out of the bathroom with her hair wrapped in a towel on top of her head, wearing another pair of loose shorts and an even looser tank top.

"I feel like I've been on a bender." She laughs, walking over to the bed. "But I didn't even go out." She looks at me and I don't think she's ever been more beautiful before. "Is that what getting old feels like?"

"Considering the fact we ate dinner at five thirty, I think we are heading into the senior citizen type of living." I laugh and take off my T-shirt. "I'm going to go take a shower."

"I'm going to lie here and pray that she sleeps all night long," she says, getting into bed and curling into a ball. Her head hits the pillow as her eyes close and she turns off the lights. "Night."

"It's seven thirty," I point out to her, laughing as I walk back into the bathroom. I start the shower and I don't even have the energy to shave. My eyes are almost closed as I walk over to my side of the bed. Sliding into it, I see her ass is in the middle of the mattress and not her pillow. I smile to myself as I lie down in the bed, looking over at her, the white towel unwrapped from her hair and tossed to the side.

I'm asleep faster than I want to admit and wake when I feel this heat over me. I try to turn over but I'm pinned to the bed. I open my eyes and looking down, I see Eva is draped over me. Her front is pushed up against my side. My arm is around her and I'm holding her ass in the palm of my hand. I'm stuck and shocked, but do you know who isn't stuck or shocked, my cock. Nope, my cock is on fucking full alert. "What do I do?" I whisper to myself while I slowly turn toward Eva.

She moans and that just makes it so much worse, because my cock now feels like a piece of fucking marble. "Eva." Her name comes out with a thickness, almost in a feral growl.

I'm facing her, and her breasts are pressed to my chest. "Eva," I say again, waiting for her to open her eyes.

But she doesn't; instead she arches her back. "Levi?" she moans out while she lifts her leg to wrap around my hip.

I look down at her in the dark, waiting for her eyes to finally open. "Eva," I repeat her name and her eyes fly open for just a second. Enough time for her to lean her head back and put her lips on mine. Her tongue slides into my mouth or my tongue slides into hers, either way I'm kissing her. My eyes close as I turn my head to the side to deepen this kiss. Fuck, I can't believe I'm kissing her. It's not a soft kiss, no, this is wet, it's hard, and it's frantic. My hands move from her ass up her back and into her hair, gripping it in my fist.

Our tongues are still fighting with each other. "Eva," I say her name in a whisper when I let her go for a minute before going back to her lips. This kiss, I can't even put it into words. I'm in another fucking atmosphere with this kiss. I have never, ever had a first kiss like this, where it was so all-consuming I would die without it. Her hands roam down my back as she arches again, pressing her tits into my chest. My hand on her ass squeezes her into me, the hardness of my cock can feel the heat from her.

"Levi." She lets go of my lips as I trail kisses to her

cheek and to her jaw, biting, sucking, and licking. Her hand goes into the back of my shorts. She uses her nails to rake the top of my ass as she moves to my hip. I'm focusing on her neck when I feel her hand grip my cock, the both of us moaning.

"Eva," I whisper her name, my eyes half closed when she moves her hand up and down, jerking my cock.

"Levi." She thrusts her hips against my cock and her hand once more. My hand on her ass is now gripping her shorts in my fingers, bringing them up and slipping under them, finding her bare. "Yes." She attacks my mouth again as my fingertips move from her ass cheek to the front of her. My fingers slip into her heat and wetness, two fingers enter her at the same time that she grips my cock hard in her palm. My whole body feels like it's about to explode as she jerks me off and I finger-fuck her. We move together. She's thrusting her hips to fuck my fingers, and I'm thrusting my hips to fuck her hand. "Yes." She lets go of my lips but doesn't move her face. Her forehead is on mine, her lips hovering over mine as my hand moves faster and then so does hers. I can feel my balls getting tight at the same time as her pussy closes around my fingers, my thumb moving back and forth on her clit. "Levi."

"Eva," I say her name, "I'm almost—" She bites my lower lip and I close my eyes because she throws her head back and comes on my fingers at the same time that I come in her hand. We ride each other's orgasm until the very last drop. I don't think I've ever come this hard before. I definitely haven't just come in someone's hand because she was jerking me off, but with Eva, I've come to realize that things aren't what I thought they were. "Baby," I say softly as her hand slips out of my shorts and she rolls away from me, my fingers slipping out of her. "I should go and…" I look down at my shorts. "I'll be back," I mumble as I walk around the bed at the same time she grabs the towel and cleans her hand, while I walk into the bathroom to clean myself up. I haven't come in my pants since I was sixteen, maybe even fifteen, yet one touch from her and I was a goner. I clean myself off before walking back out to grab another pair of shorts, finding her already snoring.

Twenty-Three

Eva

"Are we ready for daycare?" I look over at Cici as I rinse off my hands. "We are going to have a good day and not get sick, right?" I grab the dish towel and dry my hands off, while I look over and see Levi coming down the stairs dressed in a suit. I swallow back the lump that forms as I watch him.

"Okay, I'm out," he announces, rounding the staircase and coming over to us. I avoid looking at him because, how the fuck do you look at someone who you literally dry humped in the middle of the night? "Did you check her temperature this morning?" he asks.

"I did." I nod, mistakenly looking at him. The minute I do, I swear to everything my pussy contracts. He's wearing a black suit that I know is custom-made because I had to drive him once to get fitted for it. The suit is paired with a charcoal shirt and a black tie, which means he looks fucking hot. Of course, I know now what his dick feels like, so my eyes automatically go where they shouldn't before I feel my cheeks getting hot. "No fever."

"Woo-hoo." He puts his hands in the air, one empty and the other holding his jacket. "That means it's going to be a good day."

He walks to the kitchen sink at the same time I move over to Cici and take her out of her high chair. "We should get you changed," I whisper to her, and in the corner of my eye I see him coming to us. I literally, no word of a lie, hold my motherfucking breath.

"See you tonight," he says, leaning down and kissing Cici on the cheek. I think I'm in the clear, but I'm not that lucky. "Have a good day." He looks at me and kisses me on the lips before walking out the door.

I stay here stuck in the middle of the kitchen, my lips still tingling from his kiss. My heart races in my chest, while my stomach feels like it's going to come out of my mouth. I look over at Cici shocked, finding her staring at me and I swear if I didn't know better, I would think she is leering. "Don't look at me like that," I chide her, "things are a bit…" I walk to the stairs. "What did you think was going to happen after you came on his fingers?" I mumble to myself. "It's a bit blurry but it'll be fine. Everything is going to be fine." I look down at Cici. "It's fine."

I get Cici to daycare before walking into work.

Smiling at everyone, I pretend it's just another day in the office, when it's not. Nothing is like any other day because last night, in the middle of the night, I had a kiss that is—hands down—the kiss to end all kisses. It's at this moment that I would pick up the phone and call Levi to discuss it with him, but I can't.

I'm sitting at my desk, leaning back in my chair with my eyes closed, but that doesn't help. All I can see is Levi's face right before he came. My phone rings, making me jump when I think it's him and he caught me thinking about him. I look down, seeing it's Addison.

"Hello," I answer, trying to sound like I didn't get finger-banged last night. "How are you?"

"Why are you so weird?" she asks right away. "Is everything okay?"

"Of course it is." I chuckle so fake even I secretly cringe. I hear the ringing and look down at my phone. "Are you FaceTiming me?"

"Yes," she confirms, "answer."

I swallow down and take a deep breath before I press the connect button. "Game face," I tell myself as the white circle goes round and round when it says connecting. "Good morning." I smile into the camera as Addison's face comes into view.

"Good morning to you," she greets and then I hear "Good morning" being chanted from behind her. "I'm here with the girls," she explains, extending her hand so I can see them all sitting around a table.

"Hi, guys." I wave my hand, knowing I'm totally being so fake right now.

"Before we get to why you look all pent up with sexual frustration," Clarabella starts. "How is everything?"

"Everything is amazing," I chirp, the smile not leaving my face. "I'm fine, Cici is fine. We are all fine."

"Oh, my," Addison states, "you look like you are about to cry."

"I was going to say burst." All eyes turn toward Shelby. "You know those cartoons where the person is like, I'm fine, but inside they are like shaking and their head is going to explode, that is how she looks." I gasp. "But you look amazing."

"Nice save," Shelby notes. "How is married life?"

"Married life is married life." I shrug my shoulders. "It's fine."

"Where do you sleep?" Presley taps the table in front of her, hiding her smirk.

"Well, I only have one bed," I admit to them, trying to pretend it's fine. "How is everything on your side?"

"Oh, deflection," Sofia points out. "That means there is something there."

"Is there?" Addison asks, her eyes big.

"No, there is nothing there." I shake my head back and forth quickly.

"Is he packing?" Clarabella asks me, and if I could kick my own ass, I would, because the minute she says that, I feel my face flare up.

"Oh my God!" Addison says, pointing at me at the same time putting a hand to her mouth. "You had sex with him."

I slap my desk. "I did not!" I deny. "We did not have

sex."

"Okay," Shelby questions, "do you sleep in the same bed as him?"

"That's the worst question of life," Presley declares. "You sound like Amber Heard's lawyers." She laughs. "Did you drink a mega pint of beer?" She imitates the lawyer.

"I think they even objected to themselves; it was not a good day for her." Clarabella shakes her head.

"Okay, let me do this," Sofia urges. "Have you kissed him?"

"Oh, good question." Addison points at her.

"We kiss all the time." I roll my eyes.

"With tongue?" Sofia adds and now I glare at her. "That's a yes."

"You kissed him." Addison slaps the desk. "With tongue, that is, like, big."

"It's a kiss." I try not to make it seem like it's a big deal, because it's not. "It's just a kiss." I reiterate, again my voice going up a touch. "It's just a measly little kiss." A squeal comes out.

"Oh, my," Shelby cautions, "she's about to blow."

"How big is his dick?" Clarabella now sticks her face into the phone. "And you can't lie. You're under oath."

"No more court television for you," Presley hisses at her. "Now answer her question."

"We were both tired," I start to say. "It was a long day. Cici was sick and didn't sleep. We didn't sleep. She then threw up on me." I don't even give them a second. "Then I woke up and my ass was all over him."

"Yes, girl." Clarabella winks at me. "Proceed."

"And then the barrier I made in the middle was gone, I don't even know where it went."

"His dick cut through it." Presley snickers.

"And then I wake up and I'm dry humping him." My face goes close up to the camera.

"Did you guys?" Addison asks softly.

"No." I shake my head. "I woke up and I was in his arms and his hands were on my ass." They all nod like yes. "And then his lips were on mine."

"OHH," they all sing out.

"And he was kissing me and I was kissing him back—" I start to say but I'm interrupted by Addison.

"Was it weird," she asks, "kissing your best friend?"

"No," I admit and feel like I want to hit my head on the desk. "I feel like it should be, but it wasn't. It wasn't at all, it was all—" My arms extend beside me. "It was all tongue." My stomach gets fucking flutters. "It was—" I try to think of words but can't.

"It was hot." Sofia helps me out. "So you guys just kissed?"

Say no, my head yells, *say no*, but instead, I just shake my head. "He got me off using his fingers," I mumble, "while I—"

"Held his pole." Shelby laughs.

"Is he big?" Clarabella asks. "He has to be big; he looks like one of those European men. You know, like the hot guy from that movie. I think he's Italian."

"What?" Addison and I both say at the same time.

"What?" Clarabella reacts. "You trying to tell me

Stefano isn't packing heat?" Addison doesn't say anything. "Exactly. You think your father-in-law isn't packing heat?"

"He's one thousand percent packing something, that man is fine," Clarabella swoons, and Addison looks like she is going to vomit. "He is so fine. Vivienne…" She shakes her head. "It's not any woman who can keep that man, but her. She must do all the things."

"She's French," Shelby explains, "they are more open about their sexuality than the rest of the world."

"Excuse me, I would like to never discuss what my in-laws do," Addison declares, "like never again."

"I agree with her." I hold up my hand.

"Yes, can we circle back to Levi and Eva?" Addison directs.

"Oh, I have a question," Shelby says. "If you did have sex with him, would you be walking normal this morning?"

"Oh, that's a good one." Clarabella points her pen toward her. "Sneaky also."

"All I'm going to say is that I get the hype now." I close my eyes. "I was all like, why do these girls all come back and beg for more?" My stomach that was fluttering less than a minute ago is now burning. "I have no doubt if I wanted him to do me hard, I would have trouble sitting the next day. I would feel him for days."

"You need to get yourself some of that," Sofia encourages. "Trust me, the more you fight it, the harder it's going to be."

"Oh, that was a good one." Clarabella snorts. "The

more you fight it, the harder he's going to do you. If you are lucky, he's going to snap—and boom—Pound Town all over the kitchen table."

"This is why we don't eat at your house," Shelby deadpans, "this right here."

"Guys," I finally say softly. "This can't happen. He's the best friend I've ever had and I can't do that to him."

"Maybe it was just meant to happen," Shelby says. "Look at Ace and me. Best friends for so long and then, boom. You're about to walk down the aisle with another man to find out he's cheating on you and then you're on your honeymoon with your best friend." I smile. "Best thing I ever did."

"Oh, we know, you keep saying it all the time," the girls all say.

"Remember that butt dial once?" Clarabella reminds us. "Always you," she moans. "Good God, I wore earplugs for a month."

"All I'm going to say is," Addison interjects, "everything happens for a reason."

I think about her words, and when I get buzzed that my client is here, I sign off with them by blowing them kisses. I take off my necklace and then my ring, slipping it on the chain and then putting it back on my neck before I walk out and start the day.

Time flies by with my appointments being back-to-back, since I missed a day. I don't have time to do anything, let alone eat. So when I get Cici and I walk into the house, my feet are throbbing. My head is aching, my stomach is making all sorts of noise, and the only thing I actually want is a nice glass of wine. I swear my mouth drools when I put Cici on her mat in the living room before walking over to the kitchen and dumping our bags. Pulling open the fridge, I grab a half-empty bottle of wine. "You know what the best thing is?" I look over at Cici, who is playing with one of her teethers. "That first sip." I pour myself a glass and then take that first sip. "Delicious."

I take another sip when the front door opens. "Hello," he greets, and Cici turns her head toward his voice and gets all excited, making me roll my eyes. "There she is." He doesn't even take off his jacket before he walks over to her and picks her up. "How was your day?" he asks, burying his face in her neck before turning my way. His smile is still on his face, but his eyes light up just a touch more. "Is this a party?" He looks at me and to the glass of wine.

"Nope." I finish the glass. "It's just been a day."

"Yeah," he agrees, walking into the kitchen. "Do you want me to handle dinner?"

No, my head screams, *I want you to get your ass over here and kiss me and maybe, perhaps, eat me for dinner.* "Sure," I answer quickly before I word vomit all my thoughts. "I'll handle Cici, you order me a burger."

I walk over to the freezer and look at the choices. "What do you want? Some pasta or grilled chicken with peas and carrots?"

"Say pasta," Levi urges, making me laugh, "say pasta."

"Pasta it is," I say, taking it out. He looks over at me

and smirks, and the whole night is spent with us laughing and almost tippy-toeing around each other. When I'm at the sink, he walks over and gently touches my lower back. When I sit down and he has to get up to get something, he touches my shoulder lightly. It's got me on the fucking edge, and when I finally get Cici down, he's coming out of the shower.

"She down?" he asks, but all I can focus on is the two little drops of water that have fallen from his hair onto his chest. All I want to do is lean forward and lick him, fucking lick him.

"Yeah," I reply, avoiding looking at his eyes, because I'm pretty sure I'm blushing again and he hasn't said a word. "I'm going to get in the shower."

He nods at me and I'd be lying if I said I don't spend extra time in there. When I finally walk out, the lights are off in the room and he's sleeping with his back to me.

Twenty-Four

Levi

$\mathcal{S}$oft bells fill my dream until they become just a touch louder. My eyes, heavy with sleep, open slowly. I'm on my stomach with my face toward my nightstand. "Wait, is that my alarm?" I hear a grumble from beside me and get up on my elbows. "Oh my God." I turn from my stomach to my back. "That's my alarm."

"Why is it still ringing?" I look over at Eva, who is lying on her side, looking at me, this time with one eye open. "Do you need instructions on how to shut it off?"

"Eva." I twist my body to turn it off. "It's six thirty."

"Thanks for the news flash," she huffs, closing her eye.

"Eva," I call her name again and this time she opens

both eyes in time to glare at me, "it's six thirty."

"Should I alert the presses?" she asks, confused and then I lean over her. Her hand touches my bare chest and my cock is more awake than he was two minutes ago. And for everyone who knows, you wake up with a boner, but her warm hands on me make it even harder and more painful. "Oof," she groans, "what the hell are you doing?"

I grab the monitor from her side of the screen and look down at it, seeing Cici in her crib still sleeping. "Eva."

"I swear to God, if you call my name one more time," she growls between clenched teeth.

"She's still sleeping." I point at the monitor.

"Shocking," she mumbles, "I wonder what that feels like."

"Did she sleep all night?" I ask, wondering if I was just so exhausted, I didn't hear her. It's at that moment when her eyes go big.

"No." She gets up to a sitting position and snatches the monitor from my hand. "Oh my God." She looks down at it. "Did you get up with her?" Only when I pinch my eyebrows together does Eva smile. "I think she slept all night." She lifts her hand up to the side and I high-five her.

Grabbing my phone, I pull up the sleep app and gasp, "I slept over ten hours." I hold up my hand, waiting for her to give me a high-five this time.

"So this is what it feels like to be refreshed," Eva declares, throwing the covers off her and getting up. My eyes move from her eyes down to her lips, and it's no time at all before they roam down to her tits. Her nipples tease me as they tent her tank top, my tongue comes out to lick my lips at the same time we hear the first signs of movements from Cici. "I'll get her." Eva almost jumps up, making her tits bounce, and I internally groan or moan. Either way, I wish her tits were bouncing in my face so I could take her nipple into my mouth. Or better yet, I wish my dick was sliding between them while her mouth takes my dick.

"I'll get her bottle!" I shout to her retreating back. Getting out of bed, I look down at my cock who might be blue with all this non-sex that I'm having. I hear Eva from the monitor ask Cici if she slept all right before going downstairs.

I press two buttons, one for the bottle and the other for the coffee cup, both finishing almost simultaneously. I screw the top on the bottle while I start another cup of coffee, waiting for them to come down for breakfast. Last night as soon as I got into bed, I wanted to take that barrier pillow and toss it toward the bedroom door, but I also knew she was secretly freaking out about what happened between us during the night. Truth be told, she wasn't the only one. I spent the better part of the day sitting at my desk, tapping the pen on the notepad, trying my hardest not to call her. Because it was so natural to call her when these things happened. Who else could tell me what was going on, what I should do next? If I should call her or not. If I should play it cool or just ignore it and pretend it didn't happen. I depended on myself, and I decided to play it cool. But the minute I walked into the house, all I wanted to do was go over and kiss her lips. Even if it was just a small kiss on the lips, it was the only thing I wanted. However, I also know her better than she knows herself, and I knew that if I did that, she would shut me out.

"What are you looking for?" I hear Eva's voice coming from the stairs. Looking over, I see her walking down the last step, Cici in her arms, with her cheek still red from lying on it. Her eyes look all over the place until I finally talk.

"Well, look who it is." I walk toward them, Cici's head snaps, and her face fills with a big smile as she waits for me to be close enough before leaning to me. "Good morning, my girl." I kiss her cheek, feeling the warmth from her bed. "Did you sleep almost twelve hours?" I ask and she just hits my chest with her hand. "I made you a bottle," I tell her, walking over to the counter, "and I made your aunt some coffee."

Eva looks over and smiles at me. "Thank you." She grabs the cup and puts some milk in her coffee. "What are we having for breakfast?" She leans back against the counter. "How about some oatmeal with some fruit?" she asks as Cici spots her bottle and reaches for it with a whine.

"I'm going to come with you today when you drop her off at daycare," I tell her as I turn Cici on her side so she can drink her milk.

"You don't have to come with me," Eva counters, going to the fridge.

"I won't see her tonight," I remind her as I sit on the

couch with Cici on one arm, holding my coffee with the other hand.

"Where are you going?" Eva pulls out the oatmeal, looking over at me.

"I'm having dinner with the guys," I remind her. "It's Daniel's bachelor party, remember?"

"Oh, that's right," she replies, not looking at me. "I forgot about that."

"I can try to cancel," I tell her, not really wanting to go out.

"No." She shakes her head. "You have to go, you're his groomsman."

"He does have three more," I tell her, getting up when Cici finishes her bottle. Walking back into the kitchen, I put her in her high chair and then buckle her in. I grab the baby snacks, handing her a rice cracker.

"Looks like it's just the two of us," Eva says, pouring hot water in the oatmeal before adding some blueberries. "Girls' night." She smiles down at her.

The two of us don't really say anything to each other. There is a whole list of things I want to say, but I don't think we have the time to go over them. Especially the part where I want to kiss the fuck out of her.

We rush out the door with me holding Cici and Eva following me. I follow the two of them to the daycare, parking beside her. I get out of my car before Eva even puts the car in park. Opening the back door, I smile at Cici. "Who's the prettiest girl in all of the land?" I ask and she smiles as she kicks her legs.

I take her in my arms while grabbing the diaper bag,

shutting the door right before Eva joins us. We start to walk in when we come face-to-face with a man who is walking out. He looks down, but when he looks up at Eva, his whole face lights up. "Hey, Eva," he greets when we are in front of him.

I look over at Eva who smiles back at him. "Hi, Caine."

"Hi, Cici." He turns to Cici, totally ignoring me. "Is she feeling better?" He looks back at Eva while at the same time I seriously want to throat punch this guy. His eyes never leave Eva's. "She looks much better," he notes and I want to laugh because he hasn't even really looked at her. His eyes have been trained on Eva since he saw her.

"Um, hi," I finally interject, looking at Eva with a smile on my face, but it's a fake smile. It's as fake as can be because all I want to do is glare at him.

"Oh, sorry." Eva laughs nervously from beside me. Shit, is she flirting with him? Do they talk? Did they meet here? Do they see each other every morning? The number of questions I have just keeps adding up. "This is Levi."

"Her husband." I extend my hand to her. He looks at me almost with a shocked expression before turning back to look at Eva, then quickly back at me. "I'll take Cici inside, you two can catch up." I look at Eva, who avoids looking at me. My stomach gets tight with knots as I walk around Caine and away from her. I'm so fucking pissed yet I have no reason to be, really. Or do I? I walk into the daycare and drop her off with Sylvia. I'm handing her over and I'm shocked to see Eva standing beside me.

"Are you okay?" she asks, her voice quiet.

"Yup," I answer her, ignoring her as I wave to Cici. I ignore the way my heart is beating in my chest. How clammy my hands are, and especially how murderous I feel at this moment. I've never in my whole life felt this feeling. I take a second to look over at Eva. "See you later," I say as fast as I can, the need to get away from her before I say something I'm going to regret is huge. She waves at Cici and walks out with me. I've never been so angry that my whole body tremored with anger. I've never been so out of my comfort zone that all I wanted to do was to just roar out my madness. I've never been so out of my comfort zone that I felt like my skin was crawling.

"Bye," she says from the other side of my car and I think I grunt, I'm not sure. The only thing I do know is that I leave the parking lot while she is still standing there, making me feel even more like a dick. I get to work and I don't know if everyone around me knows I'm pissed, but not one person asks me anything all day. Also, I'm not going to admit it, but I spend the whole day looking down at my phone every ten minutes, waiting for her to call. The minutes turn into hours, and then at the end of the day, I'm stuck going out to a dinner I don't even want to go to.

I pull up to the restaurant, and I'm tempted to text and ask her how Cici's day was at daycare, but I don't. Nope, that would be the normal thing to do. Nothing between Eva and I is normal, especially not after that fucking kiss. Especially not after I made her come for me. I toss my keys to the valet guy before walking into the restaurant. The lounge music hits me right away as I look at the hostess who is smiling at me, wearing her hair perfect with her tits on full display, partially covered with a rhinestone bra. Her tits are so fake she can float if she falls overboard. "Welcome."

"Hi," I greet, looking around, "I'm here for Daniel."

"Of course." She looks me up and down before she smiles her seductive smile at me. "If you would follow me." She turns, and once she's in front of me, she sways her hips side to side, the black minidress barely covering her ass. We walk past tables until she walks up two steps to where a party room sits. It's four feet from the floor closed in by glass so we can watch what is going on outside. "If you need anything," she practically pants, "I'm Audrey."

"Yup." I walk past her and into the room where the guys are waiting.

"There he is," Daniel says, getting up from the couch on the side, "the other groomsman." He claps his hands, coming over to me. He holds out his hand to me, shaking it and pulling me into him. "Fuck, it's been so long," he states and I nod at him. We met about five years ago when we were working on a project together. He's a lawyer for one of the companies we audited. "Glad you could make it."

"Fuck that," Todd says from beside him, "he's the one who told us about this place." Everyone laughs and

I look around. The room has couches all along the walls with a square table in the middle of the room, with food all over it. I know that before long there will be about twenty to thirty men who are showing up for this shit.

"Hey, I've never been here. I said I knew someone who came here." I hold my hand up in defense while a server walks in from the corner of the room. She's dressed pretty much like the woman in front, except her skirt is even shorter and her bra just holds up her tits, they are fully out.

She comes up to us, handing Daniel his drink before smiling my way. "I'm Dahlia," she introduces, "I'll be your server. Can I get you something to drink?"

"I'll have a scotch and soda," I tell her before turning back to Daniel. "So how's the groom-to-be? You ready?" I put my hands in my pockets as people start to walk in and come over to us. It takes me a full ten minutes before it dawns on me that I fucking hate this. It takes me thirty more minutes before my drink comes, and I head over to one of the tables to grab a plate with some food. I look around, thinking back, when was the last time I went out to a bar? Was it only a month ago? Has it only been a month, yet feels like a lifetime ago? Did I always fucking hate it? Did it suck as much as it does today? Did I know it sucked or did I just pretend I was fine? Did I know how unhappy I was before, now that every single day I rushed to get home? Did I know my life was a shallow place whereas now a little girl holds a piece of my heart in her tiny hand and I know I would spend all my life protecting her. Fuck, what a difference a month makes.

I spend the night basically shooting the shit with the guys, not even caring there are lap dances going on around us. I ignore all the women who come to my table, trying to get me to partake in the shenanigans the other men are doing. Well, not all the men, literally the married men are all sitting on the sidelines watching. I can't even believe this is me now. Whereas before I would be the one making fun of the person I am now. I bring the glass to my lips and take a sip, my wedding band on display. The later it gets, the louder the music gets and the smokier the room gets. I decide I fucking hate this life and never, ever want to do this again. Getting up, I look and see that it's after one in the morning. "Time for me to head out," I announce to the guys. "I'll catch Daniel after." I look over at Daniel, who looks like he wants the floor to open up to swallow and spit him out. He's trying to look away and bear another lap dance they paid for him to have.

I walk out of the smoky dark cloud into the crisp night, handing the valet guy my stub. Pulling out my phone, I see she hasn't texted me. Nothing. It's been radio silence all fucking day, and I hate it.

My mood doesn't get better as I make my way home. In fact, I get more annoyed when I pull in and park beside her. The minute I walk in, it's almost as if my body does a sigh of relief. I kick off my shoes and make my way up the stairs, trying not to make any noise. I think about going and checking on Cici, but instead I walk into the bedroom.

I'm slipping off my jacket when I hear the rustle of

the covers. I stop midmovement, and when I hear her speak, the tightness in my stomach is there for a whole different reason. "I didn't think you would come home."

Twenty-Five

Eva

I hear the front door open and, no word of a lie, I stop breathing. My heart speeds up at the same time my stomach rises to my throat. I get up on my elbow, looking at the darkened doorway. Looking over to the bedside table, I see Cici is sleeping on her back, with her arms stretched out with not a care in the world. I tap my phone and see that it's after 1:00 a.m., my stomach clenches again when I hear him kick off his shoes.

I quickly lie back down on my side of the bed, my eyes closed, even though it's dark and he won't see if I'm up or not. I'm so pissed that I've been waiting up for him, even though I tried to tell myself I wasn't waiting up for him. I just couldn't sleep. I've been in bed since

10:00 p.m., tossing and turning. Looking over at his side of the bed that was empty, I wondered what he was doing at that moment. That obviously didn't help me because all I could picture was him with ten women all bouncing up and down on him as he motorboated them. Which made me even more pissed. The whole day I was on a rampage from when he left me in the parking lot of the daycare. I knew it was going to be a day. It didn't help I was pissed at him and expected him to reach out and apologize for whatever the hell happened in the parking lot before we dropped off Cici, but nothing. As the hours ticked by, so did my mood. Everyone was afraid to ask me anything, so no one did. When I picked up Cici, my mood lessened but then I fucking missed him and our routine, which was so dumb of me considering that it's all temporary. I position my head down to watch him walk into the bedroom.

In the darkness I watch him walk over to the corner, and I finally sit up at the same time as I see him shrug off his jacket. So many questions are going on in my head. Did he come here after you know what? Did he at least shower? Is he going to see her again? All of these questions, yet the only thing that comes out of my mouth is, "I didn't think you would come home."

His movement stops as he takes off his jacket. His head whips my way, even in the darkness I can see his glare. "Yeah, why is that?" He continues to take his jacket off, tossing it on the chair in the corner. The chair that not too long ago had only my clothes on it, but now it's a mix of both of our things.

His tone should make me just ignore his ass and go back to bed or pretend I don't care. But I'm out here in the middle of the ocean, in the dark, and I can hear the rumbling of the wave coming toward me, ready to pull me under. "I just figured you would be at a strip club." I don't say anything after that but neither does he. Does he really need me to spell it out for him? Now I'm even more pissed. "And I don't know, hook up with someone?"

The room that was filled with tension from us both now feels like it's frigid. It feels like ice has entered the room. I don't have to have the lights on to see his glare has turned into more of a death stare. His hands go to the hem of his shirt as he pulls it out from his pants, not even going to the closet to get undressed or even the bathroom. Instead, he stands there fuming as he unbuttons his shirt, or at this point I feel like he rips it open like the Hulk. He takes off his white dress shirt and tosses it on the chair before his hand goes to his belt. I suddenly feel like I should turn on the light to make sure he doesn't, I don't know, hurt himself.

"Was Caine going to come over?" he growls between clenched teeth.

"What?" I ask, almost breathlessly as I hear his zipper. My chest heaves as his pants fall to the floor, and he stands there in his boxers and socks. Tossing his pants on top of his shirt, followed by his socks, he walks over to his side of the bed.

"Caine," he repeats his name, grabbing his side of the covers and practically yanking them. "The guy who wants to bang you." Why would he think Caine wants to bang me?

My eyes blink as I watch him get into the bed next to me, with just his boxers. While my brain says it's only normal for me to also just be in my panties. "He doesn't want to bang me." I roll my eyes as he lies down on his back, putting his hands on his stomach.

He laughs but his laugh is anything but friendly, instead it sounds more like the Joker from *Batman*. "Oh, trust me, he wants to bang you." He looks over at me sitting here and now all I can do is lie back down, mimicking his position. "I mean, it's not his fault." He looks over at me. "How was he supposed to know you're married when you don't wear your ring?"

All I can do is gasp in shock. "I wear my ring." I hold up my hand to show him that I am wearing said ring.

"Yeah," he huffs, "like, sure, around your neck."

I open my mouth to speak but then it closes only to snap, "I wear it at night. I don't wear it during the day at work because I don't want to get it oily and stuff." It's the most beautiful piece of jewelry I have, and I would hate for it to be soiled from having to put oil and cream on my hands all day long.

"Okay," he says, which to me might be worse than telling me to go fuck myself. Then to make matters even worse, he turns over and gives me his back.

All I can think is, *you motherfucker*. "Nice," I huff, falling back to my back. "Is that all you got?" I literally slap the blankets around me to tuck myself in.

In a blink of an eye, he's turned to face me, the blanket

that was tucked around me is now all over the place. My head snaps toward him. "No, that isn't all I've got," he growls and I can feel him getting closer to me, well, more I can feel his heat. "This is what I've got."

I don't know if I lunge first or if he lunges first but my breasts are pressed to his chest, facing each other. His arms are around my waist, my arms are around his neck, our mouths finding each other. Our tongues meld together, going around and around. It's as if this is my salvation, as if one touch from him makes me feel settled. It's as if my body just does a sigh of relief with him being near me. Like my other half has arrived and now I'm complete.

Our heads move side to side as we try to deepen the kiss. We start on our sides, but he quickly pushes me on my back. My legs open for him to get between them as the frantic kiss now relaxes. He kisses me with a softness, rubbing his nose with mine before letting my lips go. My chest rises and falls as he trails kisses from my lips to my chin, my eyes still closed, feeling my body tingle with every single touch. "Levi," I say his name as his tongue comes out to trail from my jaw down the side of my neck. I move my head away to make sure he has all the access in the world. My legs wrap around his legs as his stubble prickles my collarbone, making me shiver under his touch. Down my chest, he heads toward the swell of my breast, I arch my back as my legs fall off his hips. "Levi." At this point I'm so far gone, all I know is I need him.

"Baby," he whispers so softly, his beard is rough as I

feel his fingers trailing exactly where his lips just were. "You drive me." I open my eyes just in time to feel him pull my tank top down and take a nipple into his mouth. I moan, mumbling I think his name, I'm not even sure. I might have called God; all I know is the minute his teeth graze my nipple, it sends shock waves right down to my core. My hands move to the back of his head as he works one nipple and then moves over to the other. My eyes are halfway hooded as I watch him, his eyes watching mine as he takes the other nipple in his mouth.

My head falls back, my hips thrust up, and right here, right now I'm gone for him. So gone I want to beg him to just fuck me. "Yes," I hiss and then his mouth lets me go, the cool air making my nipples even harder.

I feel him moving down my body, his hand scrunching up my tank top so he can kiss my stomach, which contracts under his touch. He drags his nose back and forth, his tongue licking down my stomach past my belly button. "Lift," he commands and I don't know what he wants me to lift. My body feels like it's on fire, and because he's between my legs, I can't close them and try to get relief. "Your ass." I move my hips up just in time for him to shed my shorts and panties. "Tell me something, Eva." His mouth hovers over my pussy, his breath landing on me making me shiver. "Was it him you were thinking about when I made you come?" I look down at him as his nose trails my pubic bone and then moves to the left side of my leg, right down the side.

"Is it him you are picturing now?" My chest swells when I listen to his voice so thick with need. "Do you want it to be him?" His voice rumbles and he stops talking when I lift my hips, hoping to get him to lick me. "Tell me who you see." He hovers right there, right where I want him to lick. Right where my slit is, my lips hiding my clit that is throbbing right now. He's spent a total of five minutes kissing me or maybe even less, and I ache for him. "Tell me."

"You want to know who I've been thinking about?" My voice comes out quivering. "You want to know who I thought about when I touched myself in the shower?" My feet move up as I place them on his elbows. "You want to know who I saw two nights ago when I came on your fingers?" Fuck, he's so fucking beautiful. "You want to know who I was thinking about all night? You want to know who's taken over all of my thoughts lately? You want to know who I dream about? You want to know who I want to touch me? You want to know who I want to slide into me? You want to know who I want to ride? You want to know whose face I want to sit on?" His eyes watch mine, my chest going up and down.

My body ready to explode, I've never been more turned on in my life. "You want to know who makes me so wet that if you touched me right now, you would feel I'm soaked?" He waits when I finally confess in a whisper, "It's you." I don't say another word because I can't. His mouth sucks in my pussy lips right before he lets them go and licks me from top to bottom. My hips thrust up, needing more of him. "Yes," I cheer when he uses his thumbs to open my pussy lips, sucking my clit right into his mouth. "Levi," his name falls from my lips.

"Yes," he declares right before he bites my clit and slides two fingers into me. I push down on his shoulder to thrust up. "All day long." His fingers move in and out of me. "All I've been thinking about is tasting you," he admits, sliding his tongue in with his fingers before his tongue flicks my clit again. "You moaning out my name is forever tattooed in my brain." He turns his hand, rubbing over my G-spot and I get on my elbows to watch him. "It's time for me to claim this pussy." He sucks my clit. "Make it mine." His fingers moving in and out of me, my hands go to my nipples and roll them. "Take care of it with my fingers." I need more. "With my tongue." I feel the orgasm coming, I've never had it build this much. It's been building for the past two days. "When I fuck you," he declares and my eyes slowly shut halfway, "I'm going to finally make you mine. Every single piece of you"—his fingers move faster—"is going to be mine." My pussy gets even wetter. "I'm going to mark every single piece of you." He bites my clit and then sucks it in. "First with my mouth." It's right there, I can feel the tightness coming in my stomach, shooting all the way down to my core, to my fucking toes. He moves his hand so much faster. "Then—" he starts between clenched teeth and I know he knows I'm close.

"I'm going to—" I say breathlessly, thrashing on the bed. My head is moving side to side, my hips come up to meet his finger.

"Then, Eva," he says my name and it's right there I'm about to jump off the ledge. I can't hold on anymore. "Then I'm going to mark you with my cum."

Twenty-Six

Levi

The minute I tell her I'm going to mark her with my cum is when she comes apart in my hand. Her pussy gushes over my fingers, my fingers riding the orgasm with her, never letting up. Her thighs close around my head to keep me there. A fucking earthquake couldn't pull me away from her. "That's it, baby," I encourage her as her pussy loosens its hold of my fingers. "So wet," I say right before I lick her, "so tight." My fingers slow down as her thighs loosen. "So fucking perfect." Her eyes slowly open, looking down at me, her tits calling my name, begging me to suck them and then fuck them.

I'm like a kid in the fucking candy story or, even better, the fucking toy store. Wanting to touch everything and everywhere. Wanting to taste everything, I have never wanted to claim someone the way I want her to be mine. The way she is going to be mine, my cock is so hard. "Good God," she moans and I kiss her inner thigh, my fingers slipping out of her.

"Levi," I remind her, wanting to hear my name on her lips. Wanting her to say my name and only my name.

"Levi," she repeats, her hand moving through my hair. Not five seconds ago her nails were almost digging into my scalp. I don't even think she knows it; she was too far gone. Taking the fingers that were just inside her, I bring them to my mouth to lick them clean. She's intoxicating. Her feet fall from my shoulders as I get up on my knees. She lies back with one hand folded under her head and the other on her stomach. "I need a cigarette." She smirks in the darkness.

"You smoke after sex?" I ask, chuckling as I get on my knees.

"No." She shakes her head. "But with you I feel like I need to."

"Is that a good thing or a bad thing?" I watch her sit up in bed.

"I'm not sure yet." She sits facing me, or better yet, my cock. "I will say I have never come so hard in my life." She gets on her knees in front of me, putting her hands on her hips. "I saw stars." She leans her head back and my hands come up to the back of her head, gripping her hair in my hands and fisting it before my mouth devours her.

Her hands go to my hips, gripping them as she tastes

herself on my tongue. She lets me go and nips my jaw before I feel her dainty fingers go inside the elastic of my boxers. Tonight, when I got undressed, I thought of putting on my shorts but I was so pissed that I just got into bed. "I want to talk about what you said." She kisses my neck. "To make sure I heard you right." Her tongue trails out at my neck, down my chest to my nipple. "Just so we are on the same page." She bites my nipple and I hiss. "How are you going to claim me?"

"I have my ways," I say, trying not to explode as her fingers grip the boxers, bringing them down and over my hips, my cock springing free.

"If you are going to claim me," she says, trailing kisses down my stomach, "do I get to claim you?"

I chuckle at her. "Eva," I say her name, pushing her hair away from her face. "You claimed me a while ago."

"Really?" She gets down on her hands and knees in front of my cock. "That's good to know." She licks from the base of my cock all the way up to the head, licking the precum off the tip. I want to watch her take me in her mouth, but the minute she twirls her tongue around the head of my cock, my head falls back and I groan.

"God," I moan when she kisses the cockhead, sucking it in a little.

"It's actually Eva," she teases, right before she takes my cock halfway in her mouth.

"I know exactly who is sucking my cock," I confirm, almost hissing when she cups my balls before letting go of my cock.

"Just making sure." She winks at me as she sucks the

sides of my cock from the base to the head again. Taking the head into her mouth once before letting it go again and then twirling her tongue around it. I move the hair away from her face so I can watch her take my cock into her mouth. Her mouth struggles to get all the way to the bottom, but she is giving it all she has. She grips my cock in the middle, her fingers can't close all the way around it. "Your cock—" she says right before she takes the tip in her mouth and her hand moves down to the base. "It's perfect." She leans forward, arching her back, her ass going high in the air as the mattress holds her up.

My hips move on their own with her movements. "Nice and thick." She squeezes the base as she says this. "Thick enough that I'll feel you the next day."

"Is that a challenge?" I ask as she swallows me. She nods, and at this point, I don't know who's enjoying this more, her or me. Probably me, but the way her hips are swaying right and left, it's a toss-up. "Then it's challenge accepted." All she does is smirk at me, and I'm done. Fucking done. "Tomorrow." She moves my cock into her mouth, her hand working me at the same time. "I want to watch you play with yourself." She moans with my cock in her mouth and it vibrates down to my balls. "Watch you finger your pussy while you tell me what you want me to do to you." Her eyes close as her hand moves faster. "Then I'm going to fuck your tits," I give her the play-by-play, reaching down to pinch her nipples before twisting them. "Fucking come all over them." I fuck her face faster. "Rub my cum into you." My balls get tight. "But tonight, right now. I'm going to mark your mouth.

You want to swallow my cum, baby?" I ask, and she just nods. "Make your tongue mine." Her eyes look up at me as I fucking come down her throat, with her name on my lips, panting. "Eva," I moan as she swallows every last drop of me. Her hand stops when she's swallowed all of me. "Eva," I call her name again as she lets my cock go from her mouth. "Where are your fingers right now?"

I can see the twinkle in her eye, even in the dark. "Right here." She holds up the hand that was gripping my cock.

"Where is the other one?" She gets to her knees, and I see two fingers are inside her.

"Here," she admits, moving them in and out. "I just need—"

My hand grips her wrist, yanking them out of her. I bring her hand up to my mouth, licking her fingers clean. "Your pussy needs to come?" I ask, and she nods. "Then I make it come. It's me who makes that pussy come." I get closer to her. "Unless I tell you to make yourself come, that's my job from now on." I slide two fingers in her, and she gasps. "Do you understand, Eva?"

She nods. "What if you're not here?" she whispers.

"Then you call me on the phone and I make you come with my words." My thumb strums her clit back and forth. "I don't care what I'm doing or where I am, if your pussy needs to come, I make it come. I own it." Her pussy convulses over my fingers. "Tonight, you got my fingers and my mouth." I move faster, her hands going to hold on to my wrist. "Tomorrow, you get my cock." She moans and I don't know if it's because she's coming again or because she wants my cock tonight. "Tell me you understand me, Eva." I nip her bottom lip, sliding my tongue into her mouth. "Say yes, Levi."

"Yes, Levi," she repeats right before she comes. I look into her eyes, watching her come apart. I was mistaken before; she might be intoxicating. But her pussy is my kryptonite. Her head falls on my chest, and I hold her up until she collapses on the bed. "I can't move," she observes when I lay her down. She looks over at me as I get off the bed to pull my boxers up. "My panties."

"No." I shake my head. "I might want to eat you again in the middle of the night." I get into bed next to her.

"Okay," she says. "I can't say no to that." I pull her to me, her ass against my cock. I kiss her neck softly. I'm almost asleep when I hear her. "I'm glad you came home," she mumbles, "and that you didn't go home with any strippers." I bury my face in her neck and fall asleep.

I roll to her side of the bed, and the coldness wakes me up right away. I blink my eyes a couple of times, seeing I'm all alone in bed. I look at the closed bedroom door before looking at the monitor beside the bed, finding the crib empty. I turn on my back, stretching out in the bed, my eyes closing again when I hear Cici fussing. I grab the covers, throwing them off me before I get out of bed. I go to the bathroom, washing my hands and face before going downstairs.

I'm almost at the last step when I see the two of them in the living room. Eva sits with her back toward the couch, her hair piled on top of her head, in the tank top she was wearing last night but with pants. She holds out her hand away from Cici, who is standing up with Eva's hand around her waist as she talks to her. "You can't have my coffee."

"Good morning," I say when I clear the last step and my two girls look at me. Cici squeals louder than I've ever heard her before. "Has she been up for long?" I ask, looking over at the clock in the kitchen and seeing it's almost noon.

"About four hours," she shares, looking at Cici. "We were trying to be quiet."

"I didn't hear her." I walk over to them, leaning down and kissing Cici on the forehead and then Eva on the lips. Before I sit next to her, Cici turns and throws herself at me. "Hi, girl," I say when she lays her head on my shoulder.

"Levi," Eva says my name and I look over at her. She looks at me with worry on her face. She's been up for four hours, so she's probably been thinking about last night for three hours and forty-five minutes. Spinning it over and over in her head, but not actually thinking about anything good.

"Don't even," I warn her, rubbing Cici's back.

"It was a mistake," she says softly and all I can do is laugh, making Cici put her head up as she looks at me smiling.

"Nope, not doing this."

"What do you mean you aren't doing this?" she questions from beside me, taking a sip of her coffee.

"It means that I'm not going to pretend it was a mistake." I scrunch my nose at Cici before turning to

Eva, putting one arm around her shoulder. "I'm not going to pretend I didn't finger-fuck you two days ago." Her eyes cloud over, no doubt remembering it also.

"I'm not going to pretend last night I didn't have the best blow job of my whole life." She rolls her eyes. "I'm also not going to pretend I don't want you."

"What are you saying?" she asks the question but avoids looking at me, instead she looks down in her lap at her cup.

"I'm saying, this changes things." I wait for her to look at me.

"What the hell are you saying?" she asks and I can see her heart is beating rapidly, because her chest is going up and down really fast.

Her breathing is coming in pants now. I turn toward her, taking my arm from around her and placing my fingertips at her throat, feeling how fast her heart is beating. "I'm saying this thing between me and you." My lips go into a huge smile. "It's happening." She sits up, shocked, her mouth opens and then closes. "I don't know what it is, but I like it." I lean in to kiss her cheek. "I like it more than that, I love it." I hold her neck in my hand. "Coming home to you." I stare into her eyes. "Going to bed with you. Doing life with you."

She listens to my words, and I can see her head spinning. "It's not that simple."

"Why not?" I ask.

"Because it's not." She throws her own hand that isn't holding the coffee cup up.

"Why can't you just go with it?" I throw her again for

a loop, but now I grab her cup of coffee and bring it to my lips. "Want to go on a date with me?" I smirk at her at the same time that Cici yells. I turn back to look at Cici, seeing her face fill with a smile. "And Cici?"

Twenty-Seven

Eva

I watch him look at Cici. "Do you want to go on a date with me and Auntie Eva?" he asks and she babbles away at him. I turn and put my back against the couch next to him. His arm going around me, he pulls me to him as he nods as if he understands what she's saying, then turns back to me. "She said yes."

I can't help but shake my head and chuckle at that. "Is that so?" I pull my feet up to the side of me, laying them on his legs.

"That's what she said." He smirks. "Did you not get that from all the babbles?"

"I must have missed it," I tease, looking at him. Last night was, well, there are no words for what it was. I have never been more turned on in my life. I've never come so hard in my life, and also, I've never wanted someone else the way I wanted Levi. I spent the better part of the morning replaying last night on repeat, around and around.

"Do you want to go for a walk?" he asks and I just nod my head. "Let's get her all the fresh air so we can have a solid eight hours tonight."

"She sleeps longer than that." I laugh, getting up.

"Oh, I know." He winks, getting up. "I meant us in bed, not sleeping."

I put my hand on my hip at the same time my pussy clenches. "Really, eight hours?"

He shrugs. "Never actually tried." He bends his head and rubs his nose with mine. "But it's worth a fucking shot."

"According to the internet, vaginal sex that lasts between ten to thirty minutes is considered a long time." I lean my head back.

"And a man from Singapore went twenty-four hours banging thirty-seven women," he counters, wrapping his arm around my waist, pulling me close to him.

"That can't be right." My arms wrap around his waist easily.

"Neither can thirty minutes being a long time." He squeezes me to him. "It just goes to show, you shouldn't believe everything you read online." I laugh at him. "Now let's get going."

"I'll go change her and then we can swap out," I tell him when we get upstairs.

"Okay," he agrees. I take her from his arms and she whines a bit. "Yeah, I know you like him."

"Is she the only one?" He looks down at me and I roll my eyes, making him laugh.

"Yes," I lie to him, "she's the only one who likes you."

"Liar," he retorts, kissing my lips softly, then cupping my ass in his hand. "Hmmm." He pulls me to him. "When is nap time?"

I feel his cock on my stomach and I want to say right now. "You can wait until tonight. You aren't going to die." My vagina screams out, *Nooooooo*. "Now go change."

"Okay." He kisses us both before he walks back into the bedroom.

I never thought I'd see the day when I'd be itching to have Levi's cock in my hand again. I never thought I'd see the day when I would get on my knees at the snap of a finger to get his cock in my mouth again. "Stranger things have happened," I mumble as I walk to the bedroom and get dressed.

The whole day drags on or maybe I'm just impatient. I'm also going out of my mind. All day long it's been the small touches here and there. The kisses that start with just a peck but then end up with his tongue in my mouth and me practically dry humping him.

At seven, Cici is ready for bed, falling asleep in record time, probably knowing her aunt's going to get laid. I walk out of the bedroom at the same time he comes out of the bathroom with a towel wrapped around his waist and another towel drying his hair. "She asleep?" he asks as if he's not just standing there semi-naked in front of me.

"Yeah," I mumble, "I'm going to get in the shower."

"Okay," he agrees, not moving aside when I walk toward the bathroom. He bends his head to look at me. "Don't touch yourself," he whispers before he kisses me softly.

"I know this is going to be shocking information for you." I put my hands on my hips. "But I think I can control myself."

"Are you telling me that if I put my hand in your pants right now—" His hand comes up and his thumb grazes over my covered nipple. "You aren't going to be wet?" All I can do is look at him, because I've been wet all fucking day long. "Exactly." He nips my lips and slaps my ass before he walks into the closet.

I take the fastest shower of my life before I slide on white lace booty shorts that really are cheeky panties, my ass cheeks hanging out of them, with a white barely there tank top. There really is nothing left to the imagination. When I walk back into the bedroom, the bed is empty and I look over at the doorway.

"Levi?" I walk out of the bedroom, watching him coming up from downstairs.

"Hey," he says and I see it's dark downstairs. "I was just closing up." His eyes roam my outfit. "Do you know this past month I've cursed every single pair of booty shorts you have?" I smile at him as he walks toward me and I start to walk backward into the room. "They were the death of me."

"Were they?" I ask when I feel the back of my knees touch the bed. His hands go to my hips. "I hate your basketball shorts," I inform him.

"Why?" He smirks.

"Because they drove me crazy wondering if you were wearing anything under them," I admit. The reason Levi and I are such amazing friends is because we never lie to each other.

"News flash." He bends his head and kisses my lips, his tongue invading my mouth quickly before he finishes his sentence. "I wasn't." He picks me up and all I can do is gasp when he tosses me on the bed on my back. He crawls on the bed toward me and I'm really fucking happy there is a soft light from the bedside table on. He's over me, his hands by the sides of my head, his knees in the middle of my open legs. "I've waited all day to do this," he says to me and I'm thinking he's going to kiss my lips, but not Levi. Nope. Instead of kissing me, which is what I'm expecting him to do, he takes one of his hands, putting it on the top of the tank top and pushing it down, my breast bare now. He bends his head, taking the nipple into his mouth and sucking it deep. My hips thrust up as he nips down on it before twirling his tongue around it.

"You know what I've been thinking about?" I ask, wrapping my legs around his thighs, shoving him to his back. He lies there with his hands beside his head. "I've been thinking of getting…" I pull down his shorts, his cock springs out and in the light it's so much better than I thought it was last night. "Yes," I cheer, putting my fingers around him. "Fuck, it's so much better than I remembered," I praise before I put my mouth over him. I take him in my mouth, stretching to take his girth in me. Feeling the veins under my tongue, his cock is so thick I really have to work it. I get on my hands and knees, jerking his cock while he watches me. He sits up, pushing the hair away from my face before his tongue slides into my mouth. He pulls me on top of him, my tits falling out of the flimsy tank top, my nipples grazing his cock as he kisses me. My hand is still working his cock as we kiss.

He sits up as my mouth falls back on his cock. "That's my girl, take me." His words push me forward. "Get me nice and hard," he urges and all I can do is moan around his cock.

He pulls me up as I kneel in the middle of his legs. His head bends to take one nipple in his mouth while his fingers roll the other one. He works me over from one nipple to the next, and I am this close to coming just from him playing with my nipples. He must sense it because he stops, my nipple falling out of his mouth with a pop before he rips the tank top over my head.

"You're wearing too many clothes." He looks down at me wearing just the white panties. His hands wrap around my waist as he flips me to my back. His mouth falls on mine before he works down to my neck, the middle of my chest, over my stomach, and right above my belly button. His hands grab the panties on the side as I lift to help him slip them off me. My legs fall to the sides as he pushes one leg up and over his shoulder before his mouth falls right on my pussy.

"Fuck." I grip the sheets beside me as I see stars. "Yes!"

"Did you touch yourself in the shower?" he asks as he slips two fingers into me.

"No," I pant out as he moves his fingers.

"That's my good girl." He sucks my clit. "Fuck, Eva." I look down at him as he watches my pussy take his fingers. "I need to get inside you."

"Yes," is all I can say. "Yes." His fingers fall out of me as he reaches over me toward his bedside table, grabbing a condom from the drawer. "When did you put those in there?" I ask as he smirks. "I don't want to know."

He stands in front of me, handing me the condom. "You want my cock?" he asks as he holds it at the base and I just nod and lick my lips. "Then get it ready for you."

I grab the condom from him, tearing the corner off with my teeth. "When was the last time you were tested?" I ask and his eyes change color right in front of me. "I'm on birth control," I start to say, looking at the condom. "And I haven't had sex in six months."

"I've never been without," he replies, his jaw tight. "You know my motto."

I shake my head. "Don't be a fool, cover your tool," we both say at the same time.

"Is this a deal breaker?" I ask and his hand cups my cheek. He takes the condom from my hand and tosses it behind me.

"I got tested before we got married," he shares with

me, and that sentence makes my stomach quiver. "Now put me in you."

"So bossy," I retort, lying back down. "You're lucky that you give good head."

"Is that so?" He hovers over me. "How good of head do I give?"

"I'm not going to boost your ego," I fire back, grabbing his cock in my hand.

"Well, you give it right back, baby." He puts his forehead on mine. "Best I've ever fucking had."

"Is that so?" I move my hips back and rub him against my slit. "I bet you're just saying that."

"Baby." He looks into my eyes. "I've never been this fucking hard in my life," he grits between clenched teeth. "Now, fucking put me in you." I place him at my entrance. "Watch with me," he urges, and we both look down at where we are connected. "I can feel your heat," he says as the tip of his head slides into me.

I close my eyes as I arch my back. "More," I pant out, holding his sides.

"No," he states and my eyes fly open. "The minute you stop watching is the minute I stop my cock from fucking you."

"Ugh," I groan, but my eyes fly down to watch him slide into me. I hold the back of his thighs, making sure I get all of him. "Levi," I hiss as half of him is inside me and I want it all.

"What do you need, baby?" he asks, his eyes twinkling.

"I need you to fuck me." I watch his cock slide more into me. "Hard." Both of us moan when he's balls deep in me. I've never been fuller in my life as his cock grinds into me.

"How hard?" he asks, pulling out until it's his tip and slamming back into me. I can't help my eyes closing as I take in the feeling of being stretched.

"So hard I won't be able to sit. Can you do that?" I tease him. "Can you fuck me that hard?"

"Eva," he snarls between clenched teeth as he pounds into me over and over again. Not once does he let up. His eyes never leave mine as he slams into me. My pussy is on fire, it's so wet from watching him fuck me. "Look at your pussy hungry for me. Taking me." He slams into me. "Swallowing my cock." Pulling out, he slams back in. "Take my cock." Pulling out and slamming back. "Made for my cock." He pulls his cock out for a second and the next thing I know his mouth is on me, but just to suck my clit and bite it, before he pushes my legs back and slams back in. "Strangling my cock, baby."

"Yes!" I scream. "I'm almost there."

"Place one of your fingers in my mouth," he orders me as he plants his cock into me until his balls hit my ass. I put my middle finger into his mouth as he sucks on it. "Now with that finger play with your clit." I shift my hips so he can get deeper into me. My hand goes to my clit. "Rub it in circles, baby." He has to have all the control. "Small circles." He pulls out slowly before slamming into me. "Fuck, I want to eat your pussy as much as I want to fuck it." He fucks me so hard. "I've never been more in love with a pussy before."

"I'm there." I close my eyes; the feeling is all over

me. My nipples tight, my stomach tighter.

"Come on my cock," he orders me, "come all over me." He doesn't have to wait long before I am coming all over him. "That's it, baby," he praises and then he groans as he throws his head back and comes in me.

The beauty that is Levi, I don't know if he just fucked the shit out of me or made love to me; either way, I want it again. He pulls himself out of me, looking down at my pussy. "Nothing more beautiful than seeing my cum seeping out of you." He takes his middle finger, rubbing around my hole before he moves up to my clit. "I want every single part of you to have me." He slips two fingers into me twice, then rubs my pussy full of his cum. "You're mine."

Twenty-Eight

Levi

I walk out of the elevator, and as soon as the phone rings from my hand, I press the green button putting it to my ear. "Good morning," Stefano greets, sounding chippier than normal, especially for a Monday morning.

"Good morning to you." I nod at the receptionist, who briefly looks up from her computer as I walk toward my office. "What's going on?" I put the cup of coffee down on my desk before sitting down in the chair and leaning back.

"Not much, was calling to ask you about Friday night?" His question shocks me.

I sit up in my chair straight, the hair on the back of my neck rises. "What about Friday?" I look toward my front door to see if he will barge in and kick my ass for sleeping with Eva.

"Word on the street is you didn't even get a lap dance." He laughs. "You didn't even go home with a stripper and you left at midnight." He lists these as if they're the strangest things in the world. "People think you are sick or have a brain tumor."

"Okay, well, to start off..." I sigh in relief that he doesn't know Eva and I had sex on Friday and Saturday, also Sunday—and fuck—even this morning. It's almost like I'm a junkie and she's my drug. I've never had so much sex in my life as I have in the past four days. If Cici is sleeping, my dick is in Eva. I just can't get enough of her. Every time I came, I wanted it to be on a new part of her body. I think at this point there are no more fluids left in my body and there is also nowhere on her body I haven't come. And let's not discuss the number of teeth marks she has on her. There will be no mistake to anyone that she's mine, or that I'm hers. "I left at one." I lean back in the chair, relaxing. "And two, I don't think it's a good thing for a married man who is newly married to get a lap dance or actually go home with a stripper."

It's Stefano's turn to laugh. "Okay, well, we know that marriage is not real."

"Well, her ring is on my finger." I look down at my hand, smiling. "And mine is probably around her neck."

"Like a noose," Stefano jokes, and even I laugh at that.

"So is that what you called me for, to shit on me? Because I didn't see you at this party, staying home like a senior. At least I showed up," I remind him.

"I figured that I would send you and no one would miss me," Stefano explains and I roll my eyes. "Clearly, I was wrong."

"Clearly. Do you have nothing better to do on a Monday morning than call and bother me?"

"I have a shitload of things to do," he replies, "but I was also calling to tell you about the sprinkle we are having for Addison."

"A sprinkle?" I question. "Like a pool party but with a sprinkler? Is that what they do in the South?" I chuckle. "Either way, I'm not coming. I don't do pool parties."

"I live in the city." He laughs at me. "No, a baby sprinkle."

"You are going to put the baby in the sprinkler?" I shout. "Is this what people do?"

"You are such an idiot. I'm going to call Eva."

"Call the wife, then," I agree, "she'll tell me where to go and what to do."

"Like a good husband." We both laugh. "Okay, I'll keep you posted."

"Sounds like a plan." I hang up on him and immediately call Eva, who answers after one ring.

"Did you just drop her off?" she shrieks. "You left home like forty-five minutes ago."

"What? No, I dropped her off ten minutes after. She is fine. She was smiling, so I think she was good."

"Why didn't you text me?" she asks and I can hear her walking around.

"You said you were going back to bed," I remind

her. "Which reminds me, should I not take Mondays off also?"

She laughs at me. "Why would you do that?"

"So we can have time together," I whisper, "uninterrupted."

"I think we have enough time uninterrupted." I hear the coffee machine going off. I pull up my schedule in front of me and see that I'm leaving on Wednesday until Friday. I make the decision right away.

"Gotta go," I say, getting up. "See you later."

"What did you call me for?" she asks.

"I'll tell you about it later." I grab the cup of coffee and walk out of my office.

"You're annoying," she huffs and hangs up on me, making me laugh.

"I'm working from home," I tell the receptionist. "I have to prepare for my meeting on Wednesday."

She looks up, and I swear she's looking at me like I have two heads coming out of my neck. I've never, ever had to give anyone a reason for anything. For anything and now even saying why I'm leaving is weird. "Sounds good." She doesn't even care, and giving her an excuse threw her off and myself also. It's almost as if I'm robbing a bank and then waiting for the cops outside of the bank with the gun.

I walk over to the elevator, hoping it opens right away and not that I'll turn around and tell her I'm going home to have sex with Eva, because at this point, who the fuck knows what is going to come out of my mouth. I look down as I press the elevator button, feeling like my shirt is getting tighter and tighter around my neck, even though I have three buttons open. When the doors open, I practically run inside, pressing the lobby button before poking the closed-door button a million times.

Only once I'm in the car do I relax, but just a little, my phone feels like a ticking time bomb. Like Stefano will call and know that I'm up to no good. I pull over at a flower shop on my way home, grabbing a bouquet of orchids in a vase. I hope like fuck it doesn't spill all over the car.

I park my car next to hers before grabbing the vase. I walk up the steps, nervous as fuck, which makes me laugh since I've never been nervous in my whole life. I've also never liked anyone as much as Eva. I've never had the sex I've had with her. It blows my mind and makes me want to kick my ass that we haven't done it before. I mean, I know why, but I don't think either of us is ready for what I have to say.

Punching in the code for the door, I walk in to find her coming out of the kitchen. She's wearing exactly what she was wearing when I left to drive Cici. A white shirt that hangs off her shoulder, showing me she's not wearing a bra. I can tell because I can see her nipples. And her famous shorts, but these are not as tight. "What are you doing here?" she asks, surprised, her eyes lighting up as her smile grows.

"Well." I walk to her, handing her the vase. "I thought I would play hooky." I lean down and kiss her neck, right before I suck on it.

"Don't you dare leave me a mark where people can

see." She pushes me away, but not really.

"You don't like my mark on you?" I wrap my arm around her waist.

"I'm not twelve and neither are you," she reminds me. "We can contain ourselves for below the waist."

"Can we?" I move my mouth lower, my chin pushing down her white shirt at the same time. "I think the best thing to do is see if we can."

"Is that why you came home?" She looks down at her breast that now has her shirt under it.

"It was one of the reasons." I smirk before sucking her nipple into my mouth. "Plus, I wanted to bring you flowers." She moans. "And I leave in two days, so we need to have sex at least four times extra."

"Is that so?" She steps away from me and puts the flowers down on the island. "That's a lot of sex." Her hands go to the hem of her shirt. The sparkle from her ring on her finger shines. "You think you are up for the challenge?" She pulls it off and tosses it on the floor by her feet. "I think you moaned yesterday that you were dead."

"No." I shake my head, shrugging off the jacket to my suit and tossing it on the couch. "I think that was you who said that." I pull the shirt out of my pants. "I think you lay in the bed and said I broke your vagina."

She rolls her eyes, which makes me know I'm right. "Either way." I unbutton my shirt and kick off my shoes. "Today we are rested." I walk to her, picking her up at her waist and she wraps her legs around me. "We've never fucked on the counter."

"Yes, we have. When I went to get water and you said you couldn't possibly wait until we got upstairs," she reminds me.

"That's because you bent over and you were naked," I retort.

"I leaned over and got on my tippy-toes," she corrects me as I walk over to the counter.

I lay her down on it, and she hisses as the coolness hits her back. "I like these shorts." Her feet drop from my hips.

"Yeah?" She looks at me. "Why?"

"Well, for one." I grab her ankle and place it on the counter, then go to the other one. "They aren't tight." I smile at her. "Which gives me easy access."

"Does it?" she asks and I look at her pussy, seeing exactly what I want.

"See," I say, moving it to the side having her open to me. "Just like this." I rub my fingers between her and feel her wetness before I slide a finger inside her. Every single time it's like it's the first. "I like having access to you any time I want." I slide another finger in her. "Like now."

"Or this morning," she pants out. "Levi." I don't know if she's asking something or just calling my name.

"Yeah, baby?" I ask.

"Can you do something for me?" She opens her legs even more to give me more access to it. I bend down and suck her clit into my mouth.

"Anything," I tell her.

"Good." She lifts her ass a bit to meet my fingers.

"Can you fuck me hard?" she asks. "Hard, fast, and raw." Every single time she says a word, she clenches around my fingers.

My hand goes to my buckle and I don't have the zipper down long before my cock is in my hand and then buried in her. "Fuck," I growl as she leans up and kisses my throat.

"I think you are the one who is supposed to fuck me." She sucks in. "But if you want, I think I've got it in me to fuck you." Her pussy clenches, I look at her and my chest squeezes. I almost blurt out that I'm falling in love with her as she lies back down on the counter. But I swallow it back when she says, "Now, are you going to fuck me or not?"

Twenty-Nine

Eva

*W*e walk out of the daycare hand in hand on the way to our cars. On Mondays he drops her off by himself since I'm off, but the rest of the week it's always the both of us. It's mundane and one of us can easily not come, but neither of us wants to give it up.

So, this is how we've been doing it for the last month. His hand is in mine as we walk to my car, and he always puts me in the car before he leaves. "Have a good day." He smirks at me, grabbing my face and kissing my lips. My hands go to his hips like they were made to be there. "I'll text you later to let you know what time I'll be home." The past two weeks he's been swamped at work, so he's been coming home sometimes right before bedtime. The good news is that he's not traveling as much, so he's home every single night.

"Okay." I look up at him, knowing he's going to kiss me again, and I'm not wrong.

He's about to let me go when a car door opening makes us both look over. Caine gets out of his car and opens the back door to his daughter. "Good morning." He looks over at us and holds up his hand.

Levi doesn't let me go, instead he pulls me toward him and puts his arm over my shoulders. "Morning, Caine." If I was a tree, I have no doubt Levi would lift his leg and pee on me.

"Have a good day," he replies.

"You, too," we both say at the same time as he ushers his daughter into the daycare.

Levi waits for him to be in the door before he mumbles, "Dick." Making me laugh.

"Are you still on that?" I ask as his hand falls away from my shoulder to my back before sweeping my ass, making my insides flutter. A month later, I still shiver every single time he touches me and he touches me plenty.

"Did he not want to bang you?" he asks the question but doesn't wait for me to answer. "Then the answer is yes."

"He didn't want to bang me, we were just friends," I refute, rolling my eyes. "Now, I have to go to work and so do you."

"That means I'm right." He laughs, kissing my lips softly before opening my door and waiting for me to get in.

"You aren't right, you're annoying, there is a difference." I pull my seat belt to buckle myself in. "Now go away."

"I'm going to have fun tonight." He leans in and kisses my cheek. "I love when I make you agree with me." The cheek he just kissed feels like it's on fire. Literally. "Have a good day, dear." He closes the door and waves before turning and walking to his own car.

He winks before he gets in, but he always waits for me to leave before he does. I pull out of the parking space, seeing him behind me, I wave one last time before I turn left and he turns right.

I get to work with a smile on my face, just like I have been for the past month. A whirlwind of a month. We crossed over the friendship into the sex thing, something that neither of us has been willing to talk about, it's just happening. Like we woke up one day and we were more than friends. Like it was always him waking me with his mouth on my pussy. Like it was normal going to bed together.

"Morning," I greet Raquel when I walk into the salon. "It's so beautiful outside."

"It's going to be a beautiful day." She smiles back at me. "Also, you have something on your desk." She can't help but smile big and I just shake my head as I walk toward my office.

I want to be surprised there is a bouquet on my desk, but this is what he does every single Tuesday when I get to work, there are flowers. Attached is always a cheesy card, pulling the white card out I can't help but laugh at this one.

I like your style
I like your class
But most of all
I like your ass
L.

I shake my head and put it back in the envelope before placing it in my drawer with the other ones. Last week's was funny also.

Roses are red
Tulips are corny
When I think of you
I get horny.

According to him, he couldn't use Cici, so he had to think of another flower, so it's always tulips like the one from two weeks ago.

Roses are okay
Tulips are fine
I'll be the six
If you be the nine.

But nothing could have prepared me for the first one.
Roses are red
Lemons are sour
Spread your legs
And feel my power.

I wonder how long he'll send them. I wonder how long this is going to go on. I wonder how long before one of us walks away. The thought makes my stomach get tight and I ignore it, pushing it deep down. Trying to live in the moment. Live for today. What no one tells you is that it fucking sucks because you don't know if you are going or coming.

My phone buzzes and Raquel tells me my first client is here, after that the only time I stop is when I walk into the café to grab myself a shake. "Eva." I hear my name and look over to see one of Levi's regular bang friends. The smile on my face stays forced and fake.

"Marianna," I say her name as she walks over to me, wearing a perfect outfit with perfect hair and equally perfect makeup. She comes to me and fake kisses my cheeks. "How are you?" she asks.

"I'm good, how are you?" I ask out of politeness, but I don't want to actually know. "It's been a while."

"Yeah, about a month," she replies, "but time to get glamified." She taps the counter with her newly manicured nails. "How is Levi?"

And there it is, the reason she came to say hello to me. I shouldn't be surprised since I introduced them. Never thinking she would be on rotation with him, also never caring, except for now. Except right now at this moment. "He's good." I don't really know what to say.

"Is he now?" she asks or tells me, she knows that we are best friends. "It's been a couple of weeks since we've hooked up." She talks as if my world around me isn't being shaken to the core. "Which is strange." She leans in. "We were a weekly thing and now it's spaced out." She shrugs. "I'm going to text him and see if we can hook up tonight." Blood drains from my body as I pretend that it's fine. It's not fine. This is what people must feel before they either have a stroke or become the Hulk. It's a fifty-fifty. Also, I've never fucking felt so on edge before, like my hand itches to slap her.

"Well, I'm sure he'll call you this week," I toss back without meaning it.

"He better." She smirks at me. "I swear he's got the best cock of life." All I want to do is fucking throat punch her.

The girl comes over with my shake, and in my head I picture throwing it in her face. "If you excuse me, I have someone waiting," I tell her, walking away from her, my knees almost knocking together.

The rest of the day is a blur, and even when I pick up Cici it feels like I'm in a daze. A text comes through from him right as I walk in the door.

Levi: *Looks like something came up and I'll be late.*

I toss the phone on the counter, not bothering to answer him. Because what am I supposed to say? Am I supposed to ask him why? Am I supposed to be all up in his business? Am I supposed to care? Obviously, I care, but I'm not this person who is going to second-guess themselves for a man. "We are going to be okay," I assure Cici as she smiles at me and babbles. She keeps saying Mama over and over again, the pain less and less each day. She thrives and I know that is the only thing Lisa would care about. "Aren't we, baby girl?"

Our night routine is a bit different now, we usually like to go for a walk after dinner, not very long but enough to get her some fresh air. I'm just getting her out from the bath when the front door slams shut. "I'm home."

I swallow down the lump and ignore looking down the stairs toward where his voice is when I walk back into Cici's room to dress her. Of course, she starts squealing for him and clapping her hands.

"There they are," he says when he comes up the stairs two by two. His jacket is off and his shirt open at the top, like it always is. I quickly look at him, wondering if he met with Marianna. He holds out his hands for her and I try to see if I smell her perfume on him, but all I smell is him. "Hi, girly." He kisses her cheek five times. "You smell clean." He looks at me. "I'm going to go get a shower and then I can put her to bed." He hands me back Cici and I turn toward her changing table.

"Sounds good," I reply, avoiding looking at him, not sure that I want to see. What if he was with Marianna? Do I have a right to be mad? Should we have discussed that if we are sleeping together, it's just us two? Should we have never slept together in the first place? Should we just end this now before it gets even more complicated? It's the questions that have been on loop ever since I spoke with Marianna.

"What's wrong?" he asks right away, catching that I'm acting strange and I want to kick myself. Here I was telling myself to act normal, apparently telling myself and doing it are two different things.

"Nothing, why?" I ask, but I'm not asking him. I'm hoping he just goes to take a shower so I can get myself under control.

"You're acting differently." I know he's staring at me because I can feel his eyes on me. I busy myself with grabbing Cici's diaper as I hand her a brush so she can play with it.

"Nope, I'm normal," I reassure him, looking over my shoulder at him and maybe, perhaps, I should just tell him that we need to talk. Maybe, just maybe, I should ask him.

"You are not normal," he says and it irritates me.

"You don't know me." I can't even believe I would say these words because even I can't help but laugh inside my head.

He laughs. "I know you better than anyone else." He folds his arms over his chest as I grab the pj's and start to put it on Cici.

"I saw your friend today." *Don't do this*, my head screams at me. *Don't do this here.*

"What friend?" he asks, and I don't have to be looking at him to know he's saying this with clenched teeth. I can feel the shift in the air from him.

"Marianna." Okay, we are doing this, I close my eyes. "She says she needs." My breathing comes out now almost in pants as my hands shake. "What were her words?" I avoid turning around to see his face but I look over my shoulder. "Yes, a dose of your dick." I pick up Cici and turn to him.

He just shakes his head and then puts his hands on his hips. I should maybe, perhaps calm down a bit before I continue. I know this, my heart knows this, but my head and my mouth, they are not down with this memo. "You know, since it's been a couple of weeks since you last gave her a taste of your dick." I try not to let the hurt get to me, but it's easier said than done.

"A couple of weeks," he repeats and then scoffs, "try months."

I don't know why but I roll my eyes. "You don't have to lie to me."

He stares at me. "I'm not lying to you." His voice stays flat.

"She said she was going to text you to hook up today." I just roll with this.

"Okay, and?" His eyebrows push together.

I'm not thinking straight, I'm thinking all over the place and perhaps, if I stopped for a second, I could see the change. "Well, obviously, that's why you were late." I stop talking right then because the lump that was in my chest is now rising to my throat, and I don't think I can get anything else out.

"Wow." He just stares at me, his eyes never leaving mine. "Is that where you think I've been?"

He shakes his head almost in disbelief.

"Well, you were late coming home." I don't get to finish because he snaps back at me.

"I had to go for a suit fitting for the wedding." It's my turn to stare at him shocked.

"Do you think I would have gone to have sex with her and then come home to you and act like nothing?" His words cut me to the core.

"I have no idea." I take a step forward as he shakes his head at me.

"Yeah, I guess you don't," is all he says before he turns and walks away from me. "I need some air," is the last thing he says before he walks out of the room and then a second later the front door slams shut, just like my heart.

Thirty

Levi

*T*he door slams behind me as I walk toward my car instead of storming back into the house. My hands are shaking but I don't know if it's because I'm so pissed or so hurt, or both.

I'm in uncharted territory, so instead of going back in the house, I start the car and head over to my place. I hold my phone in my hand, somehow wishing Eva calls me and tells me she's overreacted. To tell me she trusts me. To tell me anything, but every single step I walk closer to my place, the phone gets heavier and heavier in my hand.

I step into the elevator and then it takes seconds before I'm walking back into my place. The house feels stale, even though my cleaning lady still comes once a week. I toss my keys on the table in the entranceway before walking to the fridge, hoping that there is at least a beer in there. The fridge is literally empty with just a couple of condiments left in it and I'm in luck as the last bottle is waiting for me. "Yes," I hiss, grabbing it and twisting the bottle cap open before tossing it into the trash can, then taking a big pull before walking over to the couch and sitting on it.

I put my head back and refuse to close my eyes, because every single time I do it, I see her standing there with Cici. Her face looking ravenous and I knew the minute I looked at her and she avoided looking at me that something was wrong. I just never imagined what happened to happen. "She thought I was fucking Marianna?" I repeat to the empty room as I take another pull from my beer. I look around the room that I never really noticed before sucks. I laugh at the thought. There is nothing in this room that shows I live here, that I have lived here. That I had a life before this.

Meanwhile at Eva's, there are our wedding pictures all over the place. My sweater is thrown on one of the couches, pretty sure a pair of shorts are even downstairs. I look over at the square on the coffee table that holds a book and remotes, which is so different from at Eva's which holds a couple of pacifiers and one or two books that Cici loves to have read to her. It's home and it shows. I put the beer down on the table, this is not home. It also comes crashing to me that I hated it. How empty my life was before this. How mundane it was. How the fuck did

I think this was the good life?

I grab my beer again that is sitting right next to the phone, my hand itching to call the one person I know who would know what to say. Except she's the one person I can't call. I don't know how long I sit here. All I know is that the beer is hot when I leave and I pour the rest of it in the sink. I grab my keys off the table and walk out of the door, knowing tomorrow I'm making at least one phone call.

I make my way back home. The house is pitch black by the time I walk up the stairs and open the door. The minute I walk into the house, I suddenly feel better. The warmth hits me right away as I walk up the stairs, heading straight for Cici's room. I walk past our bedroom, seeing the lights off and wondering if she is sleeping.

I walk in to see Cici on her side in the middle of the bed, with her pacifier hanging halfway out of her mouth as she sleeps. I don't think I've ever loved anyone the way I love this little girl. She owns half of my heart while her aunt owns the other. I rub my hand over her cheek. "Love you, little girl," I say for the first time out loud. And it makes me feel as if the world is pulled off my shoulders. I smile because I can't wait for her to say it back to me. In about two years, but the wait will be worth it.

I walk out of the room with my head down and stop when I see Eva stepping out of the bedroom. "Hi," I say, looking at her with her hair piled on top of her head. Her face looks as ravaged as it was before and all I want to do is hold her face in my hands and kiss her lips, but we need to have a talk first. The talk that can make us or the talk that can break us.

"Hey," she says softly. "I'm sorry." She looks down at her hands and I can see her wringing her fingers. "I shouldn't have—"

"You were—" I take a step toward her but she stops me when she speaks.

"I was jealous," she admits, "which was dumb." She tries to brush it off and there is a tightness in my chest that makes me want to cough, it's so hard to breathe.

"Why is it dumb?" I ask, standing in my spot. My hands itch to touch her, my heart aching to tell her I'm in love with her.

"Because with us." She lifts her hands and shakes her head. "It's—"

"What is it?" I ask, waiting, holding my breath, hoping she feels what I feel for her. Hoping I haven't been just playing this thing up in my head. I hope that she felt it every time I've silently told her I love her. After all our cards are on the table, she's going to know she's the only one for me. We may have gotten here under strange circumstances, but we are here and I'm going to fucking fight to stay here.

She looks down, not willing to look up at me. "I don't know." I can hear the fear in her words, but I know I'll catch her if she falls. I'll catch her always.

"Well, I do," I reassure her and she looks up at me and I can see the tears in her eyes. "I'm in love with you." She opens her mouth, but I just continue, "I don't know when it happened. For the past month, I've been trying to show you, hoping you would see it in my eyes every time I looked at you. Hoping you would feel it in my touch every single time I held your hand. Hoping you would see it in my eyes when all I have to do is look at you and smile." She smiles as one of her tears escapes and I walk up to her and hold her face. "I'm head over heels in love with you." She laughs now. "I wish I could say I knew the moment." She puts her hands on my hips like she always does. "Maybe I've been in love with you this whole time. I was just afraid."

"Levi," she says my name softly, and before this goes on, she has to know that I've been hers.

"I've not been with anyone but you since you asked me to marry you." She gasps. "Maybe I was a little traditional that way."

"Today when I saw Marianna, I wanted to throat punch her," she explains. "I pictured throwing my shake in her face and ruining all that perfect hair and makeup." I roll my lips. "And when she spoke about your cock." Her hands grip my hips harder. "Well, it wasn't good." I just nod at her. "It was not good, and then I was." She shakes her head. "I didn't know what to say. How was I supposed to tell you not to see her when we didn't even talk about what we were?" I know her tone means she's got to get this all out there, so I just look at her while she does it. "Did I have a right to tell you not to see her? I don't know. Did you want to see her? Again, I didn't know, I had hoped, obviously," she rambles. "But was I in the position to tell you that if you touched her, I would cut off your dick and bury it in the yard?" She shrugs. "I just, it was all too much. It was like, boom, in my face I was in love with you and then I was like, does he love me? How do I tell him I don't want him to see other people? How do I tell him I don't want to see other people?"

"Well, I should hope not, you're married," I point out, "and so am I."

"This last month, the last couple of months have gone from one of the worst times in my life to the best times of my life, thanks to you and Cici." I can't keep from kissing her, so I do softly.

"Thank you for asking me to marry you," I say, smiling.

"Thank you for saying yes," she replies as I walk her backward into the bedroom.

"Thank you for driving me insane." I pull her top up over her head before I attack her mouth with mine.

Her hands pull out the bottom of my shirt. "Thank you for finger-fucking me that first time." She nips at my bottom lip.

"Thank you for jerking me off." I suck her neck.

"Hmm," she hums, stopping in the middle. "Does this mean we're, like, official, just the two of us?"

I just stare at her. "Like this isn't just a friends-with-benefits sort of thing, right?" I don't know why but I growl. "Okay, okay, just asking, you know, keeping communication open."

"How's this for communication?" I rasp. "Get on the bed and spread your legs, it's time for me to eat."

"Fine," she huffs, almost running to the bed, "but only

because I like your tongue."

I tilt my head to the side. "Just my tongue?"

"Your fingers are good also," she adds, lying on the bed and spreading her legs. "Also your cock." I chuckle. "It's a solid nine out of ten."

"Nine?" I ask, standing looking down at her.

"Well, I can't give you ten right off the bat," she goads. "You have to work your way up."

"Is that so?" I ask, my mouth watering. "It would be my honor."

Epilogue One

Eva

One month later

"Mammma," Cici starts babbling and my eyes open, looking over at the screen on my side table. Cici is standing up in her crib, holding on to it as she bounces at her knees and calls, or better yet, her voice goes louder and louder. "Mmmammmmaaaa."

"I think she's calling you," Levi mumbles, his body hugging me from the back, one hand hugs my waist, the other is firmly on one of my breasts. Instead of letting me go, he pulls me closer to him.

"She's not calling me, she's calling Lisa." I move, his hands loosen around me, making it easy to turn in his hold and wrap my arms around his neck. This is my early morning wake-up and I know Cici isn't screaming bloody murder yet, so it gives me time. But it's a toss-up if it's five seconds or five minutes, we both know it. There are times when we chance it. Not often, but today it feels like it's going to be the latter.

"Do you want me to get her for you?" he asks as he buries his face in my neck, kissing me softly. "Since she's calling you."

I roll my eyes. "All she says is mama." I lift my leg to wrap around his hip, his cock lining up with my pussy perfectly.

"How long do you think we have?" he asks, moving his hips up, slipping in just the tip.

"Not as long as it's going to take you," I moan out as he fills me, my eyes close when he rolls my nipple between his fingers.

His fingers leave me. "I can be quick." He turns me on my back, still planted in me and I chuckle. "I can be really, really quick."

I wrap my legs around his waist. "I don't know if that's a bad thing or a good thing," I joke as he slips out before slamming back into me. He throws one of my legs over his shoulder, making him go deeper in me.

"For today," he answers as he pulls out to slam right back into me, "it's a good thing." His mouth slams on mine as his tongue slides into my mouth. We're in a rush and a frenzy to get to the finish line before the wailing starts. "Fuck." He lets go of my mouth. "It's always so fucking good." He thrusts into me as he buries his face in my neck, as he puts my other leg over his shoulder, and when he thrusts into me again, my eyes roll to the back of my head. It's crazy to think that one touch from him and I'm already wet and ready to come. It's like his dick has magical powers. "You're squeezing the shit out of me." The sound of skin slapping together fills the room. "I'm almost there."

I don't say anything. "There," I say right before I moan my release. "Keep going," I beg of him so I can ride out this orgasm that feels like it's been lingering for years. As if I didn't come four times before I even went to bed last night.

"Baby," he whispers in my ear as he plants himself as deep as he can go and comes in me. Just knowing he's coming in me makes me come again, I squeeze my legs around his neck. "I take it back," he huffs as he slides out of me. "Couch sex is second to morning sex."

I laugh as I hear the whine coming through the monitor. "You only liked couch sex last night because I was riding you." He rolls out of bed laughing.

"You also sat on my face before and took my cock in your mouth." He grabs his boxers from the floor, putting them on. I stare at him a couple of minutes longer, taking him in. His muscles flex when he starts pulling them higher and then he looks at me with his hands on his hips, and my mouth waters. "Not sure I need to tell you this, but anytime your pussy is on my face and your mouth is on my cock, it's going to be high up there." He motions with his hand to the top of his head.

I roll off the bed, grabbing a pair of panties from the

floor. "Your tongue has magic powers," I throw over my shoulder as he watches me, his eyes focused on my ass. His cock that was semi-hard looks like it's coming back to life.

"I'll go get her," he offers when Cici has decided she's done waiting.

"I'll be right there," I tell his retreating back as I walk into the bathroom to clean myself up. I snap up a pair of shorts and tank top before going to the bathroom. I'm in the middle of brushing my teeth when the door opens, and I look over. "See, she's right there," he reassures Cici who has big tears in her eyes, as she smiles at me. "I told you she was coming."

I spit out my toothpaste, bending over to rinse my mouth. "What is with the tears?" I ask as I dry my hands off and then take her.

She lays her head on my shoulder as she takes a big sigh. "What happened?"

"I told you she wanted you," Levi says as he kisses my lips. "I barely got her diaper on her before she lost her shit." I smile.

I rub Cici's back. "Are we hungry?"

"I think we are hangry," Levi voices, walking over and grabbing a pair of shorts. "I would offer to take her, but she's already pissed at me." He looks at Cici, who looks at him but doesn't get up from my shoulder. "So I will make coffee and breakfast for my two girls."

"That sounds like a fantastic idea," I say as we walk down the stairs. "Everything we want on a Saturday morning." I walk to the kitchen to make her a bottle while

Levi makes me a coffee. I grab the bottle in my hand, go over to the couch, and sit down with Cici. "Good morning, grumpy pants," I say, and she smiles at me as she grabs her bottle and lies in my arm. Levi comes over with the coffee cup and hands it to me, but not before he leans down to kiss my lips.

"Nananananaan," Cici says to him.

"Oh, now we like me," he coos to her, smiling. "You get a kiss, too." He bends to kiss her nose. She drools and smiles at the same time before putting the bottle back in her mouth.

"See, all is right with the world," I state, taking a sip of my coffee when the doorbell rings. Levi stands up and looks at me.

"Are you expecting someone?" he asks, and my heart speeds up a million miles a minute. The last time the bell rang on a Saturday afternoon it was a spot visit from Josephine. It was during nap time, so she caught Levi and me with our pants down, literally. I swear my face was as red as a tomato the whole time. I even told her that we usually don't have sex during the day. At one point Levi put his hand around my shoulder and mumbled, "Stop talking."

"Do you think?" I put my coffee down on the side table, trying not to freak out. "It's her again?"

"She came two weeks ago," Levi reminds me, walking calmly to the window, where the drapes are still closed.

"Don't open the drapes," I whisper. "She might see you."

"How am I supposed to see who it is?" he asks. He's

about to look out when the bell rings again, this time followed by a knock on the door.

"Okay, it might actually be important." I'm about to walk to the door when he puts his hand up.

"Where are you going?" he asks, stepping in front of me. "Your nipples have awoken." His eyes look down to my chest. "And you are holding a child."

"Oh, good call. You go take one for the team," I tell him. "I'll head out the back door." He glares at me. "We'll never forget you."

"Just you wait," he mumbles before turning to walk to the front door, the bell ringing again. "Whoever it is," he huffs, "is going to hear it."

"Idiot." I shake my head and follow him to the front door, but not too close. Cici looks at me as Levi opens the front door. It's even worse than Josephine. "Stefano?" I ask right before he walks into the room.

"I told him to calm himself down," Addison says from behind him, "but you know him. Patience isn't his virtue."

All I can do is stand here with my mouth open, watching them walk into the room. "Jesus, did you guys just wake up?" He looks at me, then at Levi. "It's almost ten."

"It's Saturday," Levi replies, looking at Stefano, then at me.

"Why are you naked?" he asks Levi.

"I just got up. Was I supposed to wear a suit and tie?" he asks. "And why are you here so early?"

"Oh, so he didn't tell you that we were coming?"

Addison folds her arms over her chest right on top of her belly. "You had one job."

"I—" He looks at me, then looks at Levi. "What is going on?"

"I have no idea what you mean." I ignore looking at him. Levi and I have been together for the last, I don't know, two months but we haven't really told anyone. I mean, it's not like the daycare doesn't know we are together. Or that my work doesn't know, it's just that no one else knows, and by no one, I mean Stefano and then my extended family.

"Oh, shit," Addison says, "I might need to sit down."

"Um, sorry." I hear a voice from the front door and a woman with long brown hair walks in. Her big blue eyes are shocked at the scene in front of her. Or maybe she is shocked that Levi is standing there half naked. "Should I wait outside?" Her eyes go back to Levi and I am really starting to get heated. In my head, I make a new rule that he has to wear a shirt in the morning.

"No, of course not," Stefano says to her and I look at Addison, who shakes her head and mouths, "I'm sorry," to me. "This is the reason we are in town," he states, "this is Grace. She's Sofia's cousin."

She laughs. "That isn't helpful at all," she says.

"Okay, how about you guys come in," I invite to them. "I'll go get dressed and Levi can put on a shirt." I look over at him. "Then we will join you."

"I can take Cici," Stefano offers. "Come to your uncle Stefano," he urges, holding out his arms, and Cici just looks at him, then me.

"One, you aren't her uncle," Levi says, holding out his hand and Cici goes to him. "And two, stop scaring her."

"I'm her godfather," Stefano says.

"She's not even baptized." I laugh. "Go in the kitchen. We will be right back."

I walk up the stairs and feel Levi at my back. The minute we are in the bedroom and he closes the door, I turn on him. "What the hell are we going to do?" I put my hands on my head.

"I'm going to get dressed," he says calmly. "You are going to get dressed and then we are going to go downstairs and have breakfast." He puts Cici in the middle of the bed with her bottle.

"Okay, but what about Stefano?"

"What about him?" He stands there looking at me as he puts on a white shirt.

"Well, do we tell him about us?" I ask and he stares at me.

"Do you not want to tell him about us?" he counters and puts his hands on his hips. "Do you want to lie and pretend we aren't together?" He tries to hide his hurt.

"No." I shake my head. "Of course not."

"Good," he says, going to grab Cici. "Now, go change and meet me downstairs."

"Don't tell him anything until I get there," I tell him and he just nods at me. It takes me less than ten seconds to slide on a pair of gray lounge pants and matching T-shirt. I pin my hair up on top of my head, rushing downstairs.

"What did I miss?" I ask when I walk into the kitchen

and see Addison, Stefano, and Grace are sitting on the stools. Cici is in her chair as she eats some blueberries that Levi must have given her.

"I just ordered food," Levi replies to me as he leans against the counter beside Cici's chair.

"So." I walk over to grab my coffee from the side table in the living room. "This is a nice surprise," I say and feel like I'm going to throw up. Why am I so nervous?

"So," Stefano starts, leaning back in his chair, "what's the story with you two?"

He looks at me, then at Levi, then back to me. Levi's eyes come to mine before he speaks. "We're together," he says officially. He thinks ripping the Band-Aid off is better than slowly easing into it. Stefano just looks at him now. "We live together," he continues. "We share a life. We are raising Cici together." He smiles at me. "Anything you want to add into that?"

"I think you got it covered," I say, walking to stand beside him. He puts his arms around my waist. "Do you guys have any questions?"

"You bet the fuck I do," Stefano grumbles.

"Stefano," Addison says, "perhaps you should—" He looks over at her with a glare. "If you think that look scares me, think again." She gives him the same look. "I'm not Avery and you can't cut off my Wi-Fi."

"Addy," he says to her.

"No, you dragged us all this way without telling them. Then you storm into their house and are going to give them the third degree." She shakes her head. "Ethan trusted you to take care of Grace and all you've done is show her—"

"Um, sorry," Grace cuts in, "but I'm used to family squabbles."

"Nonetheless," Addison says, "you said you would take her here and show her around."

"Are you going to be moving here?" I ask, happy to take the spotlight off us even for a minute.

"I am," Grace confirms. "I accepted a position at Cottrell Group. It's a hedge fund company that started off on the West Coast, Ida and Ernie Cottrell have branched out to the East Coast. From what they said, their son is taking over for them. It's starting at an entry level, replacing his PA who is retiring." She shrugs. "I'm in school at night to get my CPA license, so I figure working for a couple of bankers would be a good idea."

"That's exciting," I say. "If you need anything while you are here, I'll give you my number."

"Thank you." She smiles. "That would be good since I know no one here." She looks at Stefano. "Which is why my parents asked Harlow, who then asked Sofia, who mentioned it to—"

"That's a whole lot of people," I joke with her.

"You have no idea," she remarks and Addison now laughs.

"My in-laws have what is called the phone chain." She rubs her belly. "And private planes, you know, just in case they want to pop in for dinner."

"My grandfather trained with the Navy SEALs for fun." Grace looks over at her.

"My uncle," Stefano adds, "pretty sure he got us all

microchipped." He laughs, then turns to us when he sees me lean into Levi. "Are you really sure about this?" he asks.

"Yes," I say without missing a beat.

"I think I always knew I'd end up with her," Levi admits and I look up at him. "Which is maybe why I was so scared to take a shot with her."

"You wanted to take a shot with me?" I ask as he smiles at me.

"Have you seen yourself?" One of his hands comes up to cup my cheek. "I was just—"

"He was banging everyone else out of his system," Stefano blurts, thinking he's going to joke about that when Addison hits his arm. "What? I'm just saying. You don't think she knows he's had sex with a million people?"

"It's not a million," Levi refutes and I just tilt my head. "Wow, you weren't Mother Teresa either."

Grace snorts. "That was funny."

"So where are you going to stay?" Levi looks at her.

"That's what we were doing here." She looks over at Stefano. "He said you guys could show me around."

"I have my condo, if you want," Levi offers and my head whips to look at him.

"She's not going to stay there," Stefano says, "it's—" He tries to find the word, snapping his fingers. "It's—"

"A brothel," I put in for him and he points at me.

"That," he agrees.

"We can have it steam cleaned," Levi says, "and painted."

"Biohazard cleaning, you mean," Stefano retorts and I ignore him.

"It's a two-bedroom condo in the middle of the city," Levi says to her. "I'm not staying there, and well, we might be moving anyway, so you can stay there if you want."

"Moving?" I squawk. "Moving where?"

"Baby," Levi cajoles, "I said might be."

"Why would we move?" I ask.

"We sleep on a queen-size bed," he explains, "and if we get a king-size bed, it'll barely fit." I don't deny this. "There isn't even a room to make an office."

"Shouldn't we—" I start to say when the doorbell rings. All three jump to answer it, leaving the two of us alone. "Shouldn't you talk to me about this?"

"I said maybe," Levi placates me. "I would like to get a space that is ours, that we can grow into." He pulls me into his arms. "You know, maybe get another bedroom or two."

"We are not putting a sex room in a house," I say and he laughs.

"I was thinking that maybe we would fill it in another way down the line," he suggests quietly.

"You mean?"

I stop there because the lump forms in my throat when Cici says, "Mama, Mama, Mama." I see half the blueberries on the floor, her fingers stained blue. "Mama, Mama."

"Get another kid who calls you Mama," Levi urges, and all I can do is put my head down in the middle of his chest and silently cry.

"You want a baby with me?" I finally ask him when they come back into the room.

"Didn't you two just get married?" Stefano yells. "How are you pregnant already?"

"We aren't," Levi denies, "but one day." He kisses my lips. "Sooner than later, yeah?" I don't answer him because his arms pull me closer to him as he bends to kiss my lips. The word "okay" is swallowed by his mouth.

Epilogue Two

Levi

Ten months later

"How does this look?" Eva asks me as she steps out of the walk-in closet wearing a one-piece white sleeveless dress. It's tight on her top and hips, then flows down and is covered in blue flowers.

"You look amazing." I look at her as I sit on the bed with Cici, who is watching a cartoon on the iPad in front of her. She's wearing a special dress Eva bought her for today and we are trying not to get it dirty. It has a white top and a full pink skirt—which she hates because it gives her trouble when she walks, or better yet, runs—a big sash in the front with a huge bow in the back that matches the bow on her headband. "But you looked amazing in the last outfit."

"I just want to look like…" She trails off. "Like I'll be a good mom." Today is the big day. She finally gets full custody of Cici; all the CPS visits are finally over.

"Baby, you are a good mom," I say softly and get off the bed walking to her. I grab her face in my hands. "You are a great mom, the best mom there is out there."

She looks down and blinks away the tears. "This is just going to make it more formal." She looks up and I see big tears in her eyes. "Like she's going to be mine."

I rub her cheeks with my thumbs. "She's already yours."

"That's actually something I wanted to talk to you about," she redirects, her voice going a bit low. "Before we leave, there are a couple of things we need to talk about."

"Um." I hesitate as she steps away from my touch and walks over to the bed.

"Cici," she calls her name and she looks up at her, "come." She holds out her hands and Cici drops the iPad and crawls over to her. "It's time for the surprise."

Cici smiles at her and claps her hands. "What's going on?" I ask, putting my hands on my hips.

"Stay there." She holds her hand up. "I'll call you when we are ready." She walks out of the room, and even though she told me to stay where I am, I walk to the doorway and out into the hallway, watching them walk into Cici's room. "Thanks for listening," she throws over her shoulder, glaring.

"I'm not following you." I stand in the hallway. "I'm making sure you guys are safe."

She laughs. "We are still inside the house."

"I didn't know where you were going, Eva," I retort, huffing. "How was I supposed to know?"

"Stay there," she orders, then looks down at Cici. "Tell him to stay." She holds up her finger.

Cici looks at me and says, "No, no, no," with her fingers shaking, because that's what we are constantly doing now that she is so independent and hates having us do things for her.

"Close enough." Eva smiles, walking into the bedroom and closing the door behind her.

I shake my head and walk over to the door, leaning against the wall facing it, and listening to the noise that is going on in the room. It's been a year since we got married, a little over a year and I've never in my life been happier. "Are you ready?" I hear Eva and I don't know if she's asking me or Cici. "Okay, I know you're outside the door. You can come in now."

I walk over and turn the handle to the door, opening and seeing Eva and Cici standing in the middle of the room. There is a streamer across her crib that says Worth the Wait. I look around and see there is a line across the room that is hanging with pictures of Cici and me from the past eight months. "What is all this?"

"Well," Eva says, then stops when her voice trembles. "Wow, this is harder than asking you to marry me." She tries to make a joke of it and all I can do is stand here looking at her.

"Best day of my life," I declare softly. "I mean one of, obviously marrying you was the best, and then when we got Cici. And then when we, you know, did the deed." I smile at her. "And then when we finally said we loved each other for real." I look at Cici. "And then when you made me do that thing—"

"Okay," she cuts me off, "let's focus right now." She picks up Cici, who is now wearing a white T-shirt. "Over a year ago, I asked you for the biggest favor of my life," she states and I can tell she's nervous when she swallows and clears the lump in her throat. "I had no idea that it would change not only my life, but yours also." She chuckles looking at Cici. "And then, well, you not only stood by my side through it all, you literally became a parent overnight."

I look at her and at the other person who owns my heart and smile at her. "There isn't anything I wouldn't do for her."

"I know," Eva replies, "she's got you wrapped around her little finger." Cici holds up her hand and looks at her finger, making us both smile. "And because of that, Cici wants to ask you something."

"Does she?" I look at them both confused.

She puts Cici down on the floor and turns her to me, showing me her shirt. And I gasp when I read it. "Will you be my dad?" I put my hand to my mouth.

"Today we are going to the courthouse and we are going to get custody of her for good," Eva explains, my eyes fly to her and I see her with tears streaking down her face. "And I was hoping you would want to adopt her."

"Eva," I whisper, my heart exploding in my chest.

"I know it's a lot to take in." She wrings her hands in front of her. She does that when she's really nervous. "But you're her dad," she finally says, "in every single sense of the word you are her dad." I can't help the tear that escapes. "You get up with her when she is sick. You soothe her when she falls down and really doesn't hurt herself, but you make sure you kiss all her boo-boos away. You teach her things and sit down with her to read to her. You protect her from everything you think will hurt her, and there is a lot on that list." She makes me laugh. "Even that little dog from down the street."

"Hey." I point at her. "That dog was without a leash and coming to her. What if he pushed her down?"

"It's a Chihuahua," she reminds me, and all I can do is glare at her. Then I squat down and hold out my arms for Cici, who walks over to me.

"Hey, baby girl," I coo when she walks into my arms and all I can do is hug her close to me. "It would be my honor to be your dad," I tell her, then look up at Eva.

She puts her hands to her mouth. "Really?"

"Did you think I was going to say no?" I ask, shocked. Picking Cici up, I walk over to Eva, pulling her to us. "How lucky could one guy be?" I look down at Eva, who smiles up at me, putting one arm around my waist. "First, you propose to me," I recap to her. "Then this girl proposes to me. I'm going to have to ask the two of you to stop stealing my thunder," I tease. right before I kiss Eva's lips softly, then turning and kissing Cici, who moves her face close to me with her mouth open to give

349

me a kiss. "I promise to forever be the best husband and father I can be."

"Shall we go?" Eva asks and I just nod my head at her.

One hour later, in the middle of the courthouse filled with all of our friends and family, a surprise neither of us knew would be happening, the three of us become a family.

Made in the USA
Columbia, SC
05 November 2023

25443397R00196